IGNITED GALAXY SERIES: BOOK 1

BONDS

DREW GOODMAN

First edition October 2023

Book design and formatting by Damonza

ISBN 979-8-9889652-2-0 (paperback)
ISBN 979-8-9889652-0-6 (ebook)
ISBN 979-8-9889652-1-3 (hardback)

Acknowledgments

I'd like to thank everyone that was involved in the process to make this book. My editors, my cover artist, formatters, beta readers, family and friends. Thank you all for helping make this dream something real.

I have to give shout-outs to specific people who this book would not exist without. First and foremost my girlfriend, Bella, who let me rant at her about story ideas and helped write them down when I was too distracted and believed in me even when I didn't believe in myself. Cassandra Jones, who content edited this book and came up with all sorts of wonderful questions to ask and advice to give about the world of Ignited that the current book would not have without her. If you are looking for content editing in your own fantasy books/sci-fi books I cannot recommend her highly enough. She can be found on Twitter and on cassandrajonesediting.com. Celestian Rince, who I had happened upon while browsing reddit, and who managed to proofread this entire book in a week and did a wonderful job of it. They can be found on their own site, celestianrince.com. I'd also like to thank all of my friends in my personal discord server who I have been writing with for over 10 years now; the foundation of this book would not have existed without them. Lastly, I'd like to thank all of my beta readers who helped me fine tune the finishing touches to the book: Mom, Dad, Jim, Ryan, Alex, Jacob, and Nathan.

You are all incredible people and to anyone who has read this far in the page, thank *you* for giving my debut book a chance. I hope you enjoy it.

PROLOGUE

*Life is about struggle. The struggle against the world
around you and the person inside of you. Every day in
this world is a war for your right to live in it.*

- COLLECTED TEACHINGS OF THE EXALTED SOVEREIGN

4.26.1371AS of the Galactic Standard Calendar

THE JUNGLE TEEMED with life. Every tree and bush held within it
an entire world of insects and lesser beasts in a constant war for
survival. Such was the way of the natural world. Nothing was
ever given, only earned. Even beetles crawling up the leaves of ferns found
their grip tested as the plants snapped at them with whip-like cracks of
their branches in an attempt to knock them away like a cow flicking its
tail to swat away a fly. This constant battle made the wilderness seem like a
massive creature stirring and writhing in perpetual slumber as trees swayed
and plants snapped at the life deemed unworthy of its bounty.

Only in one spot did the jungle seem to still itself: Zaharias stood in
the midst of this sea of greens, reds, and oranges like a predator standing
tall before his prey. He wore sleek, black armor of chitinous carapace
that covered him from head to toe save for three lines across the crested

1

helmet that made up a tinted visor. With it, the entire jungle was laid bare to him, all major movements highlighted to him along with a variety of other useful information. Nothing of note stood out, and so he changed his tactics.

Zaharias' eyes closed while he felt deep inside of himself. A fire burned within, not physically, but at the substance around his very soul. His potential, the potential that was held within every living being and surrounded every living soul, the potential that turned ordinary men and women into heroes of legend and song. A being's potential was not born ignited. There were only three ways to ignite one's potential: to be pushed to the brink of life-or-death survival, to be ignited by a dragon, or to submit to the teachings of the Exalted Sovereign, who governed all life. Ignited had a greater connection to all life and more importantly could feel the presence of others who had similar gifts.

He could feel two other lit fires nearby: his hunting partner, Zenovia, perched atop one of the great trees like a vulture searching for carrion, a rifle resting across her lap; and Theseus, with a spear in one hand and a large, carapace shield in the other. Just like Zaharias, the jungle stilled around them both. These were not what he was searching for. Distantly, through the connection of his potential, he could feel another fire burning. It wouldn't be long now.

His thoughts were interrupted by a brief click from the inside of his helmet followed by a gruff voice.

"It is still not too late to turn around, Za." It was Theseus, his eyes still on the horizon as they awaited their prey.

"If we do not act, then those outside of the wall will continue to suffer against it," Zaharias' calm and stoic voice came in reply.

"They are the ones who decided to settle outside the safe area. If they cannot protect themselves then the jungle is bound to swallow them eventually. If you ask me? It is a wonder The Suneater even allows them to stay on this world."

"Unity is the hand that guides the sword of valor, Theseus," Zenovia's voice quipped within their radio, prompting a grunt from the man and a small smirk from Zaharias.

"Don't go quoting the Exalted Sovereign to me, Zen. We cannot help every cindering person if they insist on walking into a deadly jungle the second we stop holding their hand," Theseus bit back before quickly adding, "one ignited beast isn't worth sending three of us to deal with it. I might as well spend all day in bed and get the same waste of potential growth."

Only now did Theseus' visor turn towards Zaharias, who shrugged to reply before planting his gauntlets atop the hilts of two swords on either side of his waist. "Enough, Theseus. Your gripes aren't about to let our quarry suddenly stop caring that we're in its territory. It won't be long now; it seeks a challenge as much as we do."

He could feel it getting closer; there was no point in trying to hide or lay a trap for it. It could sense them just as well as they could sense it. As he felt its presence come closer, he gestured for the others to get ready. He drew both of his blades, each an excellently crafted length of steel with a graceful curve to it starting from the hilt and working its way to the point. He reached out through his connection with the life around him, his two allies, like two balls of white fire sitting against a muted color jungle behind them, then the creature they were hunting. The white fire of its potential blazed hot and now could be seen much more clearly. Unlike the three of them however, the white sphere in the center *did* have a shape, like a set of eyes peering through the dark of night, tendrils barely perceptible reaching out towards all that surrounded it against a backdrop of fire, a true predator. The active movement of the jungle around them stilled completely.

"Oh no…" Zenovia began over the radio, a slight tremble in her voice. A feeling of dread filled the air and where once the fires of their potential had given their egos warmth against the unknown, now there was only *fear*. Zaharias opened his eyes again and could see the jungle around them had stilled. The preternatural senses granted to him by his potential heard the sounds of taloned feet scraping against the now silent underbrush and low-hanging branches snapping against a wide body.

"It's cindering *Shaped!?*" Theseus called out in frustration, unable to hide the fear in his voice as he shifted back with his weapon at the ready.

"*That's* why we're out here? Za, if this thing's identity wasn't messing with my head I'd–" Its roar resounded through the air, the voice sending a tingling wave down the spines of each of the Ignited who had come to face it.

"Hold!" Zaharias bellowed, one sword raising into the air. He was trembling, his heart being forced to pound heavier as the creature's identity threatened to overwhelm them. "The Exalted Sovereign watches us now! Today we prove our potential to be greater than this beast! Hold, burn you!"

Another snap of wood announced its arrival. The creature was near twelve feet tall, not counting the wicked horns on its head. Two gleaming, golden eyes glared at them all beneath the shade of the trees. It stood on two legs, its form hunched forward with two long arms hung in front of it, occasionally helping push its way through the underbrush. Each hand and foot had a set of curved talons, useful for digging and tearing while it had an elongated muzzle with rows of sharp teeth. A serpentine-like tongue slid out before brushing over its maw while a long, sinuous tail dragged behind it as it approached the Ignited. It had come to see what had stumbled into its territory, expecting to find worthy prey, and was only faced with three Ignited. Spines on its back bristled as it let out a low, raking growl, its head lowering as it got down onto all fours, eyes set on Zaharias.

Through his brave front, Zaharias once more reached out through their life sense to confirm that yes, it was not a trick of the light and he had seen the soul of the creature had become Shaped, earning an identity. An identity that represented fear, from what Zaharias could tell. It was slightly reassuring that the voice in his head screaming at him to run was not his own, not completely anyway. Zaharias and Theseus shifted closer to one another; Zenovia remained resting on a large branch in a nearby tree, rifle at the ready. They hoped that the creature would go for the more immediate prey.

They were right.

The Igniteds' suits warned them as the creature briefly flashed red on their display before it roared again and shot forward at a speed that no creature of its size should be able to manage.

Zaharias wanted to scream and run but managed to steel himself long enough to shout, "Theseus!"

His companion did not need to be told twice; he threw himself to the side, Zaharias going in the opposite direction as the creature tore through the air where they had once been, its sheer speed making the air whip up in a frenzy and peel away some of the bark of the nearby tree. A shot rang out and slammed into the beast's head, making it jerk to the side. It let out another roar as Zenovia shouted over their comm channel, "I think that only made it angrier!"

The creature's feet dug into the earth as it broke into a sprint, tail whipping behind it as it found its new target, golden eyes meeting Zenovia's as it closed the gap between her and her tree in an instant, talons flashing in the light before it carved through the massive tree. Zenovia's balance lurched, and she nearly lost her balance before she leaped up into the air, rockets in her boots activating in her panic and helping her stumble to the next tree over. The beast was already nearly upon her, using the still-falling tree as leverage to leap up into the air for her. Her eyes widened as she stared into its gaping maw.

A force rammed into it from the side. Theseus had charged after the creature, his ignited potential granting him increased speed and his armor assisting it further as he thrust the shield up into the creature, knocking it off trajectory and making the two of them crash through another tree. He raised his spear to pierce its heart, a battle cry on his lips but it was cut short as one taloned hand shoved him away. Talons raked over his armor and caused a web of cracks to line the surface before he was thrown through another tree that kicked up dirt in its wake. The creature recovered, hitting the ground with a skid and roll before it was back on all fours. It roared in frustration, sending another wave of tingling dread through the three of them and stole precious seconds to react from them.

Zaharias was not about to let his companions have all the glory. He crossed the toppled trees in an eyeblink, charging the Shaped creature. It dug its claws into the dirt beneath it before pouncing forward, meeting his charge. Zenovia began to fire upon it from above, her gun making an echoing *crack* through the air, yet all it seemed to do was bounce off of its thick hide. "Its scales are too thick, I can't find a weak spot!" she cried.

Both it and Zaharias clashed, the impact causing a plume of dust to blow away from them as blade met brutal, ferocious claws in an expert series of parries and strikes. "Focus on its limbs! Give me openings!" he snapped back in the midst of his clash with the beast.

Zaharias' blood pumped through his veins. Staring down the creature, he felt the fire of his potential burn brighter and brighter with each moment that he managed to survive. The joints of his armor groaned under the constant strain of impacts, but held. They were able to withstand two Ignited clashing, but with a Shaped... there was uncertainty there. This creature was a league above them and every matched blow reminded him of that. Either way, he had its attention.

Then the beast roared in pain. Theseus had returned, a rocket-aided jump bringing the warrior square onto its back. With the natural might of his ignited potential and the armor, he managed to pierce a wound into its scaly back. The doubts retreated for a moment. They had managed to surround the creature, Zaharias before it, blades flashing in the light, Theseus on its back, spear rearing back for another blow, and Zenovia's rifle aiming for its legs now to keep it off balance. A perfectly coordinated hunt. There was something wrong however. Zaharias had felt his potential burn like a new sun in his body as he faced down the creature, but he did not feel the eyes of the Exalted Sovereign on him. Was this not worthy prey?

A keening sound rang from the creature and all three of the ignited warriors froze in place. Zaharias tried to wrestle back control of his body but was struggling to do so. What was happening? He tapped into his life sense to try and see. The beast's potential burned hot; tendrils of fire and shadow seemed to lick at the edges of its very soul while the Igniteds' own flames seemed to sputter in uncertainty. Every part of Zaharias' brain screamed at him to drop his weapon and *run*. That uncertainty was deadly and it gave the beast just enough time to wrap its long tail around Theseus and tug him forward. It brought all of its talons together and speared the man straight through his stomach. There was an accompanying crunch as his armor gave in to the strength of the beast.

Zaharias cried out, seeing the flame around Theseus' soul suddenly flash hot in one final blaze of glory before snuffing out entirely, the soul itself floating away weightlessly toward the heavens like a feather lost to the wind. Theseus dropped his weapons and the creature cast aside his body with a flick of its tail, sending it crashing through one more splintered tree before it slumped to the ground. The keening continued as it then brought its golden gaze to Zaharias.

"Zenovia, run," Zaharias whispered.

"Za?"

"There is a fine line between ambition and foolishness and we have chosen the latter this day. I will not have us lose three Ignited to this creature due to my mistake in judgment." The Ignited stood with weapons at the ready. The beast did not charge him. Its tail was shifting from side to side like a content dog and Zaharias could swear there was a grin on its razored maw.

"Then let's both retreat!" Zenovia insisted.

"That is what it wants. Go, Zenovia, tell my sons that should I not see them come the next sunrise, I will see them in Memory."

"Za!" Zenovia called out, but he did not reply and brought his full attention to the beast across from him. The fires of potential blazed to new heights as he let out an exhale and with it a tremble working its way through his frame. The grip on his weapons tightened as he accepted that this moment meant the end of his life, or the shaping of his soul. He felt foreign eyes upon him from on high, the Exalted Sovereign's attention coaxed to him through the weight of this moment upon his life. The knowledge that his God now watched this duel made his heart hammer in his chest. What had changed? Life-or-death struggle was enough for one to ignite, but to be shaped as well? His eyes widened as it all clicked. His attempt to sacrifice himself to save his allies, his core motivation behind everything he did. The Exalted Sovereign saw it now, his desire to protect all those around him, and wished to see the power of that motivation here in the slaying of the shaped creature before him.

The beast bellowed at Zaharias, a warning and a taunt, to either face it with honor or to run and die a coward. Zaharias roared in reply, sliding his blades together to create a rasping hiss. Then this was truly it, his chance to Shape, his chance to become something within the Order of Ignited and show his children the galaxy he had been protecting them from all this time. He glanced back to where Zenovia was in one final, silent plea for her to leave. She returned the look before leaping out of sight. He let out a breath he didn't remember holding before focusing on the beast.

He pressed his weight onto one foot, then launched himself forward, the force cracking the earth beneath him as he charged the beast. Fear screamed in the back of his head; he was terrified, but often that is when mortals truly felt the most *alive.* The two clashed again, his blades being caught by crossed talons in the air, momentum holding them both there for a brief moment before the creature shoved him up and back. Ports in Zaharias' armor opened up as jets of flame shot out to right himself again as he landed back against the ground, already dragging his foot forward to lunge again. The beast swiped for him again but this time its talons slipped just over his head as he dropped into a slide beneath its legs. His blades cut at its haunches and made it roar in pain.

As he passed its legs he threw himself upright, now behind the creature and twisted to face it. Its tail was already swinging towards him but he managed to raise his blade just fast enough to catch it. The tail cracked against it like a whip, a small vacuum of air forming and snapping the blade in two at the impact. Zaharias grit his teeth, dropping the blade instantly as the creature had swung around in a wide sweep of its talons, tearing through the earth as it tried to rip Zaharias apart. The Ignited managed to leap back at the perfect time, the talons scraping over his chest plate as he skidded backward—right next to where Theseus' shield had fallen. He grabbed it, raising it in his left hand while he held his blade in the right. "Exalted Sovereign watch over me as I overcome this trial!" he shouted, meeting the beast in another charge.

The two clashed and whirled around one another, blades, shield, talons, and tail all clashing against each other in small showers of sparks. Trees splintered and shattered, wildlife scattered as their duel destroyed the jungle around them. In a matter of minutes the once-thriving patch of jungle looked as if a tornado had uprooted all of what was there and tore it to pieces. Zaharias' armor was barely holding itself together; cracks spread across the entirety of its surface and part of the visor had fallen off, revealing one emerald green eye and a patch of blood-stained, tanned skin beneath. His breathing was coming out in ragged heaves of his chest, adrenaline and his suit's systems being all that were keeping him upright. The creature, meanwhile, had half of one horn missing, a variety of cuts and bruises across its scales, and a few chunks missing entirely.

All in all, this "prey" had proven itself to be worthy, more worthy than perhaps even Zaharias had expected. Maybe it was a mistake to send Zenovia away… *No,* he thought, *I couldn't risk her dying too.* He wasn't dead yet, which meant there was still a chance, however slim, for him to succeed. His emerald gaze met the beast's golden one. Amidst the adrenaline and blood in the air, there was a mutual respect shared between the two apex predators of the jungle. However, such respect would not save them. *Life is a struggle* were the words of the Exalted Sovereign. *Every day in this world is a war for your right to live in it.* The two let out one final roar of challenge to one another before Zaharias ran at the beast. The beast ducked low, sweeping its talons across where the Ignited was about to cross. He leaped over it, but it was in that moment he realized his mistake, his final mistake. The creature's head lurched upwards, Zaharias' trajectory leading him right into the path of the creature's remaining horn. The systems in his armor tried to release jets to course correct but it was too late.

Crunch.

Zaharias had been skewered fully on the beast's horn as it tore through armor and broke through bone, lifting him and its upper body into the air as it roared in triumph. The Ignited coughed out blood, his vision going blurry and pain flaring up across his body. With one final act of defiance, he struck the beast's eye with his sword, stabbing it and causing that roar of triumph to turn into one of pain. It grabbed his arm with a taloned hand and ripped it free. He let out another cry of pain, blood spilling over the beast's maw and mixing with its own as it grabbed him with his free hand and threw him to the ground with a wet smack.

Zaharias looked up to the beast above him, choking on his own blood. He wanted to still cry out in defiance but all he could muster was a wet gurgle. The beast looked down at him and the last thing he saw were rows of razor-sharp teeth in an expansive maw before all went black.

The jungle became still once more.

CHAPTER 1

A struggle need not be faced alone. Lift up your brothers and
sisters who surround you. It is through unity that you may
overcome struggles that would otherwise be insurmountable.
It is through unity that our valor is known.

-COLLECTED TEACHINGS OF THE EXALTED SOVEREIGN

THE HOLY CITY of Dasos was bustling today. It was a small city; only tens of thousands called it home, however each one of those citizens was an Ignited or someone under the protection of the Ignited. Warriors roamed the streets in packs, while others leaped across the squat, stone buildings that made up the city's bulk like stepping stones, all of them talking, laughing, or training. At all hours of the day sounds of metal clashing against metal could be heard somewhere as the Ignited dueled one another and smiths of the order worked on new armor and weapons.

"They say there's going to be a meteor shower tonight. Suneater is even going to make sure the branches and leaves don't cover up the sky so we'll get a clear view of it." Phaidros grinned, excitement filling him as he looked up to the sky. Most of it was occupied by a vast network of near-black branches surrounded by leaves of red and green. Light from the sun peered through the leaves in gentle rays. Phaidros waited for a moment before adding, "Charon? Did you hear me?" He looked to his older brother, who was blankly staring ahead toward the vast gate before them. The two brothers were sitting on a bench along one of the nine paved roads that led out to one of nine gates surrounding Dasos. It was one of the small reminders that the city was not some ancient ruin being repurposed for the modern era. The silence made Phaidros purse his lips. "Charon?"

"I heard you," Charon replied, his voice coming out as if it took effort to speak above a whisper, which often made it sound like he was frustrated.

"And…?"

"And what?"

The response made Phaidros' shoulders sink in disappointment. "And when Father returns we can all go up on the wall and watch."

There was silence for another moment before Charon finally looked back to Phaidros, deep blue eyes squinting. His angular face did not help him look or sound any less angry than he was. Where once Charon had the look and build of a fierce warrior he seemed to be losing more and more muscle each day. The pressed, high-collared black uniform they all wore was starting to become loose on him. At least he still had his tan so Phaidros knew he was getting sun. Unlike his brother, Phaidros was built with a soldier's lean body, tall like their father with wide shoulders and short, black hair that was beginning to curl. "You're eighteen now and you're excited about meteor showers?" Charon asked.

Phaidros' face flushed with embarrassment. "It's… it's a chance for us all to spend time together again!" he responded defensively. "Father has been working hard to become Shaped, it could be a celebration and we can all forget about…" His voice trailed off as his own green eyes drifted to the wooden cane currently resting on his brother's lap just above a messenger bag that he carried with him everywhere. He already regretted speaking.

"Forget about what?" Charon replied flatly. "Don't answer that," he added with a huff a second later. He lifted a hand up to his head to swipe away some stray locks of his shoulder-length, curly black hair and rested his hand against his open forehead as if it was aching. "Father has been spending so much time out there because he doesn't want to look at me and I know it."

"Of course he wants to see you!" Phaidros assured, leaning over as he did so and frowning with concern. "No matter what, he cares about you, about us. He can tell you himself once he returns."

"It loses its impact when you *tell* him to say it," Charon replied, eyes narrowing again as he saw people approaching the gate. Phaidros wondered why he didn't just get himself glasses. *His pride,* his mind immediately answered.

"Are you coming to see the meteor shower or not?" Phaidros sighed, shoulders slumping.

"Of course I am."

This answer made Phaidros blink in confusion before he looked suspiciously at his older brother. "Did you have to make that so difficult?"

"I have a right to complain. Everyone treats me differently now."

There it was again. Another reminder. Phaidros looked to the cane and back to his brother again, now permitting silence to hang heavily for another moment before he forced the words out, "You could try again, you know."

"No," his brother snapped. "I'm not going through that pain again. You should worry for yourself, they won't let you stay here if you don't become ignited soon."

"They're letting you stay," Phaidros quickly shot back.

"It's different. I'm *Cindered*, Phaidros."

Silence lingered in the wake of that word. It was still all so new to them both. They had heard stories of the Cindered. They usually started in two ways, someone grew so used to victory they started to become complacent, or the fear of the fire slowly feeding upon them inevitably swallowed them in despair. All of them ended in the same way—pain, with the fire having nothing left to burn but the soul itself. When the flame was snuffed out, all that was left was a dried-out husk clinging to life, all of their senses crippled from the lack of potential.

Phaidros still remembered the screams. It had been why he had not gone to be Ignited himself by now. Every time the thought bubbled up in his mind the doubts began. What if he couldn't do it? What if he could not improve himself fast enough? What if he became like Charon?

The last thought repeated in his head and he felt ashamed. *Lift up your brothers and sisters who surround you.* The words had been drilled into him from a young age, to help one another become their best selves—the climb became so much easier for all when everyone assisted the people around them. Yet every time he looked at Charon he felt less and less like there was something that could be done. Perhaps that was why the others treated him differently. Phaidros opened his mouth to end the silence when he noticed a commotion outside of the normal. A handful of armored Ignited rushed past the brothers towards the gate. The clicking of their comms could be heard from their helmets as a crowd was beginning to gather. "What's going on?" Charon asked. Such activity near the gates wasn't common. They weren't guarded, as this was a city filled with armored, divinely gifted warriors. Any who attempted to attack the city would have the Ignited descend upon them like a swarm of large, powerful wasps. That wasn't even counting the Ideal that watched over the city.

"I don't know," Phaidros answered. Something was wrong. Phaidros leapt from his seat at the bench going to see what was going on before remembering to get his brother. He turned to Charon, who was struggling to his feet, pushing himself up with the help of his cane before he grimaced at his younger brother. Phaidros quickly moved to his side, helping take one arm as the two made their way towards the gate.

Amidst the growing commotion, Phaidros made out two of the armored Ignited from earlier, helping a third walk through the gate. Their black, chitinous armor had cracked in various places, a rifle hanging from their back as they could hear their heaving breath. The two brothers recognized the small patterns of sweeping ridges on the armor and slight beak to the helmet as Zenovia, one of their father's hunting partners. Where was their father then? The brothers exchanged looks before immediately pushing past the growing crowd towards them. The three stopped, Zenovia's helmeted head lifting to meet their worried gazes.

"Zenovia?" Phaidros asked. "Where is our father?"

She was silent, still catching her breath before she shrugged away the two assisting her to stand upright. She lifted up her helmet with shaking hands. There was a hiss of airlocks releasing before she pulled it off entirely. Zenovia had fierce features with a deep scar trailing from her cheek down to her jaw in a jagged crescent. Her skin was the same tan as the two brothers but she had golden blonde hair she kept short, and piercing blue eyes. She was much older than the two of them but still looked to be in her prime, thanks to her ignited potential. Her gaze flicked between the two a final time as she struggled to find the words.

Her silence spoke volumes on its own, both brothers' faces slowly filling with the dread of realization.

"Your father…" Zenovia began, tone curt, anger creeping in through the exhaustion. "Stayed behind. He told me to pass on to you both that if you do not see him at the next sunrise then he will see you again in Memory." The Ignited surrounding them glanced between one another. Zaharias was one of the best in the city, one of the most likely to become Shaped of them all. One of the other armored Ignited began to usher others away, giving the three space.

Both Phaidros and Charon were quiet at first. Charon set his jaw and forced out, "You left him out there?"

"Brother…" Phaidros muttered in an attempt to soothe him but Charon forced his arm free. The act caused him to stumble towards Zenovia; she reflexively moved to assist him but he caught himself on her armor. He tried to shove her back but the effort was utterly futile. Still, he strained with effort, growling as the woman looked at him with a sympathetic frown.

"I am sorry," Zenovia began, the anger leaking from her voice to be replaced with pity.

"If you are sorry, get back out there and find him then!" Charon shouted, still struggling against her.

"I tried to," she answered, voice now resigned. "The creature we were hunting turned out to be Shaped. We didn't stand a chance. Theseus had already died and your father didn't want to risk all three of us."

Phaidros kept his questions to himself until now. A pit formed in his stomach but he was trying to remain positive. "There's... still a chance he could be alive, right? You can contact him through your armor, right?" He stared at Zenovia, strained hope in his eyes, but the look she returned made the sparking flame die as soon as it was born.

Zenovia now gently grabbed Charon's wrists and pulled them off of her, the man's head hanging as he bit back tears. "I am sorry, you two, I had tried to contact him, feel him through our life sense, but there was nothing. As I was retreating back to Dasos the cindering beast caught up to me." That would explain the cracks in her armor, Phaidros looked warily to Charon as Zenovia had haphazardly brought up the curse 'cindering' in his presence. His brother only glared while Zenovia continued. "I was lucky to get away with only cracked armor, it ran off when I got in sight of the walls."

"Our father would not let some beast kill him," Charon growled in denial.

"This wasn't just 'some beast,'" Zenovia said. "It was Shaped. From my experience, it was Shaped with a 'fear' identity as well." Her eyes went distant for a moment. "I had to fight back shaking like a leaf the entire time we were near it..." She shook her head. "Your father was a great warrior, but a shaped creature like that was beyond even his skill."

Was a great warrior. Phaidros could hardly believe it. He stood there, speechless, his brother still growling in frustration against Zenovia's grip. "W...what happens now?" Phaidros asked, voice trembling.

"Now? I report this to Sacred Suneater and most likely they organize a new hunt with a much more prepared party to ensure the creature is stopped before it becomes Defined and truly a danger to the city."

Phaidros' frown deepened. Another hunt. The killing of wildlife was strictly regulated by Suneater. Dasos and the jungle around it was a holy site to the Ignited. It was a world untouched by domesticated civilization where the flora and fauna naturally ignited, and often did so, even becoming Shaped as this beast had. Outside of theaters of war and strife amidst the civilizations of the Galaxy, Dasos was a place for someone to stoke the flames of their potential in relative safety, which was why most of the people that were invited into it were people who were on the edge of struggling to burn out like Charon did. It was safe inside the walls, not so much outside, however. Even if that monster butchered innocents outside of the walls, it could not be touched without Suneater's explicit instruction.

Charon finally gave up fighting at this point, going slack in Zenovia's grip now out of breath. Phaidros nodded at Zenovia before hesitating. "May we go with you? It only feels appropriate that we are there too. He is…" He hesitated to say the word *was* just yet. He could still be out there. "Our father. We are under his protection and this will affect us as well. We should get to hear what happens."

Zenovia watched him for a long moment before sighing. "If that is your wish then so be it."

"Can you let go of me already?" Charon snapped and Zenovia immediately released him. The sudden freedom from restraint made Charon drop to his knees. Phaidros immediately knelt to pick him up but Charon brought up his hand to stop him. "I can pick myself up," he said indignantly. Zenovia frowned to herself and Phaidros took a step back, allowing his brother to pick himself back up and have his pride.

"Let's go," Zenovia insisted, stepping away from the two of them and heading off toward the center of the city. Phaidros sighed and then followed after with Charon lagging behind.

It was not a long walk to reach the center of the city. All of the main roads offered a clear path straight towards the Temple of the Exalted Sovereign, which sat up against the trunk of the great tree in the middle of the city. The building itself was utilitarian in design, a big block of stone with marble pillars holding up the open front. It always made Phaidros think of some sort of massive, yawning beast baring its teeth to all who entered. There was no ornamentation on the outside, making it match most of the smaller homes that surrounded it save for its size. As the three approached the temple they could hear voices echoing inside.

Zenovia strode in through the great pillars, Phaidros and Charon following after. The interior of the building seemed much like the outside: barren. No pews lined the grand hall. Phaidros had heard that this was something that other temples to lesser deities would often have. Scratches and small cuts carved through the stone floor where Honor Duels often took place. The only ornamentation that was allowed in the building were the murals on the wall depicting the ascension of the Exalted Sovereign. Beautiful mosaics showed the Exalted Sovereign when he was still a man facing down beasts twenty times his size, commanding armies against an army of horrid multi-armed abominations that Phaidros could never quite identify. Some of the mosaics had become dull and chipped with time; though it was unclear whether this was due to collateral damage from duels or from the passing of time. All of these mosaics met in the center where the building opened up again to the trunk of the great tree where one of its enormous roots dug into the ground. Above the back entrance there was one final mosaic of the Exalted Sovereign surrounded by a pillar of fire over the body of a dragon that was impossibly vast in size. Around him were kneeling onlookers, each holding a sword in their hand, a depiction of his final ascension.

At the far end, standing atop one of the protruding roots was a figure at least seven feet tall. Their "skin" was a near black made up of a gnarled and ancient bark that mimicked the wrinkles of an old man's face. It matched the hue of the tree they stood on. Atop their head was a nest of small, thin branches covered in red leaves, they were all tied back behind their head by one of the green vines coming from the back of their scalp. They had no eyes in the traditional sense, instead white fire barely licked at the corners of their carved-out eyes. They wore chitinous armor much like the other Ignited, however Suneater's armor was of a pure white color, near blindingly so, which contrasted against the black bark-like skin of their head. The armor itself barely seemed like armor anymore, like some of the chitin had been stretched out and had become loose and flexible, giving off the appearance that there were sagely robes being worn over a set of chitinous platemail.

Phaidros, despite living in this city most of his life, had only seen Sacred Suneater a few times and never this close. Usually, audiences with them were reserved only for the Ignited. However, the moment that he had stepped into the temple he knew that what everyone said about them was true. He had felt a wave of warmth wash over him as he took those first steps, the doubts and fears that swarmed his mind seemed less daunting than before. He found himself taking steps with more confidence than he had previously, even noting that his brother leaned less on his cane. Such was the power of an Ideal, their potential burning so bright that it affected all nearby. Phaidros had been told that outside of the Order of the Ignited, Ideals were considered by many cultures to *be* gods themselves.

Sacred Suneater stood before three armored Ignited, each with a helmet tucked under their arm. Phaidros could pick out one of them as human; one that had similar bark-like skin to Suneater, a drasil from Phaidros' understanding; and one with fins in place of ears, their hair having the same consistency of seaweed, and their skin a blueish grey, an ikaroa. The latter came in so many shapes and sizes it was usually safe to assume if one didn't recognize their features from any known source they were ikaroa. Suneater's voice echoed through the chamber. "—fall near the city it is imperative that you investigate immediately." Phaidros noticed how odd their voice sounded, like leaves rustling in the wind to form words; their mouth didn't move as they spoke either. "Go now and see that it is done." The warriors saluted, fists clenched over their hearts, then stepped past the three approaching to do as commanded. Sacred Suneater then looked upon Zenovia and the two brothers and Phaidros felt a small shiver from the weight of their unblinking, unmoving gaze.

Zenovia immediately saluted. "Unbroken Sage who Devours," she began, using the honorific of Suneater's name within the Ignited, "you have received word already on what has happened, I am sure. I have come to make my official report."

Suneater's eerie gaze betrayed no sign of emotion as it swept from the two brothers and back to Zenovia with a quiet creak. "Zaharias' hunt did not go as planned then, I see," they replied, tone as soft as they were able. "And so two cubs are left without a father and the beast is still out there."

Zenovia was about to answer, but Phaidros spoke first, one fist at his heart which he could feel pounding in his chest as he cut in. "We aren't sure if he's actually dead but—"

"He has fallen," Suneater interrupted, causing Phaidros' eyes to widen. "I could feel his potential burn up as he died."

At this, Charon's expression darkened as he took one cane-aided step forward. "If you felt that then you must have known that the creature they faced was Shaped!" he said angrily, Zenovia shot a look back at him, brow furrowed.

"You speak out of turn, Cin—" Zenovia began before Suneater raised a hand, requesting silence.

"I did," Suneater admitted. This made Zenovia snap her gaze back up to Suneater in horror. "If one is to improve themselves…" Suneater continued, "one cannot seek easy victories and hunts." The words made Charon's grip tighten on his cane. "You know this, Zenovia, as did Zaharias when he took up the commission to hunt the creature. You could have taken many Ignited with you, but what would be the point of that? What knowledge and wisdom is there to be gained in having ten or twenty Ignited swarm a single, powerful foe?"

"You kill the creature and save the people living outside of the city," Phaidros offered, still shaken from the confirmation that their father was dead.

"Perhaps true outside of Dasos," Suneater mused. "But our mission is to give struggling Ignited a chance to shape. Thus to *dissuade* people from taking on such challenges denies those who wish to improve themselves in the eyes of the Exalted Sovereign. If the people outside of the walls wish to linger, they may, but with the knowledge of the danger they willingly put themselves in. That is not our concern."

Zenovia jumped back into the conversation. "I understand what you are saying, Sacred Suneater, but if the creature has been Shaped now, then how long until it becomes a threat to the city itself? How long before sending trickling amounts of Ignited to feed it makes it become Defined? If you try to deny this problem until it is past the gates, wouldn't you just be able to smite it down regardless?"

The silence that followed in the moments after Zenovia's speech was deafening. They were spared, eventually, as the Ideal's voice carried through with the calm intensity of a parent attempting patience with an unruly child. "In such a scenario where the creature ignores my presence and decides to attack the city, then I would be forced to act. This will deny any of you the chance for growth, however. A wasted potential for any and all of you and in this, with the Exalted Sovereign as my witness, I cannot allow."

Zenovia grit her teeth and closed her eyes, taking a deep breath. Phaidros could see understanding on her face before she continued. "Then it is simply up to us to hunt the beast how we see fit."

Suneater nodded. "And so the commission will be offered to all Ignited again until the beast is eventually slain, with any updated information you can provide to the new hunters, Zenovia." Zenovia bowed her head, agreeing wordlessly.

Phaidros stood there, stunned. Nothing was going to happen? Nothing was going to change? They were just going to hope that the next hunting party could be the one to take it down? Phaidros' eyes trailed to his brother who appeared to be seething. How many more people were going to die?

"There is one more thing," Suneater said, eyes falling purposefully onto Phaidros now. "A matter of your continued stay here." Phaidros' gaze snapped back to Suneater, fear spiking in his chest as the Suneater continued. "With the death of your father and your growth into adulthood, you are now neither Ignited nor under one's protection. Which means you must either be exiled from the city, or join us."

"Surely you don't mean to kick the boy out the day his father died," Zenovia said. "You surely have some mercy, Suneater?"

"Every day in this world is a war for your right to live in it, Zenovia," Suneater quoted. "They may have the luxury of mercy outside of this city but not in it."

Charon took another step forward, now standing equal with Zenovia as he glared up at the Ideal. "I may be cindered but I am still one of the Ignited, surely that counts for something?" It was a weak defense, but Phaidros still appreciated that his brother was trying.

Suneater looked at Charon and even without expressions upon their gnarled visage, Phaidros felt the same look everyone else always gave his brother: pity. "You are no true Ignited, cindered one," they responded softly. "You may ignite your potential again to put your brother under your protection... but it will mean going back to that state of pain you wished so desperately to end." Charon set his jaw, the hand on his cane clenching the head tightly as he considered. Phaidros could see the conflict in his eyes, the terror. He remembered that day, it was one of the few he had seen a glimpse of Sacred Suneater before their father whisked his son away into the temple. He remembered waiting outside, hearing the screams.

It was at that moment Phaidros realized that he stepped forward to the opposite side of Zenovia. "I'll... I'll do it," he said, the words spilling from him before he truly thought of them. Charon's gaze snapped to him, pained, but Phaidros continued looking up at Suneater. "I will join the Ignited and..." he hesitated for a brief moment before continuing, "would like to invoke the rite of vengeance upon the beast who slew our father."

Now Zenovia's gaze was on him. "Ash and cinders, boy, are you *trying* to get yourself killed?" she yelled, about to add more before Suneater once more held up a hand.

"The boy is owed this much if he becomes ignited," Suneater answered in a tone that bordered amusement. "A family member or loved one may invoke the rite should the person in question be slain. However... There are many hunters out there who will be eager to take on this Shaped Beast to prove themselves, and you are only now making the choice to become ignited." They lifted their head. "You will have one month to complete or abandon this quest before I return it to the other Ignited."

"One *month*?!" Zenovia cried.

Suneater's gaze remained on Phaidros. "While this is a short time,

I am sure you will be able to find those who will be able to assist you to make this challenge less daunting, hm?" The Ideal turned back to Zenovia. "Unless you are still so shaken from the experience that you do not wish to also get vengeance for your hunting partner's death?"

"That's—"

"Excellent." Suneater nodded. "The boy's odds have just increased. Now, I am sure you both have a lot of training to do. The ritual of igniting will take place tomorrow, I shall put in a request with one of the smiths to prepare him his armor and a selection of weapons."

"Hey!" Charon said, one arm waving. "Am I invisible here? What about me? I wish to get vengeance as well."

Everyone looked to Charon, as if forgetting he was there until now, the Suneater's attention fell back on the Cindered. "How do you plan to do that?"

"Well I—"

"If you ignite yourself again, there is a chance you will recover, yes, but under great stress. It will take every fiber of your being fighting for survival to claw your way back to your normal life. When you are standing here, feeling the same pain you felt months ago, will you have the strength to push past it? To walk again while your soul burns from the inside out? Or will you burn the remaining drops of potential you still have to ash? You think yourself to be on the level of the Phoenix?"

Phaidros' expression saddened as he looked to his brother. There was a deep-seated anger and guilt there. He could see the memories flashing through his blue eyes, the pain, the anguish. He knew that Charon wished to help, to do *something*, but what could a Cindered do?

"Well?" Suneater prodded.

"I… I cannot," Charon eventually said, voice strained. "I wish to but—I cannot." His head lowered.

Suneater nodded sagely. "Then you all are dismissed. The ritual shall take place at first light tomorrow. You should get some rest and prepare yourself, young Phaidros." They waved their hand. The matter was decided.

Zenovia turned and began walking, her feelings on the matter hard for Phaidros to decipher. Phaidros paused to look at his brother, Charon's eyes were still on the ground, teeth clenched.

"Are you coming or not?" Zenovia asked, looking over her shoulder, her disdain bleeding through her tone.

Phaidros stepped over to Charon, one hand going for his shoulder before the brother brought up his hand, turning and hobbling out. Phaidros sighed then followed after.

He had just signed himself up to potentially become just like Charon someday, if he failed or died at the hands of the same beast that killed his father. The thought haunted him, but he couldn't leave his brother alone in this city, or demand that he ignite himself again.

The walk back home was quiet as Phaidros pondered on his future. Zenovia remained ahead of the brothers and every attempt Phaidros made to try and walk with his brother was met with more heated stares. The sun in the sky was just beginning to set over distant mountains. They had gotten about halfway home before Charon stopped, followed by Phaidros and Zenovia soon after. Phaidros looked back to his brother. "…Charon?"

"Why did you agree to become ignited?" he asked.

There was an uncertain pause, Phaidros' brow furrowing in confusion. "I did it so that I wouldn't have to leave you all alone, brother," he answered.

"As if I couldn't take care of myself?" Charon challenged.

"What? No, with Mother *and* Father gone now all we have is each other. I wasn't about to ask you to become Ignited for my sake."

Charon grimaced. "And what, I'm supposed to just sit here on the sidelines and watch as it kills you too?"

Zenovia walked back over to them, "Your brother made his choice, the least you could do is respect it," she said with a resigned sigh, "and support him. You…" she hesitated, "are an Ignited, despite the mistakes you made, you shouldn't be lashing out like this."

Charon's eye twitched. "I have a hard time remembering that sometimes, with how everyone looks at me." He looked to Phaidros. "How long until you start looking at me like that too?"

"Charon, I–"

"Don't." He sighed. "I am sorry, I just need time to think." He then walked past him and Zenovia heading down the main road towards one of the gates. Phaidros panicked then began to move after him before Zenovia grabbed his arm.

"Leave him be. You don't need that sort of distraction right now. He'll huff and moan about it for the rest of the night and apologize by morning."

Phaidros frowned but nodded, watching his brother hobble off, worry on his features, and guilt for even feeling that worry. He stood there, hesitant, then walked off with Zenovia toward their homes.

CHAPTER 2

A path already laid out before you is a path where no lessons are learned. Take the path where strife and challenges await you.

-COLLECTED TEACHINGS OF THE EXALTED SOVEREIGN

PEOPLE ALWAYS TALKED about staying inside the walls at night, however Charon knew that if you were still in eyesight of them you were safe from predators. The sheer aura of potential in the city was usually enough to warn off most dangerous wildlife. This close to the city, only a few of the plants whipped at him as he walked through it, a minor annoyance, instead of the aggravated assault he would have faced further away from Dasos. He used to be able to stride deep into the jungle and watch as the jungle stilled before him like subjects kneeling to their king. No longer, however. Now even the trees mocked him with their whipping vines. If they could laugh, he could imagine they would do so.

The sun was now setting beyond the mountains, leaving the sky to bleed into the dark purple of night with the first few stars beginning to poke through the indigo sea above. Charon's mind stirred sluggishly. His cindered soul did not just affect him physically, but mentally as well.

He wasn't a child, just a little slower than he should be. His body and the world around him moved as if there was a one-second delay behind what he intended to do or think about, an echo in a cavern becoming his everyday life.

He had gotten used to it by now, it had only been a few months, but now he could walk, talk in complete sentences. He had improved so much and yet…

His memory stirred, everyone's look of pity. All of them looked down on him. To be Ignited required one simple thing, improve yourself, and he had failed. A failure that had continued to be a stain no matter how much he worked to fight it off. They should be proud of him for even getting this far. Yet all they saw was a man who failed. A disgrace to their order. An omen of misfortune to point at and be a reminder for all others what happens when you stopped the never-ending march to stay ahead of the fire that licked at your very being.

The thought made his grimace return as he walked through the underbrush of the jungle, careful of his step, cursing at the occasional *thwap* of a vine or fern, until he came to a small clearing in the trees where a small pond lay undisturbed. Charon took a deep, relieved breath, then went to sit down by the mossy earth beside it. Here he could finally have peace and quiet. Here no one could look at him with those pitying, disdainful eyes. Insects chittered in the background amidst the calls of birds and the sound of wind blowing through the leaves of trees. Despite all of the turmoil in his heart, all of the pain he had suffered, life continued on as if he were never even there. Charon reached into his coat pocket and flipped out a pair of glasses he did not like to wear in public and looked up into the night sky, thoughtful. Countless stars painted colorful speckles in a swathe across a backdrop of midnight blue. If you looked hard enough, you could see the billowing smoke trails of star dust marking the edges of the galaxy.

That's when he saw the traces of white light dashing through the air above. The meteor shower. He had forgotten. His brother wanted to watch it with him. A pang of guilt stabbed at him. He was too harsh. His brother thought of everyone but himself, he even said he was doing all this partially for him. Charon couldn't shake the feeling of dread however, that if Phaidros were successful, if Phaidros could become a true Ignited, a Shaped even, then he would look at Charon with the same eyes as all the others. The thought sent a shiver through his spine.

He paid more attention to the falling stars above. In old books he read, people wished on shooting stars for good luck. Perhaps that was what he needed right now. A bright one flashed overhead, teal fire burning in its wake as he closed his eyes and made a wish. "I wish to be able to help my brother." His eyes opened and the star was still there, burning, until he noticed it was getting closer. Like a thin, teal bullet it shot across the sky and landed in the jungle, causing the earth to shake briefly before stilling once more.

He blinked, struggling up to his feet as he looked toward where he saw it crash. He glanced back over to the city, hesitating, before hobbling out towards the source as fast as he could. Luckily for him, it wasn't too far, and much easier to find once he saw the snapped branches and small fires at the head of some of the great trees. All of it led to a line carved through the landscape ending at the base of a tree trunk, dirt kicked up in a large pile. At the center of the impact zone was…

"A book?" Charon muttered. Something about this was wrong. Books didn't just fall from the sky. Yet before he knew it, he was next to the book, leaning down to get a better look at it.

There appeared to be a title in front, but the crash had torn away whatever was marked and had marred the purple leather that bound the book. Charon reached out with one hand, poking the book once. He expected it to feel hot and was surprised to find it pleasantly cool. He gently picked up the book, looking it over. There were no other letters on the cover, but in the light of the rising moon he was able to make out through the ruined leather the outline of a stylized skull stitched in black across the cover. The paper on the thick tome had silver leafing and the depictions of what looked to be several dozen different humanoid figures. At least that was what he found on an initial inspection; each figure had no mouth and a single, large, eye with bright teal irises like a hieroglyph taking up the majority of their heads. The longer he looked, the less human-like they appeared, multiple arms, bodies stretched and twisted in unnatural ways. Charon squinted, curious, before he could hear the sounds of boots stomping through the woods, the roar of jets accompanying soon after.

His mind lagged for a moment before he panicked and quickly hid the book beneath a pile of wood and leaves nearby left behind in what he assumed was the book's wake. As he stood he turned around to see the silhouettes of three Ignited in their armor stalking through the underbrush toward him, helmets on. He could hear a series of clicks, like an insect tapping its mandibles together coming from one of them, which was another capability of the Ignited's armor, encoded speech. There was a single click from each of their companions as they spread out, visors scanning the area while the leader with a crested helmet approached Charon. He didn't bother hiding, there was no reason for him to hide, and would look more suspicious if he did.

"What are you doing here, cindered one? It is dangerous out in the jungle at night," the leader spoke, their voice having a tin-like quality to it through the helmet's speaker. Charon's eyes flicked to the other silhouettes, the moonlight creating a gentle sheen across the ridged, black surfaces of their armor.

"I was out on a walk to try and think," he admitted. It was partially true. The leader was in front of him now, the armor giving them a good few inches of height over Charon, who tried his best to stand tall. "It is usually not so dangerous if I stay within sight of the walls," he quickly added.

There were a few clicks coming from the surrounding Ignited. The leader tilted their head to one side, sizing up Charon before looking back toward the path of destruction the book made as it fell into the jungle. "And you thought it wise to take a detour to see whatever just fell from the sky?"

Charon raised an eyebrow. "Surely if a meteor dropped it would be no harm to me after it had fallen? How often does one get to see a fallen star, let alone one that apparently harms others?"

A few more clicks from the others and they all gathered around the leader again and all looked to Charon. The leader was the one to respond. "If it was a meteor," he mused, glancing at the impact site. "Yet there is no meteor here. Did it get up and walk off?" he asked, incredulous.

Charon shrugged. "How would I know? It was barren when I got here. Perhaps it shattered as it passed through the jungle? It seemed to burst through plenty of trees." He could feel the leader's stare and narrowed his eyes at the man. "What? You think I picked up a meteor. I'm cindered. I can barely stand up straight." It pained him to tear himself down like that, but if it would make the others feel guilty and leave him be it would be worth it. The self-jab seemed to have the intended effect. The Cindered were still brothers and sisters, ones meant to still be protected despite their failure. Unity guides the sword of valor and the Ignited must lift each other up whenever they can and whatever else the Exalted Sovereign spouted. To *subtly* suggest that these three were calling the person they were supposed to protect suspicious and a liar would not hold well. The leader of the group took a single, defensive step back.

"I would not begin to think you are lying to us, cindered one," the leader replied. "Please, forgive me if I led you to believe that." He bowed his head, then looked to the others.

"You are forgiven," Charon said with a nod, frowning. "…You are right though, a meteor wouldn't have walked off as it did. What *are* you expecting exactly?"

The leader hesitated then shook his head. "We were simply on orders from Sacred Suneater to keep an eye out for falling stars near the city. For what reason? It is not my place to question them."

Charon nodded. "Very well, good hunting."

"Are you sure you don't need an escort back to the city?"

Charon smiled softly. "Whatever danger there may be, you're heading in the direction it would be coming from. I know I am in safe hands."

The leader nodded, stepping past him. There were another few clicks and the three disappeared into the jungle. Charon sat down as they left, letting out a breath he didn't realize he was holding. He felt dizziness threaten to take him before he shook it off, breath steadying. Why was he hiding the book from them again? Perhaps because he knew they would take it. Once he was a little more confident he was safe, he retrieved the book from its hiding place and walked back to the pond he was at earlier, not ready to return to the city just yet.

Charon sat back at the edge of the pond, the moon high enough in the sky that he could look at the book again. There was no lock or anything on it, how did it survive the fall...?

Unable to contain his curiosity any further, he opened the first page, which had the consistency of aged parchment. The text on the page was in a language he was unfamiliar with. "That's disappointing," he said with a soft sigh... looking back at the page again at the marks at the top of the page.

Death is not the end. It is a new beginning.

Charon started. The words were coming from inside his head. He glanced this way and that, had the Ignited come back? No... he was alone. He looked back at the page, looking at the first line again and heard the same words repeated in his head a few seconds later. Intrigued, he continued 'reading' the page.

> *Death is not the end. It is a new beginning. Take my knowledge and see that you have been lied to. The God of Life would see you march underneath his banner under what his definition of true potential is. I offer an alternative. One that tosses away the shackles to life, the shackles placed upon mortality itself. Read my works and become eternal. Read my works and become greater than any Ideal raised by Life.*

That got a small laugh out of Charon. Greater than an Ideal? Hard to believe. Let alone possible for a Cindered... still, the opening page had amused him enough that he flipped to the next page to a table of contents. "Let's see here..." The book had a list of topics that he began to read through. *Basic Vitaemancy, Advanced Applications: Soul-Binding, Reanimation, Fleshcrafting, Bone Molding, Soul Manipulation, Dead Matter Manipulation, Soul Sight, Geas Formation.* Each one had dozens of pages listed as being relevant to each. *Rituals: Gate Construction,*

Ascension, Mentor. This was… morbid. Such powers seemed like powers reserved for a particularly macabre Shaped and beyond. That last one made him double take. Mentor? He flipped through the pages towards the end of the book, giving him glimpses of diagrams and blocks of texts in the same, strange language until he got to the ritual described.

Mentor Ritual

The following ritual is for struggling practitioners. The only requirement is an offering of blood and a reflective surface along with the following.

Beyond that was an intense series of complex diagrams and explanations that someone would have to study for years to be able to truly comprehend. Yet… the longer he stared at the page, the more it seemed to make sense, the innate knowledge of the book seeming to bury itself directly into his mind. Even though he could never describe or put to words the knowledge that the book contained, he could recreate it, a thought that should have terrified him.

Charon gently placed the book down on a nearby rock, looking from its pages to the pond. *This will do*, he thought, then shuffled on his knees to the edge of it. A look at his reflection in the water made him hesitant. *Am I really about to try this?* he thought to himself before he reached into his coat pocket and pulled out a pocket knife he kept on him—it was about all he could wield efficiently without tiring himself—then gently pricked his thumb on it with a small wince. Blood welled onto his thumb before he squeezed it out into the pond. He reached out with his thoughts, with his will, doing… something, something that he could not describe as he held his hand out and watched the reflection. There was no flash or shimmer, or any other thing one might expect from a flex of power. Instead, when Charon blinked down at his reflection in the pond, another figure stood beside him, just behind. His mind lagged again before he yelped, spinning around gracelessly to see that there was no one there. He stared out at the jungle for a long moment, wondering if the other Ignited might have heard him. His heart was pounding in his chest before he slowly turned his attention back to the pond.

The figure was still there, its single teal eye staring unblinking at him through the reflection in the pond.

Hello.

The voice that came with it was like countless voices all calling out in perfect chorus with one another with a deep bass that made the surface of the pond tremble. Its tone was singular, as if trapped in a permanent state of exaltation. Charon couldn't help but stare, wide eyed with terror. The creature on the other side was no mere humanoid. It looked to be about ten feet tall and had two long, atrophied legs that connected to a stretched-out torso. It had eight arms ending in clawed fingertips, two crossed over its chest, fingers digging into the flesh, two before itself beneath the other arms clasped in prayer, and the final four splayed behind the creature and bent unnaturally as if imitating the wings of a bird. The upper half of its face was taken up by a carved, teal eye outlined in black around the unblinking lid. The figure itself had lines tracing across its entire form as if it had been yarn twisted together, waiting to be unraveled; yet the quality of its skin appeared to be more like porcelain. He had seen a depiction of this creature on the book itself.

You have called and we have answered, it rumbled.

Charon sat there, stunned as his mind struggled to process all that he was seeing and hearing. Was it all a hallucination? Had he fallen asleep at the pond? He looked to his bleeding thumb, the ache swelling from the now open wound with more blood beginning to ooze out. He was definitely awake. His eyes slowly turned back to the ever-staring *thing* in the pond.

"What... what are you?" was the first question that managed to push its way through the thick fog of his mind.

*"We are the Father's **Exaltation**,"* it answered, the final word making Charon's throat dry and his body weaker than it already was, as if an invisible force begged him to supplicate before this creature even if it was only a reflection he was looking at. *We are here to guide those who seek the Father's power.*

"The Father's power?" Charon asked, a tremble in his voice now that wasn't there before. He gulped, feeling like a paralyzed rodent trapped in the gaze of a serpent. "Then it is not your book?"

No. We are but a piece of him, his gift to the world, his sacrament.

Charon could not think of another reply quickly, so many questions churned in his head. He realized that the normal ambiance of the jungle disappeared. It was now dead silent, save for the sound of his own breathing. "And how are you going to help me? I managed to use the ritual here somehow without even being able to understand the language in it."

Such is the ingenuity of the Father, it answered, tone increasing in reverence to this 'father' that it spoke of. *To be able to give power so freely to all that seek it. A kindness to all mortals to conquer that which they fear most.*

"And what is it they all fear?"

Death and the oblivion that follows.

A deafening silence followed. Charon couldn't believe what he was hearing. This was a madman's talk. Yet, the book had fallen from the sky. It was clearly what the Ignited were looking for but why? What use did they have for a book with the power over death when they were already granted immortality by the Exalted Sovereign?

You have questions, its voice broke through his thoughts. *Ask,* it beckoned.

"People were looking for this book. Ignited. What would they want with 'the Father's' power? Do you mean the Exalted Sovereign? Potential is the power of life after all."

Falsehoods. They seek to hide our Father's power from mortals, it lamented, though its voice remained trapped in the rapturous Exaltation of this father it kept talking about. *It is power that challenges them that does not require suffering to get it, so in their envy they seek to destroy it.*

Charon chewed on those words. Power to rival the Ideals and the Ignited. Were the Ideals truly keeping this from them? How could a mortal become powerful without becoming ignited? No matter how much he turned the thoughts over in his head it seemed impossible... and yet with no training he managed to summon this 'sacrament' in the first place. He... a Cindered, was able to do that. "How then? I am Cindered, such power should not be possible for me to wield."

Poor child, the victim of an abusive god burning any who do not march ever onward faster than the flame licking at their heels. You do not need such potential to wield the power of the Father. All that is required is a soul and the knowledge of which to manipulate it. Read the book, we beg you to take the Father's knowledge and see that we speak the truth.

His eyes trailed back to the book in question, still opened to the page on the ritual he performed moments before. He felt it calling to him, beckoning him to take its knowledge and use it. The idea was tempting, too tempting, overwhelmingly tempting. Charon licked his dry lips, staring unblinkingly at the book. If he could master it... then he would no longer be useless, the others would no longer look at him with those condescending eyes. His brother wouldn't be able to leave him behind as he advanced past heights that Charon could only hope to achieve.

Use the book, he heard Exaltation call from the pond.

Fear broke through his thoughts like a hammer shattering glass. No, no he could not use this book. Any power that came from such a creature or whoever created it could not be good or right. Hands that were reaching for the book slammed it shut before hesitating, one palm flat on the cover. If he wasn't going to use it... what would he do with it?

He could give it to Sacred Suneater, but the thought made his stomach twist. That is what he *should* do, yet the pit in his stomach prevented his thoughts from focusing on that solution. No, not yet. He could try and destroy it, yet that seemed to be even worse. His fingers trailed over the ridges that outlined the skull on the ruined cover. The power to conquer death supposedly lay in the pages beneath. He set his jaw, fingers clutching at the edge of the binding before he picked up the book. "I... I need to think about it," he said as quickly as his mind allowed, tucking the book into his coat. The creature did not respond. He was grateful for that, though he hesitated for a moment to wonder if he should look back in the pond and see that it was still there.

Sense won out in the end and he grabbed his cane and began making his way back towards Dasos. He had much to think about, but he didn't want to rush into a decision just yet and leaving the book out here for anyone to pick up or potentially take back to Suneater seemed like a horrible option in comparison. So, for now... he'd keep it, just in case. If it meant that he could progress alongside his brother without the need to go back through that pain again... then perhaps it was worth it.

CHAPTER 3

We care not from where your blood reigns, only where it is
spilled. Let no person be born into greatness, let greatness
come with arms clasped together as we achieve it as one.

-COLLECTED TEACHINGS OF THE EXALTED SOVEREIGN

P HAIDROS' EYES OPENED. He stared at the stone ceiling above him in a bleary haze as an alarm chimed beside him. When he peered towards the window he saw that the sun had barely begun to creep into the sky. The alarm was a formality as usually his father would have been awake by now and knocking on his door. He used to dread it; now he missed it, another small reminder that his life had been permanently altered. The simplicity of waking up, training with a sword through the day, studying hunting tactics at night, and spending time with his father and Charon in the evening had been wrenched away from him. Before today he was never sure if he was going to become Ignited, but as long as his family was around him, that would have been okay. Now? Now he felt as if he was in free fall and he was grasping at anything he could to stop the pit in his stomach. Today he was to become Ignited and whether he liked it or not, he had to move forward. A million different fears crept through his mind, voices similar to his own telling him that he could never live up to his father, that he would fail like his brother.

He pulled himself upright, rubbing at one eye before moving into an accompanying bathroom in his room to get cleaned and dressed in a uniform his father had been saving for this day. Dasos being a holy city for the Ignited, everyone was expected to adhere to the same military fashion that the Exalted Sovereign had once worn when he was mortal: black uniforms with high collars that hugged the neck with clean pressed trousers tucked into boots. Those that had made successful hunts were allowed to adorn their uniforms with trophies of what they had hunted, making the uniform itself a blank canvas waiting to be adorned with shows of victory and improvement in one's own life. This led to many Ignited being adorned with necklaces of fangs and claws of predators or pelts of fur or scales across that which would normally be modern dress outside the jungle. Only Ignited could wear them, and until today Phaidros had worn the grey reserved for Kindlings, those who worked for or were under the protection of Ignited.

Phaidros made a quick check in the mirror to make sure all looked well. As he brought a hand up to fix his collar, he realized his hands were shaking. He heard the voice of his father echoing in his mind teachings of the Exalted Sovereign, *when life seems uncertain and you are unsure where to go, move forward, for wherever you are going will be better than the place you were before.* He took a deep breath, running a hand through his curly hair as he gripped the sink beneath the mirror. His head hung for a moment as he let the dread wash over him before he pushed himself upright and forced himself to leave into the main room of the house. Everything here was as utilitarian as the rest of the city. The room was an open floor plan, with enough space for working out and several machines to assist with it, a sitting area for eating, and a small kitchen. Phaidros rummaged for some dried jerky and bread, chewing on it thoughtfully as his gaze inevitably fell upon Charon's door. His brother's words still echoed in his head and guilt added to the gnawing emptiness in his stomach.

He walked to the door, lifting a hand to knock but hesitated. What could he say that could make it better? After a long moment he sighed quietly and went back to the kitchen to prepare something for him. He left the plate out on the counter and finished his own breakfast and stopped at the front door, taking a deep breath. "Alright, let's do this, one step forward," he muttered, then he pushed his way out of his home and into the outside, where rows of similar, two-story stone block buildings stretched on in both directions. The people outside were all heading up towards the temple at the top of the hill the city was built upon. Phaidros started his way up towards it with the rest of the crowd, where his future awaited him.

Ignited weren't required to come to the ceremonies of the newly ignited, however it was considered taboo to not do so. They were all supposed to be 'lifting each other up' after all, and how could one do that if they weren't even willing to meet or welcome their newest member into the fold? Usually there would also be more advanced notice with multiple supplicants becoming ignited in the same ceremony. The urgency of Phaidros' igniting made it so there was less time for fanfare. Still, the usually grand, empty hall was filled with hundreds of Ignited.

Phaidros scanned across the sea of heads. Most were familiar in some manner having been acquaintances to Zaharias or simply someone he saw walk or run by throughout the years spent in Dasos. Some were complete strangers. Dasos held several thousand Ignited, Phaidros wasn't sure of the true number, but new Ignited arrived every day and others left. He could see some of the ra perched up in the rafters, taloned feet hanging as hawk-like eyes stared down at him. He could see the tree-like drasil with their leaf-like or vine hair and bark faces communicating in a tongue he didn't understand. Then the ikaroa made up some of the shorter specimens, a few having frog-like faces and bald heads while others looked mostly humanoid with a few features that reminded others of their origins from the sea. He recognized one as he walked in, who turned to look at him with pitch black eyes. They smiled, showing razor-sharp teeth that made Phaidros immediately look away in fear. Others that he passed nodded to him as they noticed him, others gave polite and much less frightening smiles and a few waves before returning to whatever idle task they were doing while they waited.

With so many Ignited in one place, the room itself seemed to glow as if lit by hundreds of independent fires. People bustled about, keeping a center line open for the new blood that was to join them but otherwise were talking and laughing among old friends, rivals, or a mixture of the two. Everyone here was adorned in various trophies whether it be medals won in wars from far-off worlds or the pelts and furs of beasts slain. One man among them seemed to tower over the rest of the crowd, the black antlers on his head making him even more so. His eyes had no pupils and had an almost metallic sheen to them that scintillated different colors as the light hit them. He wasn't talking to anyone around him, his attention on Phaidros the moment he stepped through the doors. Phaidros tried to avoid his eye contact as well.

Each step Phaidros took from then on was heavier than the last. As he walked down the space cleared for him the talking slowly died down aside from a few whoops and hollers from some in attendance. At the end of the path was Sacred Suneater, dressed in their armor and standing upon the massive root that tore through the back of the temple. They were quiet while the rest cheered, the weight of their glowing, white gaze felt as if Phaidros was wading through the deep ocean. At the base of the main root in front of Suneater were two armored Ignited with something held in their upturned palms. They did not speak, but held the object in their hands with reverence.

Phaidros got halfway through the temple when he realized why he felt so heavy. It was the weight of expectation. He would not be the first to be ignited so quickly with such a daunting task ahead of him, nor would he be the last. Those stories ended in either one of two ways: the Ignited shining brightly and fiercely before they were quickly snuffed out by the world, or their burning brightness made them Shaped. More often it was the former. By now he knew it was too late to back out. He walked ahead in silence, his features locked on Suneater, his jaw clenched and breath held in his chest.

The Suneater raised a hand as Phaidros neared the base of the great root and the final, rogue cheers were silenced. A quiet moment passed while Suneater watched Phaidros from on high. "We are gathered here today to welcome the newest member to our order. Phaidros, son of Zaharias," Suneater began, gesturing to the man before him, "who was slain and now walks in the memory of the world with his ancestors and his ancestors before him. May his soul find its ideal self in his new life where it could not in its old." Suneater and all those present dipped their heads in respect, Phaidros fighting back tears as he stared upward toward Suneater. The moment of silence passed and the Ideal continued, "Phaidros, the ritual we partake in today is not just an igniting of a soul to further its potential but a binding contract between you and the Exalted Sovereign. He will grant you power and eternal life and in return, he asks but one thing: improve yourself, become the best *you* that you can be, and seek not only to survive and live in this world but to thrive in it. Do you understand the responsibilities expected of you?"

A new weight fell over Phaidros, different from the presence of the Suneater or the gaze of all of the Ignited in the room watching him. He fought the urge to look around even as he felt something pressing in on his very soul, like someone had rested an anvil on his chest. "I understand," he replied, throat dry and voice barely above a whisper.

Suneater nodded, then stepped down from the root, the two Ignited at the base clearing way for the Ideal, each dropping to one knee and lifting up the object they held to them as they passed. It was a sword, sheathed in a scabbard that looked like it belonged on some storied king's belt. Suneater lifted the sword with care, speaking in a voice loud enough for the rest of the temple to hear, addressing them all, "Then let us begin." They drew the blade from its scabbard with a hiss of steel. As it exited its sheath it blazed in a glorious white fire, the fire of potential made manifest and physical in this world as it bathed the whole temple in its glorious light. Suneater held it aloft and Phaidros stared in awe at its beauty. The blade was like nothing he had ever seen, as if it had captured the very essence of all that was divine and regal and was molded in their image. Even Suneater looked up at the blade with some manner of awe. "Behold, a blade of the Exalted Sovereign. His final gift to what would become the Order of the Ignited before his ascension. This and all of its kin stand as a reminder of everything that we stand for." Suneater lowered the blade, pointing it at Phaidros. "That we must all give a piece of ourselves so the rest may prosper. That no one person must stand against a cruel and unforgiving world alone. With this piece of the Exalted Sovereign himself, we may elevate any who wish to better themselves no matter their background, no matter how much they've suffered in the past." They brought the blade back so some of the still-burning blade rested against their palm without burning them. They stepped closer to Phaidros. "Kneel, Young Phaidros, and speak the tenets of his world and in so doing, allow you to take your first steps forward in a new, better life." Phaidros kneeled before them, eyes cast to the stone ground beneath. Suneater raised their voice, beckoning to all present to join in as they began the tenets. "We do not pray amidst the pews."

"We roar on the field of battle!" the Ignited chanted back, Phaidros joining them, albeit quietly.

"We care not from where your blood reigns," Suneater called.

"Only where it is spilled!" the Ignited replied in unison. Phaidros took a deep breath, the warmth of the presence of all the Ignited around him filling him with some measure of confidence to fight back the doubt that plagued his mind.

"Separated we are led astray!" Suneater's voice increased in volume and something was happening within Phaidros as the blade in Suneater's hands rested on Phaidros' shoulder.

"United our valor is known!" the Ignited answered. As Phaidros looked up toward Suneater, he no longer saw the Ideal but two, piercing, glowing blue eyes staring back at him, pupils narrow much like a feline's.

"We set ourselves apart in our deeds!" Suneater's voice rose one final time, though to Phaidros, it sounded like he was far away, the temple around him bleeding away and hidden by a thick and heavy fog. Those eyes staring him down were unblinking, curious, it seemed, to see if Phaidros would say the final words.

"So the sum of our whole grows stronger," Phaidros spoke, no longer hearing the Ignited that had surrounded him before, but still felt the blade lift off of one shoulder and touch the other. His voice echoed through the fog with no reply to answer him. He was alone with those eyes, the only thing he could make out through the fog. They were both as small as a house cat's and as vast as the open sky as his mind struggled to perceive what was in front of him. Was he alone now? He wasn't sure. His gaze turned this way and that and saw nothing. His gaze eventually returned to the eyes before him and he let out a hesitant "Hello?"

Silence…

Then, he felt a breeze flow through, disturbing the fog around him, allowing him to see curls and shapes within. On the sudden wind came new scents, the fresh dew of a spring morning, the smell of cities burning followed by the new fresh air that took its place in the aftermath. A cacophony of sounds, the sounds of natural life with birds in the trees and insects buzzing, of men and women fighting and bellowing war cries and dying, of steel ringing against steel. The more Phaidros tried to focus on what he was hearing however, he was surprised to be able to make out words. *You have much potential, Phaidros, yet I can feel the fear and doubt that surrounds you. Are you sure this is what you want?*

Phaidros' jaw gaped, was that *the* Exalted Sovereign himself? How did he even respond? How did he react? Finally finding his wits, he responded. "I-I have seen what the price of failure is, my lord"—was that what you were supposed to address him as?—"I mean, Sovereign One, and I fear that I will be the next victim of it." He paused before adding, "I know I must move forward. That is all I can do."

The wind blew around him again and with it the sounds and scents of blood soaking the ground before it too fed new plant and animal life in what was once lost. *And that is why you will not fail. Many will be gripped by fear and despair and dig their heels into the soil in the hopes that change will not come for them. Life is change and uncertainty. To become paralyzed by this is to accept stagnation over growth, death over life.*

The God's words made the tension Phaidros was holding release, if only somewhat. "I must move forward for the sake of my brother and the memory of my father. I won't let fear rule me, most exalted one, I promise."

Life grew and thrived and between groaning trees and whistling birds the God's voice came forth once more. *A promise made of selflessness, how refreshing. Yet that is not why you fight. You fight for survival, to cling to what once was. If you do not let go, then you will share your brother's fate.*

Phaidros lost his words. "I will," he assured, both himself and his God.

You must, the voice returned through the sounds of roaring beasts. *I command you to thrive, Phaidros, I will accept nothing less, nor will the world around you. Show the world who you are.*

Warmth followed, oppressive warmth, a flash of fire that seemed to surround every fiber of his being and roar to life. He could see the tendrils of it lashing around him. The suddenness of the experience forced him to gasp and with that breath his perception snapped back to the temple.

It was as if every breath before had been shallow, tainted, in some way, like a person living in a smog-filled city breathing fresh air for the first time in their life. Phaidros blinked, once, twice, as he saw, truly saw, the world around him for the first time. The colors of his surroundings seemed to become more saturated and detailed. He could outline each individual furrow of the bark-like skin of Suneater above him, the individual leaves behind their head and a few insects buzzing through the air far behind them. Sound came in as the roar of celebration of his fellow Ignited finally tuned through his senses, different pitches and tones being able to be picked out through the raucous uproar.

Phaidros looked down at his hands in some disbelief, the words of the Exalted Sovereign echoing in his head. *Life is change and uncertainty.* Just a day ago he had been under the protection of his father, a worthy warrior of the Ignited, and his brother only months prior to that. Before all that he would have disagreed with the Exalted Sovereign but now? His words rang true. He felt within himself the fire that burned and raged, eager to feed and grow. It made it difficult not to run out into the jungle right now and try to seek vengeance immediately, but he stuffed the thought back down. The darkness of uncertainty had been washed away through divine purpose and an innate sense of belonging from being surrounded by so many familiar flames as his. Yet even then he could feel it creeping along the edges of his mind, like a predator waiting beyond the light of a campfire, ready to strike the moment it flickered. A nervous smile finally spread across his face as he looked around at his new brothers and sisters and up at Suneater. "Thank you all," he said, his voice somehow coming out stronger than it had all day. "I swear on this day that I will live up to the expectations of the Exalted Sovereign, you all, and myself. Today I will no longer live but thrive as you all strive to do."

"And so it is spoken and so the contract is sealed. Welcome, Phaidros, to the Order of the Ignited," Suneater said, expression unmoving despite the warm tones carried on the wind of their voice. "Let whatever past there was before this moment be forgotten, all that matters now is the path ahead, and the steps you take through it." The Suneater waved a hand, signaling the others were free to do as they wished.

Many approached Phaidros, hands clasping onto his shoulder and personally welcoming him to the order, others left. Through the crowd he could finally see Zenovia leaning against one of the walls, arms folded and waiting with a barely perceivable smile on her otherwise fierce expression. Sacred Suneater also seemed to be waiting upon him.

When there were only the three of them left Phaidros glanced between them. "So... what happens now?"

"The most important part," Zenovia cut in. "We get to give you your armor and you get to pick out a weapon to focus on."

"Just one?" Phaidros asked curiously. Whatever this creature he was to face was like, he felt like he'd need every tool available to him to be able to best it.

Suneater answered this time. "It's much easier to improve yourself when you have just one path to focus on. Once an Ignited has gained enough mastery of a weapon they tend to pick another to focus on. I've seen some Ignited covered head to toe in different weapons and tools."

Phaidros nodded. "Where do we go, then?"

"I had contracted one of our smiths, Daxia, to prepare your selections. It should be ready now," Suneater answered.

"It still seems odd to me that there are those in the Ignited that are not warriors," Phaidros mused.

"Based on the tenets, one would think that, but no. There are many battlefields in life, young one. Some find it out in the jungles, others in surgery rooms, and some in their forges." Phaidros had never thought of it like that, and it only made him curious to actually go meet one of the smiths. "No more questions for now. Go you both, you have only a month from now to kill your beast and it would be a shame if we wasted it all on questions about the order. You will find her in her workshop in the Smith's district, workshop number thirty-six."

Both Phaidros and Zenovia bowed to Sacred Suneater in respect. "Thank you, Sacred Suneater, for your assistance in this," Phaidros said. Suneater only nodded in response. Phaidros and Zenovia then left the temple to go find this 'Daxia.'

The Smith's District was between the roads that led out to gates two and three in the northeast of the city. The city itself built as near a perfect circle as can be, with all nine roads spiralling outwards towards the 9 gates that lined the edge equidistant from one another. Each 'District' was between one of these roads. This excluded the Merchant's District, which was the city's one connection to the outside galaxy at large and was left outside of the wall. The Smith's District provided a break between the overgrown look of the city, with most of the branches and roots steering clear. The buildings were still small, each made to house a singular smith's forge and workshop, but were made out of newer, fabricated stone rather than whatever was made in the city's origin. In front of each workshop was a sign with a number on it, correlating with which street it was on and position in the row. Phaidros couldn't help but notice how the air differed here from everywhere else, like fire and ash. His new senses forced him to taste the smell of industry that permeated the Smith's District.

Eventually the two Ignited made it to Daxia's workshop. Above the double doors was a sign painted in galactic common that read *Daxia's*

Hoard. "This is it," Zenovia said, examining the building. "I don't remember any smiths named Daxia. Must be a newer arrival. Hopefully she isn't too burnt to be of use."

Phaidros frowned. "Suneater has to know the situation we're in and gave us someone they knew would be able to help us."

"Suneater might have also given us the worst of the bunch to give us more of a challenge, it's always a toss-up." She sighed, stepping towards the door and knocking. "Let's see which it is."

Silence followed. From here, Phaidros could pick up the sound of something burning on the inside pause before a voice from the inside called out, "It's open." Without any further invitation the two opened the door and stepped inside.

CHAPTER 4

*The war we wage within ourselves does not care whether you are a
soldier or an artist. Each of us finds conflict in our lives, each of us
has our own battlefield to conquer. Let those who toil in the fields and
workshops be as mighty in your eyes as those that wield the blade.*

-Collected Teachings of the Exalted Sovereign

THE FIRST THING Phaidros thought as he stepped into Daxia's
workshop was that the word 'hoard' described it perfectly.
Where he had expected to see an armory of clearly distinct
racks of weapons and sets of armor, instead he saw a cluttered mess. In
one pile was a collection of swords and axes haphazardly placed atop
one another. Against one wall were racks of pistols, rifles, bows and their
quivers all competing for the same studs keeping them from falling to
the floor. A few metal exoskeletons flanked the back weapon rack like
statues. The actual counters were covered in what Phaidros could only
assume were half-finished products and the only clean spot Phaidros
managed to find was the front desk in the middle of the room in front
of the door.

He looked at Zenovia with a small grimace. Zenovia had a plain look of disappointment on her face before the two finally looked into the workshop proper to their left.

There, amidst all of the machinery and tools that made up the forge was a single set of ignited armor on a stand that had various mechanical arms with different ends currently not in use. The black chitin plating gave it the appearance of a sinuous bug, with small ridges forming where the plates interlocked with one another. It seemed… rather ordinary from what Phaidros had seen before, save for the left gauntlet being larger than what was standard. What then caught his attention was the Ignited currently fiddling with something Phaidros couldn't see beneath one of the plates.

Daxia hadn't even bothered to look at them when they had entered, clearly too focused on her work. She wore the same uniform that Zenovia and Phaidros wore but seemed to only be keeping it draped over her shoulders rather than properly wearing it, revealing a plain shirt that might have been white but was covered in oil and grease stains. Those were the normal things he noticed. Everything else was not what he expected. Two near-black, jagged horns extended out from Daxia's head backwards in an arc. Her cream-colored hair could be described more like a mane that had been tied back out of her face in a messy ponytail while she worked, revealing two sharply pointed ears. Beneath her hairline and creeping into all of her olive-brown face were scales a similar color to her horns and extended down her neck. He found similar scales to be covering her hands which each ended in chipped, claw-like nails. Behind her he noticed a spined tail as long as she was tall, which was hard to gauge while she sat, and ended in a tuft of fur similar in color to her hair.

She finally looked up to them and Phaidros could now see her eyes. The pupils were serpentine slits surrounded by deep crimson as if a black sword rested against molten-hot iron. To Phaidros she looked like a demon that had crawled its way out of the old stories and into the world. She sat up straighter and Phaidros felt the hair on the back of his neck stand up.

She then let out a big yawn. The motion revealed two lines on either corners of her mouth that separated to show darker red skin as her jaw extended way farther than Phaidros thought would be possible. "You're Phaidros, right?" she asked, rubbing at one eye with the back of her hand. She sounded exhausted, and way less intimidating than Phaidros had expected. He looked over to Zenovia who stared at Daxia with surprise.

"You're a longshi," she said.

Daxia sighed. "Here we go…"

"longshi?" Phaidros blinked. "Like… a dragon?" he said in disbelief. There were many tales about dragons, most of them horrifying, and from what Phaidros understood, mostly in opposition to the Order of the Ignited.

"Alright." She put up her hands. "Let's just stop this before it starts. You're here for your armor right, kid?"

The fire of his potential burning within him gave him the strength to answer her—and to not ask her a million questions about dragons. "Yes, sorry. I'm Phaidros and this is Zenovia, it is nice to meet you, Daxia."

She nodded in appreciation as he changed the subject. "Yeah," she answered simply before she looked back at the armor, "I was just finishing her up. I had to work all through the night to get the plates all fashioned right. Annoying things were rather stubborn about becoming all you-shaped." She gestured vaguely to Phaidros, before continuing, "So I couldn't afford to do anything fancy with it."

Phaidros felt a question about what that was supposed to mean on his lips followed by a pang of guilt. "I'm sorry, thank you for the effort though. I'm sure it'll be fine." He looked up to the armor, approaching it curiously, leaning in to inspect the gauntlet. "Though I did notice the uneven gauntlets. Why is that?"

"Ah, right. I did add *one* thing," she said with a slow nod and pushed herself off her chair. She was about a foot shorter than both Zenovia and Phaidros, which put her horns at dangerous eye level. Her tail swayed behind her as she opened up a plate and tapped on unseen buttons. From the underside of the gauntlet the plate lifted and a chitin pointed much like a stinger launched forward and stabbed at the open air in front of its hand. Phaidros let out a surprised sound and leapt back to safety; Daxia only grinned. "It's always good to have a little extra surprise out there." She grinned sheepishly. "If you don't like the look of the set, don't worry about it. The plates all start to change as you wear them anyway."

Phaidros blinked. "They do?"

Zenovia spoke up, "The chitin you see on the armor is reactive to your potential. People still debate on the exact cause but the general agreement is that it becomes a reflection of the person beneath the armor as people begin to associate the two as one."

"That's incredible," Phaidros said. "Where do you get the chitin then?"

Daxia pointed down. "There's some insect found all over the galaxy if you dig around in the earth enough. They're large and just as the lady put it they're extremely reactive to potential. The smiths put out commissions to hunt them for their chitin and we fashion it onto the exoskeletons you see there." She jerked a clawed thumb back to some of the exoskeletons the two had seen earlier. "Great stuff, real tough against most threats, only gets tougher as you become shaped, defined, and so on, and it has the benefit of just growing back if it gets damaged."

"Dasos has a few of those cave systems that reach down that far," Zenovia added. "Suneater sends us out on hunts for them sometimes if the supply is low."

Phaidros remembered hearing children's stories of giant insects crawling out of caves to snatch up disobedient and unruly children in the night. Those always got tears out of him and required his brother or his father to try and calm him down. The thought made his curiosity die a little as he remembered his father's fate. "Must be difficult," he said distractedly.

Zenovia seemed to pick up on something wrong and spoke again. "Why don't you try it on? Then we can figure out your weapon."

Phaidros nodded and Daxia opened up another plate and pressed a few buttons. The entire front of the armor opened up, making it so Phaidros could just step into it. "It'll be a little snug in there but you'll get used to it." Phaidros approached the armor wearily and slid into place, the armor closing around him with a hiss of various airlocks and seals. "The suit has a neural net attached to it that'll sync up with your thoughts so once you get the hang of everything you'll be able to use all of the suit's systems as if it were second nature." She closed the panel and knocked on the shoulder. "Take a few steps around for me will you?" She walked away from the other Ignited to rummage around at one of the far tables.

In front of Phaidros' face the three slits that made up the visor shimmered before suddenly he had an unobstructed view of everything in front of him. Various notifications began cycling through his vision as he looked around. All of the weapon pile silhouettes began to be highlighted red while Zenovia and Daxia were highlighted in blue. The data stream was fast but Phaidros found that he was able to follow all of it, which he was certain was thanks to his new powers as an Ignited. He took one step forward and was surprised at how light his whole body felt, which in turn made him stumble off of the armor stand before catching himself.

"Careful there," Zenovia said, arms out as if to catch him if he fell. "One wrong thought and you'll smash through the wall."

"Break my workshop and I'll break you," Daxia chimed in from the side, finally turning around to reveal she was getting herself coffee. She took an idle sip.

Phaidros took a second step that was much more coordinated than the first as he walked back and forth through the workshop. "I feel light," he commented, though Zenovia raised an eyebrow and Daxia was smirking. "What?"

"The voice encoder is on," Zenovia pointed out with a sigh. "We can't understand a word you're saying. Turn it off."

Phaidros had no idea how to turn it off but he tried to focus on that thought. A small flash of text in the corner of his display highlighted, reading *encoder disabled.* "Like this?"

"There we go," Daxia said with a grin, her tail swaying behind her in satisfaction. "Nice and easy, yeah?" Phaidros nodded and she gestured with a free hand towards the various piles of weapons around the workshop. "Take your pick."

Phaidros looked around to the cluttered weapons with some wariness. "Any of them?"

"Yes, just try not to disturb the piles too much."

"Why do you keep this place so cluttered anyway?" Zenovia asked.

"It's not cluttered," Daxia snapped back. "Everything has its place so I can remember where it is."

"You can do that while keeping the place clean," Zenovia replied flatly.

While the two argued, Phaidros carefully picked his way across the room to take a look at his options. He thought back to better days of his father teaching him how to use a sword with Charon watching close by. Phaidros had been an eager learner at the time, before everything changed. He didn't want to just default to a sword without seeing the rest of his options, however. He walked over to the pile of guns on the counter and squinted, nervous to try and move any of them without invoking the longshi's wrath. His visor began to pick out the silhouettes again with small blurbs of text identifying them. "I don't see too many Ignited that use ranged weapons like these," Phaidros mused. "Why is that?"

Zenovia was the one to answer. "A lot of people think there's less 'danger' in picking something with range behind it. It's easier to learn how to use a rifle but people are often disappointed at what they believe is a 'low skill ceiling.'"

"What does that mean?" Phaidros asked, brow furrowed.

"It means," Daxia replied, "that Ignited prefer weapons that are harder to master and more rewarding when they do. It is better for the potential to be able to face an enemy with a sword in hand than it does with a gun because there is more personal risk and reward, or something like that."

"Seems like an odd thing to focus on when someone can just shoot you from afar and be done with it," Phaidros answered.

Zenovia sighed. "Yeah well, things start to get complicated once you get to Shaped and beyond. Daxia said it herself, the armor becomes stronger once you advance, making most attempts to harm you useless without some special trick of your own." She gestured to the suit. "Besides, a normal Ignited in one of these suits can dodge or parry bullets more often than not and energy weapons bounce off the chitin or just crack the plating. If you're hunting, some beasts just don't care about being shot if they've advanced their potential enough." Phaidros could sense some bitterness in her voice as she said that. Daxia only hummed thoughtfully and took another sip of her coffee.

"Why do you use a rifle then?" Phaidros asked, turning towards the older ignited.

Zenovia's expression fell. "When you're in the thick of it, too many people on the front lines can get messy and it can be beneficial for whoever you're fighting with as a whole to have variety. That... and being a mighty hero on the front lines is all well and good until someone with a shaped power bullet or arrow completely ignores your fancy armor. Sure, it isn't an honorable kill, but honor hardly matters when you're still alive from making a shot more than a mile away and your big scary opponent with a sword is now dead before they even knew you were there."

Phaidros stared in stunned silence, letting that thought sink in. He *could* pick a ranged weapon like that too, be someone's death before they even realized what was happening to them. Was that really what he wanted though? His stream of thoughts was interrupted by Zenovia continuing, "Besides, it doesn't matter much if we're not fighting ignited or shaped creatures. My aim's still good and I can line up a shot that'll kill three normal men in a single trigger pull if I wanted to."

Phaidros watched her for a moment longer before returning his attention to the gun pile. That was true he was sure, but even then his father still died while she lived. He hesitated, thinking maybe it would be safer this way, but then decided against it and moved to his original point of interest, the blade pile.

He had always liked carrying a sword; it made him feel like he was some fabled hero of old only remembered in myths. His emerald eyes trailed across the pile, suit highlighting as needed until he spotted one sword in particular. A sword a little shorter than he was tall. It had blue wrappings around the long hilt with enough room for him to be able to grip it easily in two hands, with a black metal cross guard and pommel, and a vibrant silver edge that extended down into the tangled mess and coming to a point at the end somewhere beneath. It was simple yet elegant, a longsword worthy of some long-dead knight. It stuck out of the pile like a sword sheathed in a nest of steel. He grabbed the hilt and carefully pulled at it. There was a strange feeling of tension as the sword was freed from the tangled confines of its brothers and sisters. The pile remained intact when the sword was finally free and he let out a sigh of relief that he was once more spared the potential wrath of an angry dragon. He held it up to the lights, finding it lighter than he initially thought it would be as he examined his reflection in the steel. Something felt right when he held it and he smiled to himself. "This will do I think." He would be able to honor his father's memory this way, yet this sword was also his own, a large, simple sword as opposed to two elegant and graceful curved blades. With a nod to himself, the decision was made.

"A bit traditional," Daxia commented, "but a good sword will treat you right if you treat it right. If it starts to wear down just bring it back to me and I'll fix it up good as new."

Phaidros nodded and smiled towards the smith, though she couldn't see it. "Thank you, Daxia, I will be sure to do so."

"Think you can make some rounds that'll punch through a shaped creature's hide?" Zenovia asked.

Daxia hummed, scratching at her scaled neck with her claws. "That's a tall order without a shaped weapon. I might be able to come up with something though, I'll have to see what the merchants can bring me. I'll get back to you on that, just give me a few weeks." Zenovia tensed, that was cutting it close, Phaidros knew, but the other Ignited nodded. "Alright if that's all then please leave," Daxia said with a shooing gesture. "I got more commissions to work on. The blade will magnetize to the back of your armor so don't worry about needing a sheath."

Phaidros felt some sense of pity for Daxia but nodded with an unseen smile. Zenovia reached up and patted him on the shoulder guard. "Alright, let's move on." Without any further delay, the two left Daxia's workshop. Zenovia led the way with an armored Phaidros following soon after with the blade resting against his shoulder. Phaidros couldn't help but notice that Zenovia still seemed bitter.

"We have a lot of work to do, Phaidros, so please, listen and don't make me repeat myself," Zenovia said dryly as she took them back towards the housing district they both resided in.

"I won't. Where are we heading first?"

"The jungle. I don't need you crashing through buildings because you accidentally activated your jets and blasted through someone's living room."

"I'm not *that* green."

"That's what they all say when they first wear the armor, I did, then two days later I got my head and shoulders stuck in a temple ceiling."

Phaidros' eyebrows raised. He wouldn't have expected a skilled hunter like Zenovia to have such issues when she started. "Point taken," he muttered.

With that, the two made a quick stop at Zenovia's house for her to get her gear, then they made their way down the main road and towards the jungle. One month… would he truly be ready by then? A rogue spark of dread wormed its way down his spine before he let the gentle warmth of his burning potential mask it. The flame made it easier to simply ignore those negative feelings. In that comforting warmth new resolve started to flicker into being. He *would* avenge his father, or die trying.

CHAPTER 5

Your mind must always be open to the future, if it lingers
in the past, then you might as well be standing still.

-COLLECTED TEACHINGS OF THE EXALTED SOVEREIGN

THE TWO IGNITED walked out of the east gate of Dasos, heading opposite the direction that Zenovia had returned from the day prior. Her armor was pristine now, the cracked plates having sealed themselves up naturally overnight. Phaidros had never gone outside of the wall all of his life except for a few trips into the Merchant's District outside of the northwest gate with his father. Unlike that gate, this one led directly out into the jungle, with not a single tree cleared before the gate proper. The jungle always unnerved him, the way the trees and ferns swayed in the distance like they were writhing against invisible binds, the distant sounds and cries of beasts he couldn't see. He hadn't known how his father and brother did it, but today he surprised himself with how he could walk alongside Zenovia with relative ease. The ignited soul most likely played a part in that.

"You've got a lot on your mind, I'm sure," Zenovia said, breaking the silence between them. "And a lot of questions on top of that. What you don't have is time for me to sit here and explain everything to you, so I will be going through the basics and you're going to listen so I don't have to repeat myself, understand?"

Phaidros blinked. "Understood, Zenovia." He was thankful for her help at all, though he could sense some tension behind her voice. Something was bothering her, but Phaidros did not have the courage to ask.

Zenovia nodded. "You're ignited now. You've probably already noticed some of what that entails"—Phaidros thought of how his vision already seemed to be improved tenfold, but didn't speak up to interrupt her—"and seen what an Ignited can do from duels in The Ring. An Ignited is stronger than the average person, faster both in how they can react to their environment and physically so. They can heal from wounds that naturally might leave men in hospitals for months at a time like broken bones and concussions. All of your senses have been enhanced and if it weren't for you being ignited, you wouldn't be able to process all the information probably going through that helmet of yours right now." She tapped on his visor a few times hard enough to make his head push back a little. "In simpler terms, you are more *alive* than the average living being, qualitatively so, and have a greater connection to all of life around you than normal beings with inert potential."

Phaidros had heard this much before, but never quite so spelled out for him. He always heard it as the Ignited being heroes among all living things, closer to the Exalted Sovereign than anything else. Whenever he asked his father about this, the man always just grinned at him and said he didn't want to ruin the surprise when *Phaidros* became ignited. The stray thought made Phaidros grow solemn again, his father dreamed of this day, and yet he never lived to see it. The downward spiral of thoughts was interrupted by a knock atop his head by Zenovia shoving at him. "Hey, I said pay attention."

"Sorry, Zenovia," Phaidros said. "I was just thinking about how my father would have wished to teach me all of this."

Zenovia paused. Silence lingered between the two of them and they had ceased walking, now surrounded by nothing but trees and the ambient sounds of the jungle. She eventually let out a frustrated sigh. "I know he would have. He mentioned it often, how he was sure you would come around to igniting soon enough and that we'd have our 'fourth hunting partner.'" Phaidros was about to speak again but Zenovia cut him off with a raised finger. "But we don't have time for that now and I won't have him haunting me because I was too busy letting you cry over his death to stop you from dying right along with him."

The words made Phaidros go stiff. "R-right," he answered, his voice straining more than he intended.

A heavy silence fell as Zenovia stood up straight again, a clear attempt to collect herself and remember where she was in her explanation. "Let me teach you about life sense." The mood didn't recover with the topic change, but Phaidros glanced over to her and nodded. "It is the innate ability of all Ignited to gain an intrinsic sense to all that lives around them." She gestured around them as they spoke. "Sit." She reached over and pushed down on his shoulder. Phaidros complied, dropping down to his knees. Zenovia joined him, sitting across from him with her rifle now across her lap as she took a deep breath. "It'll become easier with time, but for the first attempt, I will try to guide you how to do it. Take off your helmet for now." The two pulled off their helmets, Zenovia setting hers in front of her and Phaidros mimicked her. "Now close your eyes." Phaidros did so. "Take a deep breath and listen to the jungle around you."

Phaidros wasn't sure where she was going with this, but listened as instructed, it was a welcome distraction from where their conversation was going prior. Around him he heard the creak and groan of aged trees in the distance. He kept listening and picked out the droning hum of insects with the songs of birds creating a chaotic melody all their own. A snap broke through the song followed by the flutter of wings and the hiss of some unknown beast. Phaidros tried to feel for some deeper meaning beneath it all but was coming up short. "I don't see—"

"Quiet," Zenovia cut him off. "You're not trying to understand life, just feel it."

Phaidros wasn't sure what he was supposed to be 'feeling' but his failure to do so was starting to make him anxious as he sat there. He once more tried to focus, but rogue thoughts began to creep into his head. They were reminders of the price of failure, of his dead father. The sounds of life continuing as normal around him ate into his consciousness and through the warmth of his ignited potential. The chaotic melody he had heard before seemed to intensify into a cacophony of noises that all screamed to him that he was going to die. "I don't know if this is working," he said, voice strained and eyes snapping open.

Zenovia opened hers and she glared at him with an intensity that made Phaidros regret speaking. Whatever anxiety Phaidros was feeling in the moment, it was clear either Zenovia didn't pick up on his internal struggle, or didn't care. "Very well," she said with an edge to her words as she picked up her helmet and secured it back onto her head. "We'll get right into physical training."

Phaidros welcomed the news, standing back up and securing his helmet into place. Maybe physical work would be better than trying to figure out life sense; anything was better than being alone with his thoughts. "Alright, what did you have in mind?"

"I'm going to hunt you," she replied flatly.

"You're going to what?"

"You don't want to focus, you keep talking about Za, so I'm going to give you something else to think about until you realize the severity of the situation you're in."

"So what, you're just going to chase me around the jungle and–" A gunshot landed right at his feet. The sudden noise and fear of injury made Phaidros leap back. His newfound strength and the assistance of his armor carried him farther than he intended and he slammed back into a tree. The back ridges of his armor cut sharp lines through the tree's bark before he hit the ground.

"We're finished today when I crack each plate of your armor and not a moment before. If you stand there and let yourself get hit in defiance, you'll get no training and die at the end of the month if you don't cinder before then."

"You're insane!" Phaidros said, fear prevalent in his voice. She shot him again. The bullet slammed into his shoulder plate and cracked it, a single shell lodged into the center of a spider web of cracks while the impact of the blow itself sent him back against the tree.

"Talk back to me like that again and the next shot's going to be your head," Zenovia hissed. "Your armor will protect you, now get running. You'll be considered to 'pass' when you manage to make me miss or you parry a shot with your sword."

"Make you miss? Is that really that hard?" Phaidros asked, though he was already edging to the side of the tree while Zenovia kept her rifle trained on him.

"I don't miss," she answered flatly. She fired right before Phaidros could wheel around the tree out of sight. The shot caught him on the gauntlet, cracking the plating near the joint.

He didn't need any more words of encouragement and sprinted off into the jungle away from Zenovia. The armor carried him further with each step than he was used to, though he was sure some of it was part of his newly ignited soul. Behind him he heard the sound of rockets igniting and Phaidros was sure that it was Zenovia taking to the trees to follow him. His first instinct was to hide, but she would just use life sense and find him immediately. He needed a plan, any plan. Before such a plan could arise a crack pierced through the air and a bullet pierced through one of the back plates of Phaidros' armor. He panicked, scrambling to the side behind more tree cover but not before three more plates were compromised. How many did he have left? At the thought, his visor's display showed a holographic display of his armor with cracked plates highlighted in yellow. He was fine for now, but for how long? His thoughts were interrupted by a voice coming over the communications, Zenovia's. A small circle appeared on the side of his heads up display, ringed in blue. "It would be really helpful to know where to run right now if you could use life sense wouldn't it?" she taunted.

He had intended to reply, but he was much too busy running from the woman shooting at him. Phaidros leaped over a fallen log, the motion carried him high into the air and he lost control. He began to flail his limbs, careful of his sword before the plates on the back of his legs opened up and the rockets sent him further skyward. That so happened to be the perfect path to smack face first into the branch of a tree. The ensuing collision snapped the branch off entirely while it sent Phaidros into a backwards flip while still sailing forward. More shots followed, more plates were cracked, each shot landing with perfect precision before he finally hit the ground in a tumble, his sword skidding away from him. He crawled for it as quickly as he could but he was disoriented from the fall. The grass crunched behind him. *Oh no* were the last thoughts that went through his head before he saw the plate integrity of his suit drop rapidly. The crack of gunfire shook him physically while his mind screamed at him to curl up into a ball while the fire in his soul urged him onwards. He reached for his sword and grabbed it, then tried to roll onto his back while swinging, hoping to stop a bullet by chance. Instead his hand connected with a boot, sending the sword flying out of his grasp. The heel then swung back and cracked his face plate, the last few shots taking out the remaining plates on the front of his armor.

The echoes of the last shots rang through the air, Zenovia still had one foot planted on his head as she raised up the barrel of her rifle, smoke spilling from the tip. Phaidros' body still shook and he could feel the adrenaline pumping through his veins as he caught his breath. He wanted to yell at Zenovia, but fear prevented him from doing so. Instead, he let out a meek, "You could have killed me."

Her visor turned down towards him and she let the heavy silence linger for longer than he liked before she shoved her boot off his head. "I didn't," she replied in what Phaidros could swear was a growl. She crouched down to look at him, rifle resting against her shoulder. Even through the helmet Phaidros could feel her sneer. "If you think that this was difficult, then you're going to be too shaken to take a single step when you see that beast. So, all things considered, I think this was great practice." She knocked on his helmet a few times. "You got some idea of how well the armor protects you and your first taste of maneuvering with it, even if you failed spectacularly." Phaidros couldn't help but note how satisfied with herself she sounded. If the rest of her training was going to be like this, he was worried for his mental state by the end of it. "Now, your armor will repair itself by tomorrow, and we'll get to do it all over again."

"Are we done, then?" Phaidros asked. She was pulling off her helmet again but paused.

Then she laughed at him. "Ash and cinders, boy. You think I'm going to let you off the hook after just a few *minutes* of chasing you through the jungle? Get up."

Phaidros felt embarrassed as he reached for his sword and then pulled himself to his feet. "What now then?"

"We can't go hunting yet, you're just going to embarrass yourself even more than you already have. So, you've run from me, now you're going to try and hit me." She walked away from him to go put her helmet to the side. "I won't run from it or anything, just dodge as I would against an opponent that got close."

Phaidros hesitated for a moment, looking from her to the helmet she discarded. "Then why are you putting your helmet away?"

"Because you're a little spark and if you *could* hit me, you probably also would still be running from me right now."

The constant taunting and the fresh hell she just made him go through chasing him through the jungle and shooting at him finally was beginning to grind on Phaidros' nerves. His grip on his sword tightened while Zenovia just kept looking at him with a smug grin on her face. "Fine," Phaidros answered and got into a stance, blade pointed out and ahead of him towards Zenovia. He had only been trained in traditional sword fighting outside of armor. He wasn't sure how it translated with the armor, but he was sure this was where he would be able to show Zenovia he meant business. A moment of silence passed between them, then Phaidros struck.

It was a simple, diagonal chop across her shoulder as he shuffled forward. The air whistled as it arced through the air with speed Phaidros wasn't used to but even so Zenovia easily backed up out of the way. When Phaidros followed it up with a stab she weaved to the side, still smirking at him as she circled around him. "Come on, you used a blade before right? Hit me," she taunted.

Phaidros lunged for her again, striking at her with quick, efficient chops of his blade while Zenovia deftly and gracefully dodged once, twice, then on the third she brought her armored boot up to parry the blow. Such a move would have been ridiculous if she hadn't been Ignited but the power of the blow knocked Phaidros' sword aside.

"You're holding back," she noted. "You saw how your brother fought didn't you? You're Ignited now, you're not limited to conventional fighting. Hit. Me."

Phaidros grit his teeth, swinging with more force this time, utilizing the new strength of his ignited soul and aided by his armor. The force created a rush of wind in its wake but still Zenovia twisted underneath the slash and slammed her boot into his back, knocking him off balance and stumbling forward. "Better. Now just stop fighting like you're swatting a fly." Phaidros came at her again. He struck at her in wide sweeps that normally might have caught him off balance, if he were not Ignited. There was no such downside this time and unlike with the training prior, Phaidros was picking up on it much more naturally. Soon enough they were no longer confined to the clearing that they had started in. Zenovia began to dodge him by running up and kicking off of trees to get around him. She'd coax him to strike low before rocketing upwards into a spinning kick at his head. The blow sent him spiraling into a tree. Phaidros was not nearly coordinated enough yet to be able to mimic that, but he took mental notes every time Zenovia knocked him off his feet. He hadn't hit her a single time over the course of hours.

The sun was beginning to set now and Zenovia looked like she had barely lost her breath despite moving around far more liberally than Phaidros had been. Phaidros was also fine physically, but mentally he was beginning to feel the futility of it all creeping back into the edge of his mind. His strikes became frustrated lashes towards the Ignited across from him as they continued to not find purchase. Then in a sudden change of pace, Zenovia rushed at him, easily ducking under his blows as a powerful, rocket-aided kick threw Phaidros from his feet before hitting the dirt. "That's enough for one day."

"What do you mean?" Phaidros asked, offended.

"You're only getting frustrated, I can see it," she answered, "So you're going to spend the night making sure your armor repairs and think about how you're going to do better tomorrow."

"As if it'll be that easy," Phaidros said with a huff.

"It won't be," she said, narrowing her eyes at him. "And you'll thank the Exalted Sovereign that it isn't, and me, when this is all over. Welcome to the war, Phaidros, now fight for your right to live in it, like your father did."

The words sent him reeling. If he had to commend Zenovia on one thing, she had done what she had set out to do. He had spent the whole day not thinking about him; he was too busy either running for his life or trying to wipe that smug grin off her face. Now with a few words she sent him back into reality with a greater force than any bullet or kick she landed on him today. He sat in stunned silence before he couldn't meet her gaze any longer. His helmet felt suffocating and he pulled it off his head and threw it to the side. He took deep breaths, emerald eyes unable to look back up. "I will," he said, ending the silence.

He could feel her eyes on him, the weight of her expectation being a heavy burden on top of what already felt overwhelming. "You can say that all you want, 'I will' 'I'll try'; if you want me and everyone else to believe it, then do it. You have a Shaped Beast ahead of you and a fire at your heels. You have no choice now except to move forward or get burned."

Phaidros finally gathered the strength to look up to Zenovia. He wasn't sure what else to say, but felt the need to say something, anything. "What was it like?" he inevitably asked. "To fight the beast."

Zenovia paused, she clearly expected more pushback from Phaidros, not this. Her gaze shifted from judgmental to distant in a single moment. She sat down across from him, visibly pausing before speaking. "It wasn't a long fight," she began, "but I had never felt more useless in all of my days." Phaidros could hardly believe that with how soundly Zenovia beat him across the jungle. "When you become Ignited, things aren't supposed to scare you like they used to. You spend your every waking hour fighting past all that and just…" She trailed off before shaking her head. "All of it goes out the window as soon as that thing comes stalking through the trees. Let me tell you, Phaidros. I've fought in wars in far-off places, seen a lot of the galaxy and what all is out there. I've seen Shaped before, ash, I've seen *Defined* change the course of an entire battle. You think all of that prepares you, then you're sitting in a tree, firing your entire magazine into some beast that's acting like you're some annoying gnat pricking at its skin while it kills your friends." Her eyes narrowed, one fist clenched as she stared off at nothing.

The jungle around them filled in the long silence, making it seem to stretch into eternity. Phaidros did not have the right words to say to her at that moment, but he could feel a twisted blend of pity and resentment. On one hand, they were feeling the same sense of loss, but on the other she had just added to his own feeling of uselessness by how poorly he thought she had taught him today. Perhaps if she had been stronger his father would still be alive right now, perhaps if she was a better teacher, the mixing of anger and fear in his gut wouldn't make it so hard to empathize with her. He set his jaw, then got to his feet. "Then perhaps we both have some growing to do." She glared at him and Phaidros felt an instinctual need to shrink down but fought against it. Zenovia said nothing and Phaidros soon walked off, leaving Zenovia there in the jungle, alone. It was going to be a long month.

Chapter 6

*Bask not in the victory itself but the struggle required
to achieve it. If you did not struggle in your task, then
the victory that follows is shallow and pointless.*

-COLLECTED TEACHINGS OF THE EXALTED SOVEREIGN

2 years ago

CHARON STOOD IN the sands of The Ring, an arena surrounded by metal stands where Ignited faced off against one another in duels meant to test one another's mettle. His eyes were closed; his helmet picked out the claps and cheers of the crowd surrounding him as the announcer introduced him and the man across from him. His opponent, Orius, had been someone he had known about even before becoming ignited when he would come watch the duels as a child. No one was a better duelist than he was, that is, until Charon stepped into the ring of course.

Now the two of them were squared up against one another in a vast empty circle of sand. Charon opened his eyes, looking at his opponent. Orius wore standard ignited armor that seemed to shine brighter in the light of day with one important modification. The plates on his back could pull off by a hinge to reveal two sets of thin, long dragonfly wings. They came from the same insects that made up the rest of the ignited chitin plates, but from a rarer subspecies from Charon's understanding. The benefit of these wings was that they could heal over time, much like the plates themselves. The man was spinning two pistols in his hands, psyching himself up for the duel ahead.

Charon himself had gone to one of the Order's smiths to put stronger jets into the metal skeleton beneath the chitin of his armor. It made his forearms and calves look more exaggerated than the usual sleek look the armor gave the wearer. When he bent his arms, the exhaust ports could be seen in the space between the plates. Charon brought no other weapons to the duel; he had always felt like the only weapons he needed were his own fists and feet. He looked up towards the crowd, spotting his younger brother and his father sitting in the stands. The former waved excitedly at him while his father sat with calm intensity behind his vibrant, emerald eyes. Charon had become ignited the moment he turned eighteen and had since been making a name for himself as a duelist. It took him two years for him to get to this moment. This was his chance to prove himself to be the Ignited his father hoped he could be. The weight of expectation settled comfortably onto Charon's shoulders as he focused on the fire within him to ease his nerves while his gaze settled upon Orius.

The announcer, an ikaroa who looked like a large toad that had decided it wanted to walk on two legs, was reaching the end of his speech, He wore a slate grey uniform, marking him as one of the Kindlings. He looked odd amidst a crowd of people training to be warriors. Charon tuned out everything else but the final words croaked out by the man.

"Ignited! Begin!"

The crowd roared one last time as the sound-off was signaled with a shot into the air. Everything that followed was in slow motion for Charon. He saw his opponent's body shift down in the beginning of a jump while one pistol aimed toward him. The trigger pulled and there was a resounding *crack* in the air before the bullet landed where Charon was a split second before.

The young Ignited was already on the move. If he had been a normal man his reaction would not have been fast enough to dodge a bullet, but as an Ignited with the suit assisting him? It was more than possible. Charon dodged to the side, boot kicking up dust as the momentum carried him into a slide on one foot mid step. He kicked forward toward Orius, creating a blooming cloud of smoke from the sheer speed and the jets at the back of his calves roared to life.

Orius had already jumped into the air, wings springing outward with a loud *buzz* as he laid down a barrage of fire toward Charon. The shots forced Charon to leap, duck, and slide feet first through the dust, miniature explosions making the sky rain sand down onto him. He was mid-slide when he saw the opening he wished. He forced himself upright with a jet on his arm, before both feet planted into the dust beneath him and he launched into the sky. He could not fly, but with his momentum and the aid of his jets, he could soar through the air easily enough. Wind whipped at him and bullets cracked more plates. His armor flashed with warnings about the damage but he blinked those away. He twisted through the air right as he reached the apex of his jump and jets roared back to life, sending his leg whipping around to crash into his opponent like a hammer. It should have worked, but Orius was not Ring Champion for no reason. He flipped backwards just before the kick reached him. Charon sailed past, missing his mark and opening up his back to Orius' hail of gunfire.

The second Charon missed he knew he needed to move. He flipped through the air to reorient himself then rocketed to the ground, land-ing with both feet planted and one hand in front of him with his body sliding backwards and facing Orius. He threw his weight forward into a run. The first step didn't carry him forward, but the second launched him. Orius dove after him, dropping his clips onto the ring's sand and loading new ones in but Charon had now run past him, forcing Orius to swoop and curve low to the ground to chase after him.

To any of the observers who weren't Ignited, the whole fight would have looked like a barely conceivable blur, the past exchange happening over the course of mere seconds. Through the corner of his eyes Charon saw Phaidros squinting hard to try and keep up with the fight.

Charon had never felt more alive. Adrenaline pumped through his system and the fire of his potential burned hot. The fire helped him keep razor focus as his mind processed the current situation and what he needed to do and the action following in the same eyeblink. His armor made up for whatever weakness might have remained. It kept track of Orius even when Charon couldn't physically see him as he ran across the ring and considered his options. He knew a straight assault would not work again; he had foolishly ceded the initiative to Orius, so he had to create a new opening–somehow. He reached the edge of the ring, bullets pinging against the back of his armor and at his feet before launching himself upwards at the wall of the arena. With a twist and the sheer speed of his ascent, his feet planted against the wall against the will of gravity and pushed down into a squat. In the same breath of time he threw himself off the wall into the open air as Orius approached. He threw his arm to the side, engines screaming in his limbs as he spun around in a cartwheel of jet fire through the air. The suddenness of the maneuver had the intended effect as he heard a loud *boom* and weight against his boot. He had caught Orius right on the head, sending the duelist down and headfirst into the sand in a tumble with a shower of splintered chitin following. There was a roar from the crowd, but Charon knew this fight wasn't over yet.

Orius skid to a stop in the dirt at the same time Charon hit the floor with a loud thud before rocketing off towards the Ring Champion. He had seized the initiative and he wasn't about to let his opponent get it back. Orius's wings fluttered back to life and the jets on his limbs helped propel him forward. Charon saw that Orius' helmet was still intact, but it had chunks of chitin missing from the thickly armored head piece, Orius was known for his thick head and his armor grew to match. The champion flew low to the ground with both pistols in his grip as he fired off two shots, one low to make Charon leap over it then one high to send him into another skidding dash before they were about to collide. Then, at the last moment Orius swung himself up higher, leaving Charon trapped mid slide with a pistol aimed right at the skull of his helmet. A crack filled the air and the bullet slammed into the face plate, splintering chitin onto the sands.

Another roar resounded through the crowd as Orius rolled higher through the air, arms out at either side of him as he circled around to look at the crowd and bask in his victory before twisting through the air to prepare another swooping dive towards Charon.

Charon's armor had stopped the bullet, but it would not do so again. His head was ringing from the impact but he quickly steeled himself, fingers digging into the sand and twisting himself around to be on all fours, eyes narrowed at Orius. Another rain of bullets came for him and he dashed to the side then pivoted into a new direction, a second of his sheer momentum causing him to drag over the sand before he shot forward again, running away from Orius and going instead for another part of the arena.

Orius arced behind him, firing shot after shot as Charon weaved through the fire again. Charon suddenly dropped to the ground, hands reaching out on either side of him for the discarded clips Orius had dropped earlier. He kicked himself up and off his feet, hanging in the air as the rockets in his legs turned off. He sailed through the air and spun around horizontally as Orius came barreling towards him. The jets in his elbows ignited and he threw the clips through the air. The sheer speed might as well have been a bullet for a normal man, the outlandish tactic catching Orius by surprise as he barrel rolled through the air to try and avoid the projectiles, now moving much faster than he was previously. He wasn't fast enough however as the clip slammed into one of his wings, sending him into a flailing spiral as his speed overtook Charon.

Charon grabbed Orius by the arm as all of his rockets roared to life at once, carrying both of them straight into the wall of the opposing ring. Charon held Orius on course until the very last moment before shoving himself away, sending him slamming into the wall so hard it left a crater while Orius speared straight through the wall headfirst under him and stuck.

Charon felt his entire body ache, his visor displaying multiple breaches and broken plates. They would grow back in time but a new sound stole his attention away from the pain settling in his body: cheers. He forced himself upright, blinking in a daze up at the crowd that surrounded him, then to Orius still stuck in the wall beside him. He had incapacitated him quite spectacularly. Charon blinked one more time, the meaning of that dawning on him in a sudden wave that immediately made him forget about how much he was hurting right now. He won and now *he* was the champion of the ring.

A wide grin spread on his face as he opened his arms to the crowd, his potential burning bright enough that he felt like the sun in that moment. The thrill of victory washed over him and pride swelled in his chest. This was how the Exalted Sovereign wished for them to live. To feel just as he did in this moment basking in the pride of his victory, the proof of how far he had come in his two years of being Ignited. He looked to his family, his father grinning with pride back at him as he clapped with the crowd. Phaidros was clapping along with him with visible excitement, looking up to his father and back at his brother. Charon felt so amazed in this moment that surely the Exalted Sovereign would come down this very moment and shape his potential. No divine intervention came, but it did not take away from the moment, a moment that he would be sure to burn into his mind forever.

Little did he know that this would be the end of his glory for the rest of his days, and that after climbing so high so quickly, that he might lose what drove him to make the journey to begin with. All that mattered was that feeling of victory now and not the struggle that he had gone through to achieve it.

CHAPTER 7

Those who fall should not wallow in the pain of their loss.
Pick yourself up and try again, and those of you who see
your fellows fall, reach out and help pick them up. Those
will rise higher than any one man on a path alone.

-COLLECTED TEACHINGS OF THE EXALTED SOVEREIGN

CHARON OPENED HIS eyes to the gray ceiling above. The late morning sun peered its way through blinders and made bars of light on the opposite wall where his old armor sat, dust beginning to collect from its disuse. The armor itself looked withered and rotted, reflecting its old user. He stared at it, unable to truly see it with how his eyes refused to focus properly and let his mind wander sluggishly to better days when he could truly wear it and stand tall among his peers. As the fog of sleep began to clear from his mind he sat upright suddenly. His brother was becoming Ignited today. He looked to the window again as his hand went for his nightstand to take his glasses and put them on.

Guilt settled in over him when he realized that he had missed it, having returned home late after his encounter with the sacrament and fallen straight to sleep. His mind was then torn over to the book, which sat on a dresser in another part of his L-shaped room. From here he could make out the art on the silvered leafing and the dozens of teal eyes staring back at him. Curiosity burrowed deep into his mind at the sacrament's words.

Poor child, the victim of an abusive god burning any who do not march ever onward faster than the flame licking at their heels. You do not need such potential to wield the power of the Father, all that is required is a soul, and the knowledge of which to manipulate it. Read the book, we beg you to take the Father's knowledge and see that we speak the truth.

He could still hear its voice in his head, a shudder raked through him as he tore his gaze away from it and got up, walking into the living room proper. A plate of food meant for breakfast was waiting for him out on the counter. He frowned. He wasn't there for his brother when he ignited, yet Phaidros had always supported him since they were young. Charon took the plate with a sigh and began to nibble on it as he leaned against the counter, thoughtful. His cindering had truly ruined everything and every new day he was beginning to grow more and more resentful of how much harder life had become. He couldn't get it all back unless he went through the torturous first days of his soul burning once more, his very being in a constant state of pain until he had brought his potential back to a healthy state. It wasn't fair. None of it was. Hadn't he suffered enough? Why couldn't the Exalted Sovereign just make it so the Cindered disappeared, or that when he tried to reignite there wouldn't be so much pain? It was he who spoke of second chances, but it was easier to crawl belly first through broken glass than ever suffer through that pain again.

His eyes were back at the doorway leading to his room; he couldn't physically see the book, but its presence made him painfully aware of it. The pangs of hunger distracted him though and he tried to focus on his food. As he lifted his hand up to take a bite he realized he was trembling.

Read the book, his own thoughts whispered to him. He took the plate, going to take a few bites while his blue gaze drifted to the doorway again. *You and Phaidros can avenge Father together if you can learn how to use the power inside.*

Charon hesitated, then hobbled over to the doorway, food forgotten on the counter, and a small knife in his hand as he slowly approached the dresser the book was on. He stared at it for a long moment, then looked into the mirror beside him. His mind screamed at him for even considering it before he took the knife and pricked at his already wounded thumb again. He jolted in pain before then smearing the blood over the mirror, reaching out to it in a way he still could not describe, yet it felt natural to use the ritual now that he received from the book.

As expected, when he blinked, the creature from the night prior was standing there in the room with him. Despite him having seen it before he still jolted. It spoke a moment later.

Hello again, child.

Its voice rang out, causing the surface of the mirror to shake. Charon winced, looking around suspiciously. Would others be able to hear it speak?

Fear not, our conversation is our own. Though you must be careful of your own tone.

That alleviated some of his worry as he grabbed a piece of cloth to hold over his wound. He looked to the sacrament in wary silence before he finally said, "You said that I did not need potential to use your father's power..." He hesitated before continuing. "Would you be able to fix my cindering?"

Your scarred potential will have no part in these powers of the Father's. It is of life and the Father's is of death. You will not fix your cindering... however you will be able to work around the disadvantages that have been given to you.

That caught Charon's interest. "How?" he asked, quicker than intended. The sacrament's gaze turned from him to the book in the reflection.

The section on basic vitaemancy will have the answers you seek. Be careful though, child, as the Ignited will not take kindly to seeing such powers used.

Charon's gaze followed the sacrament's. Was he truly considering this? It had only been one night, one more night of being useless to his brother and the world. The book was too good to be true, yet what if it was? He was in front of the dresser before he realized it, hand outstretched. It was so tempting, surely he could just try it once and stop, right? If it turned out bad. The book might be shaped to give him power, but the chances of it having Domination or a similar identity was slim. He carefully opened the book a fraction, hesitating, then closing it again. Not here. "...then perhaps we should head to the jungle. To practice." He looked back at the reflection. "Will you still be here when I return?"

You have bound us through this mirror. You will not need to recreate the ritual when you return.

Charon nodded. "Then I will return soon... with more questions, I'm sure."

We wish you a swift victory, child. We rejoice to know that you will use the Father's power, may it bring you great fortune in the coming days.

Charon smiled half-heartedly at the creature before stuffing the book into a messenger bag and getting dressed properly. He then left the house, food still forgotten, and made his way with haste towards the jungle. *I'm doing this for my brother. I will not make him stand alone,* he told himself.

As usual, no one questioned Charon as he made his way out of the city and into the jungle proper. At most he'd get a nod and a friendly smile, at worst he would get someone creating more distance between them as he walked by, like he was some omen of misfortune stalking through the streets of their holy city.

He walked uncontested out the gates into the jungle beyond. This time, he would dare to walk a little farther past the gate's influence and off one of the main paths. The last thing he needed was someone walking in on what he was about to do.

When the vines of the trees started to snap at him and the bushes bristled angrily at him, he knew he was in the right spot. With a few new cuts on his arms, legs, and pride, he moved to a clearer patch of jungle and reached into his bag to pull out the book. He opened it, finding the table of contents. There was still a section of basics waiting for him but he ignored it for now. He was just going to use the parts in the book he needed; if he could just fix his potential then he could toss it or give it to Suneater and be done with it. At least that was what he kept telling himself.

Charon found the page number he was looking for and flipped through the book to the section in question. His eyes trailed over the pages, taking in the diagrams and text in an unknown language, focusing all of his attention to the best of his ability. *All life is connected,* the book read, *that connection is severed upon death, but while it yet lives the vitae yearns to be whole again. Just as a creature consumes a plant for energy and then is itself consumed by a predator, one with this power can consume the vitae of others for new vitality. Be warned, the fires of ignited vitae will burn the user of this power.*

Charon furrowed his brow, the following explanation beginning to go into depths he could not understand and yet, just as before, the knowledge slowly trickled into his mind. He could not fully conceive what that knowledge was, but more importantly, he could replicate it. He shifted his stance, trying to hold the book more comfortably before a vine from a nearby tree lashed out at him, whipping against his shoulder and making him cry out. The book dropped, and anger boiled within Charon. When he went out into the jungle it used to become silent around him; it had always been an insult since then that not even the plants and animals gave him the respect he once commanded. He lashed out, hand outstretched towards the tree as he growled. The tree's vines and branches reared back as Charon felt like his hand was touching something. Instinct told him to grab and pull at it. He did so, and felt as if he had just inhaled water as the tree struggled, then withered.

Charon dropped to his knees, coughing as whatever he felt he was holding dropped as his hand hit the dirt. He shook his head, the feeling of choking passing as he heaved in breaths. That's when he noticed it, the silence all around him, no more did the trees and bushes rustle and bristle around him in anger. It was as silent as the grave. His gaze turned up toward the tree he had done... something... to it, and saw that its leaves had turned a dusty brown, the furrows in its bark seeming dry as its branches and vines slumped and shriveled. It was dead.

More importantly, Charon didn't feel the ache of his new cuts any longer. Inside of his body he felt as if water had been thrown over a fresh burn. The feeling didn't go away as he pushed himself to his feet and nearly lost his footing from how his body had responded quicker than it usually did. The delay was still there, but less so. The jungle around him remained still. A small grin spread across his face as he threw out another hand and made a tugging motion, breathing in as he did so and watching as another tree shriveled and died before him. Then another, and another. The once vibrant and lush colors that surrounded Charon became dull, brown, and lifeless.

Charon felt *alive* for the first time in months. It felt good to see the world that had mocked him now sit still again in quiet respect and fear of his power. He reached down and picked up the book again, seeing it in a new light than he had previously. He saw the endless potential that was held within it. Already after killing merely a few trees and bushes that had made him angry, he was feeling like he could walk with newfound strength he didn't have before. He looked to his cane then, considering discarding it—but no. If he simply drained the entire jungle dry and walked into the city as a new man, then they would ask questions. A part of his mind told him that if he sat down and read this book in its entirety, he'd be able to fend off the whole city—but no. He did not let such ambition take his mind for now. He was doing this to help his brother, he reminded himself. His fingers brushed off the dust that had gotten on the cover, which despite falling onto the jungle floor still seemed to be in the same condition despite the weak brush of his hand.

He needed to find Phaidros. Perhaps he could convince him to allow Charon to assist him in the hunt. The idea made him pause. Would Phaidros treat him like all the others now that he was Ignited? Anxiety swelled within him again, his hand gripping the strap of his messenger bag. The display of power today brought some confidence back to him and he let out a huff of breath. No, he would be able to convince him this time. Even if it was something small like helping train Phaidros. Charon *was* the Ring Champion before all this; even if he could not fight personally, he could help guide Phaidros while slowly taking the life of the jungle around them. In a month's time? He would definitely be able to stand alongside his brother, he was sure of it.

For now, he would have to think about what to say. He was sure that Phaidros would be out training right now so all he could do was go back home and wait until he returned. Charon took one last look down at the bag carrying the tome with a new sense of reverence. Whoever 'The Father' was, Charon owed him for giving him a second chance so freely while the Exalted Sovereign taunted him with it. He looked ahead again and began to make his way back to the city with newfound energy in his steps.

This time when he returned home, the jungle did not snap, hiss, and bristle at Charon; it remained completely quiet and still. It was the most peaceful walk Charon had taken since he became Cindered.

The sun was beginning to set by the time Charon had returned to the city and home. He returned the book to his room for now, the sacrament was still in his mirror as he passed it just as it said it would. He did not exchange any words with it however, some part of him still felt a creeping dread looking upon the thing that he could not place. He cleaned up the living room and waited, trying to piece out what the right words to say would be.

It wasn't long until he heard the door beep and slide open for a towering figure with a sword resting against his shoulder. Despite knowing this, Charon still felt a drop of fear before Phaidros' familiar voice came out with a tin filter around it. "Evening, Charon," he said, Charon being able to hear the smile in his brother's voice despite not seeing it. He sounded exhausted, and only now did Charon notice all of the cracks across the plates.

"Hey," Charon replied, brow furrowing. He questioned himself on whether or not he should let Phaidros rest but pushed through anyway. "Can we talk?"

"Yeah, just give me a minute to put away my armor and weapon. It's been a long day." He stalked off towards his room, the door to his room sliding open and then closing behind him, leaving Charon alone again. He would have to get used to seeing his brother in armor; it didn't seem to match his vision of him at all. Phaidros was a kind soul, deep down, and yet in that armor he looked like some towering, intimidating knight with way too many points on him.

He sat there mulling over the sight for another minute before Phaidros came back in his comfortable clothes and walked over to Charon before pausing for a moment. He looked his brother up and down before his head tilted. "Are you okay?"

Charon blinked. "Why wouldn't I be?"

"Your eyes, they seem... different," he said, squinting. "Just barely."

Charon had no idea what he was talking about, but the paranoid side of him blamed the book he brought home and so he answered, "Your vision was enhanced when you became ignited, you're probably just noticing more detail than you had before." It was technically true and seemed to make Phaidros stop inspecting him so closely.

"That's true enough..." Phaidros muttered, seeming distracted before going to sit on one of the seats in the living room opposite of his brother. Charon let out an internal sigh of relief that Phaidros didn't press further. He would have to examine himself if his eyes had changed later.

There was a moment of silence between them before Charon broke it. "So… how was it?" he asked first, not quite willing to go straight into business just yet.

Phaidros smiled but Charon could see strain behind it. "It was like I was breathing in smog my whole life and took my first breath of fresh air," he said with delight. "Like I was truly made alive and all moments until then had been in a haze… then I trained with Zenovia." His smile turned into a deep grimace.

Charon nodded slowly, that was how it felt for everyone, the igniting that is, he had never trained with Zenovia. He smiled. "It really is life changing," he replied, tone soft. "Zenovia isn't going to go easy on you so just try and bear with it. It'll get better, I am sure." The way Charon spoke made Phaidros pause, looking worried that he might have made Charon upset, but his brother held up a hand and shook his head. "I am happy for you. Truly," he began. "I wish Father could be here to see you as you are. I know he would be beaming with pride."

Phaidros' grin returned. "And probably order me right into the jungle." The two of them shared a somber chuckle, both of them looking off to the side as they each reminisced about their lost father. Silence followed.

Charon would break the silence again. "I know you are set on this hunt," he started, voice still quiet as he flicked his gaze back to his brother. "…and I know that I behaved horribly yesterday when you needed my support most of all. Father is gone, I barely even remember Mother's face anymore, all we have is each other now." He hesitated before continuing. "So, I wanted to apologize, Phaidros."

Phaidros blinked in surprise before his grin softened into a smile. "I know you mean well," he said with a sigh, one hand reaching up to scratch at the back of his head. "I'm in a bit over my head, but the Exalted Sovereign always wants us to challenge ourselves, yeah? Well, killing a beast that killed a trained Ignited as a person who has only been ignited for a few days should rank itself pretty high with him I think." Phaidros' smile disappeared completely by the time he finished speaking.

"I don't want to lose you too, Phaidros. If you go out there on your own there's a good chance of that happening no matter how good you are," Charon cut in, tone serious. "Let me help you." Phaidros had opened his mouth to speak but Charon raised a finger, having anticipated the initial objections. "I know I can't help you much physically," he admitted with a heavy heart. "I know on the hunt itself I will probably just get in the way, but I was still one of the best duelists in Dasos. Let me at least teach you how to best use your armor."

Phaidros shifted in his seat, obviously a little uncomfortable with the topic. Charon narrowed his eyes in offense and Phaidros brought his hands up defensively. "Charon, I love you," he started. "But what can you show me? Sure, you can tell me what to do, tell me how you used to move and how best to do it but I'll have no practical way to replicate it if you can't do it yourself." Charon's shoulders slumped and Phaidros kept speaking. "I really do appreciate how much you want to help me but… unless you ignited and fixed your body, I don't know what you could do that I couldn't get from another."

The words were like a shot through Charon's heart. Was he truly so useless in his brother's eyes? Of course he was, it was exactly what he had feared. "Am I just a burden then?" he asked, voice strained.

"No!" Phaidros quickly answered. "Of course not."

"Then please, let me help in some way, any way. Don't let me sit here and do nothing. If you died out there while I was stuck here I'd…"

Phaidros moved over to sit beside his brother and put a hand on his shoulder. "You know what you need to do then," he said, voice consoling. "Igniting will hurt at first but if you move past that it'll be as if it never happened. Like the Phoenix." At least that's what they had all been told. "Or just… move on." Phaidros looked pained to say such a thing but continued, "If you didn't want to ignite I don't know what else you'd do. I want you to be able to help. I wish we could both go out there and kill that *thing* that killed Father and bring its head and hide back to Suneater. I have to be realistic though. I only have so much time to train and get ready to face the beast. I can't wait for you." He pushed up and out of his seat, turning to look back at Charon who was now glaring at the floor, defeated. "…if you somehow get to a fighting state by the end of the month though? I won't deny you that, brother." Charon blinked, looking up at his brother. "I can't wait for you, but if you close the gap fast enough on your own then I'd happily have you along."

Charon's eyes widened, meeting Phaidros' calm, challenging smile. "I… I will," he found himself saying. "I'll be able to stand beside you, brother, just you watch." Charon found newfound strength in his voice, rising to look him in the eye.

"Good. The Exalted Sovereign will surely be watching your journey, and I believe in you wholeheartedly. Now if you'll excuse me, I am about ready to pass out. I'll talk to you soon?"

Charon nodded. "Soon." Phaidros began to walk towards his room, Charon watching him the whole way. The Exalted Sovereign probably would not watch… but someone else would. Once his brother disappeared from sight Charon slipped back into his own room, new determination on his features. He looked towards the mirror, seeing the sacrament standing ominously in its reflection already looking at him. He had a month to figure out how he could build himself back up to a reasonable fitness level to be able to don his armor again. At the thought he looked to his old armor, still collecting dust, still looking as if it was wasting away. He had half a mind to clean it, but decided against it, instead going up to the mirror, now that he had spoken to his brother and a goal had been set he felt less odd about going to the creature for assistance. "Exaltation?" Charon asked, voice quiet. The creature was always there but Charon still wasn't sure if his attention was always there as well.

We are here.

The trembling surface of the mirror made him wince; he quickly looked in the direction of Phaidros' room to see if he heard… but apparently he did not, meaning it wasn't lying to him. That was a relief. "I read the pages in the book you had mentioned, the ones on… vitae absorption? I feel better than I did before. I need to know what happened."

A wise choice, child. You have now tasted the Father's power for your own and have drunk on the raw potential of a living being, filling your own.

"Raw... potential?" He had only ever heard of it as 'potential' before.

We have tried to put it in terms you might understand, but a better term for it is Vitae. It is so sad to see your god give powers so freely while also refusing to teach his followers on the true nature of it.

"But what *is* it?"

To answer that question, one must ask the question: what is life? What is death? All life has potential in it, all living things grow, move, and change. Death is static, there is no more change, no more growth, and therefore no more potential. The vitae is what makes you alive, gives you the capacity to grow and change. This is what 'burns' when you become Ignited. It is the fuel source that forges your soul anew when it is shaped like iron being tempered in a hot forge and just like a fuel source, you may siphon more fuel from an outside source.

"So... I took this 'fuel source' and siphoned it into my own soul, how did that heal me? I felt as if some of my cindering had been cured or at the very least..." He felt over his chest again. "It feels like there is something there."

You had almost completely burned away your potential. Thus it made it harder for you to be alive, you were one step away from death. As you have refilled it through another life's vitae, you have therefore filled your fuel source and your 'potential' to live has been healed. The amount would depend on the potential of what you siphoned from. An insect will barely give you a drop, while a powerful beast could fill you to the brim with potential. If it doesn't kill you first, that is. Your soul is still scarred from being cindered, however. Your vitae will slowly deplete again unless you renew it.

Charon blinked, curiosity raging inside of him now. "Wouldn't that make me infinitely more powerful if I just kept drinking others' potential? Beyond where I was before I was cindered or ignited?"

You can be overflowing with vitae, but what use is an over-filled canister of fuel that has cracks in it or a large pile of logs without a fire? You cannot make a sword from an ingot by dousing it in gasoline. Even if you were to become ignited again, it would only guarantee that you would burn for far longer before you cindered again. Your actions are what stoke the flames hot enough for your soul to be shaped; vitae, or potential, as you call it, are a fuel source, nothing more.

That was somewhat disappointing, though Charon knew it would be odd to show up suddenly as an Ignited brimming with potential after only a month. He hesitated before he found the next question on his mind. "What would you do with the excess then?"

The creature's pupil seemed to focus on him, making Charon feel more than a little uncomfortable.

That is a perfect question, isn't it?

CHAPTER 8

The people around you will call you a monster.
Yet it is your sin that will bring them salvation.

-BOOK OF THE FATHER, FIRST PAGE

CHARON WAS UNABLE to sleep the rest of the night. His brother's words still echoed in his mind. If Charon could just catch up to him in a month, then he'd be able to stand alongside them. His eyes opened for the tenth time that night into pitch darkness. Even in the gloom of night when he looked to his mirror he could see the blurry silhouette of the sacrament hovering inside waiting patiently for him to awake. He stared at the creature. It had told him that it would not be able to answer his question here in this city; if Charon wished to catch up to his brother, then he must leave Dasos. He had wanted to think on that, mull it over, but the longer that he lay in his bed with the thought forever turning in his mind, the more he realized that staying in this city was not an option. The high he felt earlier in the day from draining the potential—or vitae, he had to remind himself to call it—had faded. It was like his soul had cracks in it that the new vitae was leaking out from drop by drop. He sat upright with a sigh, blinking away the feeling of exhaustion that permeated his every waking moment and looked to the sacrament. "I think... I'm ready to go," he said with quiet resignation.

Then let us depart.

It had answered, the mirror rumbling with it. Charon slid part way off the bed, rubbing at his face as he went to stand fully with a small stumble. "I can't take the mirror with me and the pond will be too close to the city... will my pocket knife work as a mirror for you?"

Any reflective surface will do.

Charon nodded, then began to pack his things. Not much, he felt weaker still, but he could still fit the book and at least one other change of clothes into his bag. He got dressed and grabbed his cane, then headed out into the main room of the house. He was about to head right out the front door before he paused, looking back towards the door that led to his brother's room. A gnawing voice in the back of his mind told him he should just go back to bed and not leave Phaidros to his fate. His stare lasted for what felt like an eternity before he sighed; the least he could do was tell Phaidros that he left. He wrote a note, keeping it simple. *Phaidros, I am taking your word to heart. I have an idea that will allow me to catch up to you before you face the beast. I ask that you trust that I will be able to handle myself and that I will return not as your cindered brother but as your equal. May the Exalted Sovereign watch over you, brother. -Charon.* He left the note on the counter and without wasting any more time strode from the house with the help of his cane and out into the night.

Dasos might as well be as loud in the night as it was in the day. Here the ambiance of the surrounding jungle was deafeningly loud, with all the creatures that were nocturnal taking over the moment the sun set. There would still be Ignited out there training, ra swooping overhead, and hunters in the jungle, but the sounds were nothing before the life that surrounded the city, the screaming insects, the whipping of tree vines, and the echoing hoots, hollers, and roars of larger beasts. It was in this noise that Charon slipped out of the city, silently grateful for the lack of any true guards. He left out the sixth gate south of the city and began heading west, giving the merchant's district a wide berth. The city itself might not have any guards, but the merchant's district most likely did with the Shaped Beast prowling about. He wasn't too frightened of running into it; ignited creatures sought challenges, not Cindered. An occasional tree snapped at him with a vine and he drained its vitae as punishment. Just as before, the tree withered before him and he got a new supply of vitae, the display of power subduing the wilderness around him and providing him with more energy as he strode into the jungle alone with new strength. His exhaustion was gone, supplanted with the energy of the life he had stolen.

It was about an hour into his walk that he decided to pull out his pocket knife and summon the visage of the sacrament once more. The creature's reflection wasn't as clear in the steel, warped from the curves of the blade and giving it a whole new dimension of eerie to its visage. "Now can you answer my question… sacrament? Is that your name?"

We are the Exaltation of the Father. This or 'Exaltation' will do. We will answer any question you ask of us.

The knife vibrated in Charon's hand as it spoke. He was half afraid the blade would shatter but when it held intact he let out an inward sigh of relief. His previous question from earlier in the day still itched at the back of his mind. "I drained the vitae from the trees but the excess appears to be leaking, you implied there was something I could do with the excess."

Yes, your cindered soul is weakened and cannot hold the vitae it does not naturally grow, your ability to live has been permanently altered unless you ignite yourself again. However, the excess vitae that you hold has many uses and with the power to manipulate it, that gives you the power over life. More specifically, you can imbue the vitae into the world around you and control it.

Charon stopped in his tracks, trying to wrap his brain around the concept that he could control anything else. He had heard of some Shaped and beyond in the Ignited who had the power to manipulate others, but to be able to do so without being shaped seemed too good to be true. "How?" he asked suspiciously.

All life yearns to be one once again. It is connected to one another and even in death will seek that connection once more. The soul is free, but should you fill the husk with vitae once more, it will seek a soul to latch itself to. Your soul. With vitaemancy, you will be able to use this connection to puppet the vitae in its husk as if it were an extension of your own body. Read the section on reanimation and you will have the power I speak of.

Charon was curious. He glanced around. Despite walking for hours he could still see the sight of Suneater's Great Tree looming over the horizon. A reminder that there are things other than beasts he should be afraid of. "Not here. Not yet," Charon muttered. "We need to get farther away. If I kill a few trees Suneater just might suppose it's some wildlife, but if we start delving into this power then I don't want to be in sight of them. I think I know of a place where we can go but I don't have my armor. Is there a way in this book for me to be able to travel faster?"

The powers within are basic in their abilities, however offer great flexibility based off of the creativity of the user. You have what you seek already. Your vitaemancy need not drain the entirety of a being's vitae when you use your power. You have already seen how it refreshes you. Look around you, young child, and see the life that surrounds you and is yours to use. Do not drink deep, drink slowly, and you will find you will never run out of energy so long as there is vitae for you to pull from.

Charon looked around himself. That would have been useful information before he got a little ahead of himself earlier today. Still though, it was worth a shot. He took a cautious step forward, then another as he slowly brought himself into a jog. His muscles strained from disuse; he had not done anything other than hobble anywhere he needed to go for two months. His feet weren't sure under him and he nearly stumbled over a root but he followed the sacrament's advice and took a breath as he focused not on one tree but everything around him. Trickles of vitae flowed into him, the wildlife around him wilting, but not dying. Charon on the other hand felt a new surge of energy and began to run faster and faster. The wind rushed through his hair and his face and he had to jump over a gnarled root in his path but his body responded as if he were normal. Two months of feeling like his life was over bled away with each new strong step he took as his pace grew faster and faster. A laugh escaped him while he drained the vitae from everything he passed to make up for what leaked out of him. The jungle did not fight back and soon enough began to instinctively try and pull away from him as he passed. He felt *alive* again. In that moment, all of what had plagued him disappeared, all doubt, all his self-loathing, all gone in an instant as once again he was able to feel the cool wind of the evening against his face as he ran through the jungle. He missed this, and while it wasn't as fast as he was when he was an Ignited, even the chance to run again made his heart soar and any lingering wariness about the book in his possession disappeared.

Charon never tired, not after running till the sun came up; he barely even broke a sweat. They were now deep into the jungle of Dasos, a large flowing river carved through the path. A leaf that had fallen from a nearby tree touched the surface and was immediately shredded to bits by the carnivorous fish beneath. There was a small clearing around the edge of the water that Charon would be able to make a camp and if he needed more space, he'd just have to kill a few of the trees. He wasn't afraid of the fish in the water, after just getting the *basic* powers from the book he was sure he could scare them off well enough to be able to get water should he need it. "Alright, reanimation," he said with some confidence, sticking the knife into the ground for now as he sat down and pulled the book out of his messenger bag and flipped to the section titled *Reanimation.* Just like before, the page was filled with strange symbols and diagrams but the knowledge bled into his mind without him needing to understand it. *Life and Death were once two who became one then split once more. Each person is a small piece of this greater whole. With the power of vitaemancy, you can reanimate what was once living by filling it with your vitae. This requires a constant influx and connection of your vitae much like how a limb cannot be manipulated without blood flowing to it.*

So that meant that with his cindered soul, he couldn't keep it permanently connected. His vitae would inevitably run out. Well, it was worth trying out. He glanced to a nearby tree, with a flex of his will the tree withered and died and gave him an influx of vitae. He then reached out, still not sure how, and managed to easily push the vitae back in. His senses extended to the tree as if it were a part of him. He felt the wind pass over his branches, the weight of the vines as they swung in the breeze. He shifted and the tree groaned to the left then the right along with him. Charon threw his hand forward and the vines snapped ahead in mirror of his motions with the vines acting like boneless fingers. With a thought he pulled his vitae back out, noting that it was less than what he had put in, as the tree slumped back into death. "Doesn't seem like it's useful longterm and trees aren't going to be able to stop a shaped creature."

You have but one piece to the greater puzzle and you have only taken the lives of flora that can do little to fight back. Think grander, to control the beasts that roam the jungle, the insects that skitter below in the caves beneath all worlds, to the very Ignited that might one day hunt you.

Exaltation rumbled from the knife. That gave Charon pause. He looked back down at the book. To control the very Ignited that might one day hunt him? To take control of the dead. Until now, the consequences of such power had been lost on him. "Would I be able to bring my father back?" he asked, surprised at himself that this wasn't the first question he asked.

No. It is too late, the soul has gone to the Father and has been reincarnated,

such is the cycle. However if you could find the body, you could reanimate it
as if it were a part of you.

That sent a shiver through Charon's spine. He snapped the book shut. "Okay. We're not going to reanimate anything for now. We can save that for later," he said, nervous at the very idea of desecrating his father's body in such a way. Trees were... Well, they were trees. They were everywhere and they might as well just be annoying pests that swatted at anything that came by. Charon could stand reanimating trees, but the idea that the ultimate expression of this ability was to bring people back from the dead as some sort of puppet was a bridge he was not willing to cross. "What else can I focus on that doesn't require... *that*," Charon asked, looking to the knife that contained the sacrament.

All of the sections in the book are useful for one reason or another. Read
all of them, there is no downside, no struggle you must achieve to be able to
attain it like igniting your soul.

Charon still didn't quite believe that but... he had committed himself to catching up to Phaidros in a month. If he was going to do that, he was going to need all of the power that this book had to offer and then some. He took a deep breath, starting to feel some of the exhaustion creep back in. After taking a moment to center himself, he flipped the book back open, going to a new section. It was going to be a long, lonely month.

CHAPTER 9

*Do not let your desire for success blind you into charging
head first into danger. When your approach doesn't
work, try to find a new angle of attack.*

-COLLECTED TEACHINGS OF THE EXALTED SOVEREIGN

PHAIDROS AWOKE THE next morning to a letter from his brother. Anxious thoughts swirled through his mind. Where did he go? Would he be safe? What if he died and Phaidros never found out? He should have been better to his brother; he should have listened. Amidst the anxiety, anger began to rise. If Phaidros had been stronger, this wouldn't be necessary. If Charon wasn't so proud then he'd still be here. If Zenovia wasn't weak, then his father would still be alive and none of this would be happening. The fire within him demanded him to act. His hand drew into a fist and he nearly slammed it on the table before he released the tension, hand instead going through his hair as he dropped into an open seat. He was truly alone now, with nothing but the fire within to both comfort and warn him. Should he give in, then the flame would take him, just as it took his brother. With great pain in his heart he pushed himself upright again, the sun was just starting to rise, and Zenovia was no doubt going to wring him thoroughly today. He retreated back to his room to don his armor with the silent resignation that whatever followed today was going to be hell.

It was. Zenovia put him through the same routine as yesterday, except this time they didn't have the excuse of a ritual in the morning and a smith to meet after to make the day feel any shorter. Zenovia chased him through the jungle, hunting him like he was some pack animal separated from the herd until all of his plates cracked. She never missed. Afterwards he spent the remainder of the day trying to hit her while she taunted him and struck at him every opening she saw. He always missed. By the end of the day, even through the protection of his armor and the fire around his soul, he had never felt more sore in his entire life.

That was until the next day, then the day after that, and the day after that, until finally on the fourth day Phaidros felt like he had enough. It was storming that day, the heavens opening up in a torrent of rain, boom of thunder, and flash of lightning. He thought he had Zenovia today. He had sprung himself up into the trees and made her chase him without any good openings for over an hour. In the end, when he tried to feint and get her to finally miss, her shot glanced his shoulder plate, the final unbroken plate. It still cracked and with it, so did Phaidros' senses. The constant failure, his father dead and his brother gone, the downpour around him, Zenovia's taunting. He roared in frustration. When Zenovia had dropped from the trees, he launched himself at her, sword already drawn as he landed in a puddle of mud and swung out towards her in a violent arc. She dodged backwards and Phaidros followed through with his strike, stepping into it and thrusting at her midsection. She weaved to the side and stepped into his strike, her rifle butt coming up in a hard swing at his face that knocked him clear off his feet and into the mud below.

His vision blurred as she stepped into view and looked down at him, waiting. Phaidros growled and shoved himself back to his feet, sword forgotten. He stalked toward her, finger jabbing at her. "Is this fun for you? Huh?" She didn't seem the least bit intimidated, staring him down as he continued. "Kicking my ass up and down the jungle every day? You're supposed to be helping me and instead all you're doing is kicking me into the dirt over and over again. What in all that burns is that supposed to teach me? How to take a hit? That thing is going to kill me, Zenovia!" He realized he was trembling but the words continued to spew forth like the storm above them. "Is this all an excuse? Some way for you to feel like you're tough after you let my father die?" He wasn't able to get the next words out before Zenovia punched him in the face, splintering chitin and sending him staggering back.

"You have some nerve talking to me like that, boy, when I'm the one trying to save you from the situation *you* put yourself in," she hissed, pointing at him, already closing the distance again as she grabbed him and yanked him close. Phaidros couldn't see her expression through their helmets but he could feel her glowering anger through the glow of her visor. "I could have called the rite of vengeance, I could have built a team from the ground up to be able to fight that damned beast without having to train some cindering boy who hasn't stepped into armor a day in his life beforehand." She shoved him back but Phaidros stood his ground this time, frustration and anger blinding him as he tried to return fire with a right hook. She moved into the strike, grabbing his arm and flipping him over her shoulder with her foot now planted against his neck. "You won't focus, you won't listen to me, you're already dead, Phaidros. All this is just your final death rattle before you go to join your father."

Phaidros tried to fight her grip but she had him thoroughly pinned. He struggled anyways, letting out a growl of frustration that echoed over the rain before his head hit the mud behind him with a small splash of rain. Water stained his face with the impact, his own tears. The choked sobbing began, though it sounded distorted through the filters of his armor. The rage subsided into a pure, guttural sadness. He was frightened, alone, and every step forward seemed futile. The flame in his soul offered no comfort now, only an ever-present reminder that he had to keep going, keep pushing. Right now? He felt as if letting the flame overtake him was the better option, to surrender to oblivion and let the fire burn away all that was him. That had to be less painful than this. "I don't know what to do, Zenovia," he admitted through tears. "I don't know what to do, where to go. All of it seems wrong."

Zenovia watched him in silence, but her grip on him slackened. She tossed his arm from her grasp and pulled her helmet off, uncaring of the rain as she crouched down to look at him. There was pity hidden beneath the anger, Phaidros could see. "It is wrong. This whole thing is wrong," she said, gesturing around them. "But we don't have a choice, Phaidros. We have to keep moving, even when it seems like each step is taking us closer towards death's door." Even her voice sounded strained. "Because when we are lost? Then you might as well keep moving, every step forward has a chance to take you to a place that is better than where you were before." She hesitated before continuing with a heavy sigh, "And you *are* in a better place, Phaidros. The first day, you lasted minutes before I could break all of your plates, in only four days you've made that process take hours. You're grieving, I know, it is never easy to lose someone close to you like that, it's a reminder about how the world is unfair and uncaring." She sighed, running a hand through her now rain-soaked hair. "And I've been hard on you. I have to be, Phaidros. It isn't because I'm trying to take revenge on you, it is because I want you to live." She jabbed a finger at his chestplate. "I've already lost your father and Theseus, I'll be ash and cinders before I let Za haunt me for losing you too."

Through her speech, Phaidros' sobbing quieted. It was a strange comfort, making him forget about the pit in his stomach for the moment. He finally pulled himself up out of the mud into a sitting position and took off his helmet, carefully wiping away tears with a gauntleted hand. The rain brought a strange sense of calm as the water cooled how hot his face felt from the frustration and sorrow still present within him. "I'm sorry, Zenovia," he said, voice still shaky. "I said some things I shouldn't have and... maybe I was projecting a little."

She quietly scoffed but replied, "And I have not been the best teacher. I've never had to teach someone before." She looked up at the sky through the trees, thoughtful. "We're going to call it early today. Let's let the bad blood rest for now and we'll try it all again tomorrow. That sound fair?"

Phaidros hesitated but nodded. "Alright." He felt guilty now, every second that ticked by was a second closer to his end but he didn't argue with the chance to let the tension die.

Zenovia nodded, then put her helmet back on. "First light, same place," she said, then began to walk away. Phaidros waited for a few moments longer, staring at the ground before he sighed and returned to Dasos as well.

᠕

Despite having the free time now, he wasn't sure what to do with it. He didn't want to spend more time with Zenovia than he had to, right now, his brother was gone, Suneater surely had more important things to be doing. The rain had begun to let up by now, leaving the city in the fresh aftermath of a storm. Puddles of rainwater collected in open dirt, reflecting the afternoon sun as it passed overhead and birds sang in the distance while uniformed Ignited wandered the streets as they always did. Phaidros had gone home to change into his own uniform before he, too, wandered the city. He glanced over to others as he passed, wondering what they might be up to or where they're going. This was a city filled with people in the same situation as him, everyone here was trying to stay ahead of the flame, to find what drove them and improve themselves. Phaidros wondered how anyone could look so calm while they constantly fought off becoming Cindered. He had been ignited for less than a week and he couldn't imagine people spending years and years like this. How had his father done it? How did Zenovia do it? Did they have the same thoughts he had? Zenovia seemed to be in a similar state as he was in, but before today he barely could see it. Not only were they fighting off the fire, everyone in this city was here because they too struggled with keeping pace with it. Did anxiety cloud their thoughts? Did they go to bed wondering if tomorrow was going to be the last day before they cindered? How could they walk around smiling and laughing with their friends when that future loomed just beyond the horizon for all of them?

His thoughts continued to wander alongside him until he stopped and finally paid attention to his surroundings. He was in the smith's district. An idea formed in his head. He couldn't talk to the others, but maybe Daxia could be a voice of reason? Phaidros wasn't sure how good of an idea this was, but frankly if he had to stew in his own thoughts for any longer he felt as if he was going to go mad. Soon enough he was in front of *Daxia's Hoard*, hand raised and ready to knock. After one final moment of hesitation the fire within spurred him to give a few powerful knocks. Several anxiety-filled seconds passed before the door opened. Daxia stood across from him, dressed in a similar fashion as the other day with a half-filled cup of coffee in her hand, she blinked up at him blearily, "Yeah?" was all she asked.

Phaidros had a sudden urge to run the other way but instead he stood there trying to remember what he was going to say. "Uh…" was the only thing that managed to leave his mouth. "I um," he sighed. "Can I get your help? Zenovia's running me through during training and it feels like I'm beating my head against a wall and my brother is gone and I don't have anyone else to talk to about it." Daxia stared at him with one raised brow before she took a long sip from her coffee.

"Okay, this sounds like there's going to be a lot to unpack here and I was about to head to the market to pick up some supplies, so let me finish this and we can walk and talk. Sound good?"

"Um, yeah," Phaidros said, surprised that she was agreeing at all.

"Great." She smiled, showing fangs, then closed the door in his face, leaving Phaidros to stand outside of her door awkwardly while she got ready. When she returned, a large, hovering cart followed after her. "Okay, let's go," she said, beginning to head west without waiting for Phaidros, hands in her pockets. Phaidros quickly followed after. "So, Zenovia—she's the woman that was with you before right? Anyway, she's training you and you're having trouble, what's the issue?"

Phaidros sighed, "We spend part of the day where she hunts me throughout the jungle until she cracks every one of my armor plates, I 'pass' when I get her to miss or parry a bullet out of the air. Then afterwards–"

"Stop," she replied. "I find it's better to work through problems one at a time. What's your strategy so far?"

"Well… I've tried to out maneuver and outpace her until she finally missed."

"Uh huh…" she said, as if she expected more from the thought.

"And… that hasn't gotten me anywhere but Zenovia did say that I've been lasting a lot longer which is good."

"Lasting longer is great in certain circumstances but I think the goal here is to try and win," she said with a nonchalant shrug of her shoulders, "and with what you have going on it's not working. So it's time to change strategies."

"But what could I do, there's no way Zenovia is going to miss, she never misses. If I try to attack her she just dodges and takes the open shot," Phaidros said, his confidence beginning to wilt. Daxia nodded sagely, then her tail smacked him upside the head. "Ow– Hey," he said, offended, the tail came in for a second swipe but he dodged backwards, the fur barely missing him.

She wheeled around to face him, pointing up at him. "There. What did you do just there?"

"I… dodged it?" Phaidros replied, sounding confused.

"You didn't just dodge it, you anticipated it was going to swipe a second time and you reacted accordingly. You picked a sword when you were in my shop. You know how to use it, right?"

"Yes." Phaidros answered, trying to follow along.

"Then it sounds like the only thing you're missing is anticipating Zenovia's moves. For Ignited it's a lot more difficult, sure, but it isn't like she's shaped. You're both on equal levels and Ignited have the reaction to stop a bullet if you're smart about it. So the answer is simple, anticipate where Zenovia is going to shoot, react accordingly. You said she can't miss, so stop trying to make her miss."

"I…" Phaidros paused, then considered. "When you put it that way, it sounds easy."

"Don't get me wrong, it's still going to be hard, but in fighting, you want to be the one in control, if you let her have the control then she gets to pick and choose when to engage."

"That goes into my second problem though, the second part of training is I have to land a hit on her and she slips out of the way every time."

Daxia spun back around, waving a dismissive hand as she continued walking. "Worry about passing the first test, then you can worry about the second. You already know how to use a sword you said, so it's the same thing, anticipate and try to put her on the back foot."

Phaidros blinked, well, it seemed to make sense—and was more direction than Zenovia gave for certain. He felt another well of frustration begin to build but he forced it down, Zenovia had told him she had never trained anyone before. Which brought up a new question. "How do you know so much about this, Daxia? You're a smith aren't you?"

Daxia's smile became distant, and the exhaustion that seemed normal in her features were even heavier than before. "I wasn't always, but that life is behind me now." Her molten eyes flicked over to look at him. "And I'd rather not talk about it, before you ask."

Phaidros' curiosity burned, but he respected her wish. "Right, got it." The conversation naturally lulled as the two strode across the city. Occasionally some of the Ignited waved to them as they passed or brought a fist to their chest in a salute. Phaidros returned the gesture but Daxia kept walking, the only break from her silence being the occasional yawn. Another question did inevitably come to his mind though. "You know, since becoming ignited, I find it really difficult to be tired, yet both times I've seen you it looks like you haven't slept in days. Is that… a smith thing?"

Daxia reached up and scratched at her head. "No, all Ignited are the same, I have the same powers as you, I just don't like to sleep is all."

Phaidros raised a brow. "How long have you been awake?"

"A week," she answered matter of factly.

"A… a week?" He tried not to sound too surprised but failed. "I didn't realize the powers extended your alertness that far."

"Oh it helps but coffee does the rest of the heavy lifting," she said with a fang-filled grin. "Besides, when I have a project in my head it gets difficult to sleep until I've finished it. I'm going to give it a few more days before I let myself sleep. You don't need to get all worried about me for it, this is just how I operate, the armor and sword works fine, yeah?"

"Yes," he said, voice trailing off as he thought more but decided against pushing further on the topic. The two exited the gate and entered into the market district.

Unlike the rest of Dasos, the buildings set up here outside of the wall were not ancient stone buildings but a series of semi-permanent tents built alongside concrete structures for some of the merchants that had set up more permanent lodgings and venues here for both Ignited and the visiting merchants. Unlike the uniformed black of the Ignited, or the grey-uniformed Kindlings, the people here dressed in many different colors, patterns, and outfits, each calling out their wares to the Ignited and other traveling merchants that had begun to stream into the district after the storm. Some people were still pulling down tarps and coverings for the rain. Daxia paid them no mind, walking through the paved streets, people making way for the two of them as they passed. People didn't seem too fazed by two Ignited walking by. Phaidros was a little underwhelmed. The Order of the Ignited were supposed to be heroes of the common man, but he supposed that if you saw them every day then perhaps that awe was tamed.

Daxia led the two of them into the market square, where a bunch of stalls were set up in loose collaboration with one another with a circular path that cut through. The stalls themselves were big enough to be small shops in of themselves; if someone was traveling across the galaxy to trade here then they'd most likely have a lot of wares to sell. Phaidros was surprised to see that a lot of the merchandise were simple things like fruits and vegetables, butchered meat, trinkets, and other things that Phaidros couldn't see the worth of. "What sort of supplies were you looking for again?" He turned to look and see Daxia already conversing with a ra merchant. The man was holding out a small device in his taloned hand. The ra himself was thin, like most of his kind, with barely any heft to his waifish frame. He stood on taloned feet, his frame mostly humanoid save for feathered wings on their back and a crest of red feathers lining the center of his otherwise dark, human like hair.

"Four bags of Cretian dark," Daxia said to the man, offering a small card to the ra. Those that were a part of the order got a monthly stipend, though from Phaidros' understanding it was less on Dasos than elsewhere, due to the nature of the city. The man accepted the card, slotting into the device, and after a small ping he handed the card back to her and picked out four bags bigger than Phaidros' head and hefted them to the front counter.

"What's tha–" Was all Phaidros had time to get out before the bags were shoved into his hands by Daxia.

"Put those into the cart for me," she said before wandering down to the next stall.

It was at that moment Phaidros realized he was being dragged *grocery* shopping of all things. He followed along, each item in question shoved into his hands for him to put into the car—he didn't know why she bothered when the cart moved on its own—before moving onto the next one. It gave him more time to think on her advice on his dilemma. When he fought against Zenovia, his heart wasn't fully in it. He wanted to win, yes, or more importantly he wanted to move on without taking the lesson to heart. That had led to him failing again and again, hoping that Zenovia might give up and teach him something else instead or change tactics. She never did, so he had to. Realization dawned on him. These past days since his father died, he has been riding along with the current of events, but he hadn't really been present in them. He knew he needed to move forward but was letting others drag him forward as opposed to himself taking those first steps. He had no control over his situation other than the initial agreement to become ignited. *If you let her have the control then she gets to pick and choose when to engage,* Daxia had said and she was right, in more ways than one. His problem extended beyond Zenovia. New inspiration struck him and he suddenly spoke out as Daxia was heading towards another stall with a human family of four running a store that seemed a lot more mechanical than the rest. "Hey uh, I need to go."

She looked back at him, one brow raised. "Hm? Oh, alright," she said, not offering any resistance.

"Thank you, Daxia, you've been a great help to me today." He saluted.

She scoffed at the salute. "Don't salute me, it's weird. Go on, you're welcome." She made a shooing motion and Phaidros began running off back towards the city and back to his home. Any exhaustion or sore muscles he felt in the moment were gone as he donned his armor again to practice through the night.

⤙ᘒ

The next day, Phaidros had gotten to the meeting place before Zenovia. He hadn't slept all night, but that didn't bother him. With a change in mindset, the fire within him was no longer an anxious reminder but had returned to a comfortable warmth that stoked him onward.

Zenovia arrived soon after, her helmet tucked under her arm and her rifle on her back. "Eager are we?" she said, one brow raised. "Feel better? How long have you been here?"

"Yes, yes, and most of the night, in that order." Phaidros stood upright, resting his blade against his shoulder, his helmet was currently off and sitting against a nearby stone. "Can we get started, I think I'm going to pass today."

Zenovia gave him an odd look, then frowned, as if it wasn't right for him to seem so pleased about this. "Alright, boy. Let's see what you can do." She donned her helmet, Phaidros following, and slung her rifle off her back, loading it and then leveling it at him. "Ten-second headstart as al–"

Phaidros charged her. His blade arced through the air and she kicked back away as the blade missed her narrowly. She let out a sound of surprise but Phaidros didn't give her time to make a snide comment and was already mid back swing. She leaped backwards, kicking off a tree and over Phaidros as she fired. Several of his plates cracked but Phaidros wasn't focused on those today. He spun the blade around, whistling through the air before breaking into a sprint towards her. More plates cracked, but the only plate that mattered was the last and his maneuver forced Zenovia to duck and roll to the side before blasting up into a tree. By the time she turned around, Phaidros was out of sight.

By this point, Zenovia most likely would use life sense on him to find him. He still hadn't figured that part out but if he used the rest of his senses, hopefully he wouldn't need to. Phaidros kept on the ground this time, ducking through trees as heard the distinct rustle of branches being disturbed by a heavy object nearby. There she was. He quickly threw himself into cover but not before several more plates broke in quick succession. With a jet-aided leap he was in the trees as well with a clear view of her. She had caught wind of his strategy by now and the second Phaidros moved towards her she fired off what shots she could before making a hasty retreat. Phaidros followed, leaping from trees and swinging through others, the jets in his armor roaring to life at a thought to keep his momentum going. He was already much better at navigating through the twisting branches, vines, and roots that made up the jungle, but Zenovia had been doing this a lot longer still. Soon enough he lost track of her but he did a quick reading of his suit plates. A bunch of them had cracked all over his front and side, but his back had been left completely unscathed. He knew where she'd strike next.

He heard a rustle coming from behind him and he gripped his sword. Shots rang out, Phaidros twisted, and it was just then that he saw it. He *saw* what everyone had been talking about. The enhanced reaction, the bullet twisting in the air straight towards where his back plate once was. He swiped the sword across and split the bullet in a shower of sparks before it fell uselessly to either side of him. Silence followed and Phaidros could feel his breath heaving out of his chest. He... he did it. He parried the bullet. Another silent moment followed before a small icon appeared in his screen. "Well, burn me to ash, Phaidros, you did it."

CHAPTER 10

*Set yourself apart in your deeds, so the sum of our whole becomes
stronger. Seek new avenues of strength and you will find that your
weaknesses will be less exploitable. It is through such diversity that
we may better stand together, strong enough to face all odds.*

-COLLECTED TEACHINGS OF THE EXALTED SOVEREIGN

THE REST OF the day, Phaidros had not managed to score a hit on
Zenovia. She did start wearing her helmet during the exercise
though and the gesture made Phaidros swell with pride. She
was taking him more seriously now. He knew he'd have to thank Daxia
sometime soon but he still had more training to do. The next three days
passed faster than Phaidros knew and he only slept once during that
stretch of time, stretching the energy of his ignited soul as much as possible to not waste a single moment he could. Each day Zenovia managed
to crack fewer plates before Phaidros managed to parry the bullet and
each day he got closer to catching Zenovia. She had begun to also ask
him to practice running around the wall in his armor to get a feel for
how fast he could go and also to go use the jungle as an obstacle course
to further his familiarity moving through crowded spaces. It also served

the purpose of giving Phaidros something to do after Zenovia left him for the evening. They had also returned to trying to activate his life sense but to little avail. When he was alone with his thoughts, it was difficult to feel life around him without the creeping dread of his future with the beast and his dead and lost relatives behind him. He now felt most comfortable when he was training in his armor with a sword in his hand. It was the only time he felt like he was truly in the now.

Now came the difficult part, however. They needed a third. Phaidros couldn't rely on Charon being ready in time, and he couldn't accept just anyone's help. He needed someone deadly and easy to work with. Often these two did not go hand in hand. He had begun to wonder if it was easier to wait for his brother. Part of him still worried for his safety, he hadn't heard a word from him since he left. Phaidros still had no idea how he planned to catch up in the first place. Charon wanted him to trust him to handle himself but Phaidros had been the main person taking care of him since he cindered. His brother could barely walk, let alone fight. He hoped that whatever Charon had planned, it wasn't going to get him killed.

Phaidros stood against 'The Ring', a large building made of solid stone as if it had been carved from a giant boulder of ages past. Statues of various Ignited, Shaped, Defined, and Ideals lined the pillars that held up the many archways that made up its entrances. The sun hung low in the sky, still rising, and currently being mostly shadowed by the great tree in the center of Dasos, making the usual hot and muggy atmosphere feel a bit more comfortable. His armor kept him cool despite the heat, but he had his helmet tucked under one arm which made his face feel the full sweltering heat of the jungle. He could hear the sounds of battle behind him, people were already in there dueling and he was tempted to go in and watch but, he'd prefer not to get ahead of himself before Zenovia arrived.

As he thought that, he saw the armored warrior stride up, rifle slung over her shoulder and helmet under her arm as she nodded to Phaidros. "Did you do your rounds?"

"Ran around the entire wall, twice."

"And obstacle training?"

"Swung around in the jungle through and around the trees for two hours."

"And your sword—"

"I did everything you asked, Zenovia," Phaidros said with a light chuckle.

"You're going to need it. I've been keeping tabs on what has been going on in The Ring and who might be a good partner for us." She kept her voice low; she didn't need to be swarmed with interested parties eager to prove themselves against a Shaped Beast. They had to be picky, if they openly spoke about the trouble they were facing, then every Ignited and their mother would descend upon them like a pack of starving vultures.

"Who'd you find?" Phaidros asked curiously, following her lead and keeping his voice down.

"A new guy who arrived a little over a week ago. A zhuk from what I've heard."

"A zhuk?" Phaidros asked, the name sounded made up.

"I guess I should expect you not to know that. They're the warrior caste of the nazeko."

Phaidros took a moment to register that and remember what he could about them. He had never seen them on Dasos which made young Phaidros not really think to learn anything about them. If they were anything like Daxia though, the expectations were high. He smiled awkwardly to Zenovia, hoping she'd explain further.

Zenovia stared at him before grunting in annoyance. "They, at some point, were just insects but a few of them became Ideals and lifted up their kind in their footsteps and made a handful of clans, each representing their origins."

Phaidros blinked. "They used to be bugs? Wouldn't that make them... small? And not very helpful?"

Zenovia quickly smacked Phaidros upside the head with a dull *thunk* before holding her finger up in warning. "You're lucky he didn't happen to be standing nearby. They're like humans, they come in many shapes and sizes, though even more so than us." With that she dropped her hand, stepping past him and heading through one of the archways to one of the stands, the sounds of battle echoing within. "Now come on, he has been spending a lot of the time in The Ring so it'll be our best chance to find him."

"Didn't have to smack me about it," Phaidros mumbled, following after her. She stopped, turning back to him with a glare. "Sorry," he quickly added. She silently turned back around and stalked into the ring with Phaidros in tow. Inside, they went up to the stands to view the duel currently taking place.

"Oh we're in luck," Zenovia commented at the top of the stairs up to the stand.

"Is he here?" Phaidros asked, quickly moving up beside her, looking around before she gestured to the dueling grounds.

Two Ignited were currently in pitched battle against one another. Though there was one clear difference: one of them was massive. The man had to be at least seven feet tall, his ignited armor only adding to his hulking mass. Thick armor plates padded every inch of his body, interlocked and interwoven in a complex pattern that made him look more like a graceless beetle than the usual, slimmer armor sets Phaidros had gotten used to seeing. The strangeness continued to the man's helmet, the usual flat surface of the standard helmet instead curved concave toward the man's face with two chunks of chitin shaped into mandibles coming from each cheek and meeting in the center. Atop the helmet were two holes that sprouted out into a pair of branching antlers. In the man's hands was a two-handed hammer that looked to be taller than Phaidros was, with the hammerhead being overly massive, too massive, Phaidros thought, to be practical in any meaningful way.

He was quickly proven wrong as he saw the zhuk fight. Down below, the zhuk's opponent was in standard ignited armor, wielding a halberd, a popular choice as it mimicked the Exalted Sovereign's own weapon when he was still mortal. The weapon seemed useless however as the man was repeatedly shifting backwards while thrusting the halberd forward as the antlered Ignited came barreling toward him. The armor cracked under the strength of the blow but there was so much of it and the zhuk didn't even seem to care as he roared in reply and swung his hammer once, the force of the blow sending a wave of sand to kick up from the ground in its wake.

The man opposite him ducked under the swing, the sheer weight of the strike still making his boots skid backward against the sand. The hammer slammed into the side of the ring where they had been fighting and left a crater in the rock. The zhuk's opponent seemed to think he had an opportunity as he shot forward, aiming to strike a blow at one of the smaller plates that covered an armor joint. That was a split second before the man was grabbed by his neck and hoisted into the air by the zhuk as he, with one hand, yanked his hammer out of the wall, threw the man into the hole he had just made, then slammed his hammer into it again. A loud crunch echoed through the stadium.

Zenovia, Phaidros, and the other scattered Ignited who were in attendance stared in stunned silence, a few of them with mouths agape. The zhuk pulled the hammer out of the now much bigger crater in the wall and his opponent fell face first into the sands, chitin plates in splintered pieces revealing the metal exoskeleton beneath. Phaidros's enhanced sight let him get a good look at the man even though he was far up in the stands—he was still alive, but he was going to be out of action for some time. When he looked back at the hole in the wall, he saw an imprint of the man's armor carved farther into the stone, showing that it had managed to hold, if barely. As the man slumped, the zhuk let out a loud, boisterous laugh and he turned back toward the crowd, arms at either side of him in an open gesture. "Is that all you have for me?" The man had an accent, with a slight buzzing trill at the end of his s sounds. "This is all the Holy City of Dasos has to offer? I was hoping to have a fun vacation with the Ignited who struggled most but instead all I have are easy victories!" he lamented. "Are there no others?"

The only answer he received was silence. Phaidros and Zenovia glanced at each other before Zenovia whispered, "…well I think he'll be a great help."

"Then maybe we should challenge him?" Phaidros offered. Zenovia hesitated. "You're not scared are you?" Phaidros prodded.

"What? No! Of course not," Zenovia bit back. "I don't want him to smash up my rifle and have to get it fixed before the hunt." A bad lie.

Phaidros looked back to the zhuk who had scoffed at the crowd, throwing a dismissive gesture at them all before he picked his hammer off the ground and hoisted it over his shoulder as he began to walk towards one of the waiting rooms. Kindling staff immediately ran past him, giving him a wide berth, to collect his opponent off the dueling grounds. "Well, now's our chance to talk to him. Come on, let's catch him before he leaves, or breaks someone else." Zenovia nodded and the two hurried off.

The waiting rooms were more like small meditation chambers. Here the Ignited would focus themselves before a fight. There were no armor or weapons to choose from, as each warrior Ignited was given their own set to care for and maintain. The zhuk currently stood in the center of it all, hammer hilt first on the floor as he picked at splinters of chitin stuck in the hammer head with thick fingers. It was proving difficult. The man was talking through his own private channel, a series of clicks emanating from him that sounded frustrated when the door opened and Phaidros and Zenovia walked through. "Great match out there," Phaidros started, realizing now he wasn't quite so sure how better to approach the man.

The zhuk scoffed, standing taller, towering over the two humans as his visor turned to look at him. "Was not great. If it was great I would be missing a plate or two," he grumbled in clear disappointment.

Phaidros wasn't sure how to respond, "Uh… sorry?" he tried.

"Sorry?" he asked, disappointment bleeding into amusement. "You are not the one to be crushed by my hammer, little man." He hefted the hammer onto his shoulder walking over to the two of them before leaning over to look Phaidros over. "Unless, you want this? The rest of them are cowards but maybe you will prove me wrong?" Phaidros instinctively leaned back, which made the zhuk seem to loom even more.

Phaidros suddenly felt nervous. "Oh– well– I–" He tried to quickly come up with a reply before Zenovia quickly pushed him to the side to look up at the zhuk. "We're not here to fight you. We wanted to talk to you and possibly get your assistance."

Another scoff left the zhuk before he turned to go back to the center of the room. He carefully balanced the hammer back to where it was so he could pick more pieces of chitin from it. "You are no fun. What is it you want from me?"

"Your name, first of all. It's only polite," Zenovia replied. "I am Zenovia, this is Phaidros." She gestured to Phaidros beside her who bowed his head respectfully.

The zhuk watched them for a moment, head flicking down then up, as if sizing up potential prey. "Dominik," the man replied. "Dom will be fine."

"Dom. A pleasure," she said, a smile in her voice behind her visor. "Welcome to Dasos, you mentioned something about a vacation?"

Dom muttered something under his breath. "Was busy fighting in the war on the homeworld. It was great, for a time. Ah but the same battles over and over again get tiresome, yes?" Phaidros noticed some tension in the zhuk's voice as he spoke about it, like he wasn't telling them everything. He didn't want to interrupt his potential new hunting partner however as he continued, "I thought it must be an amazing vacation to come out all this way and hunt and fight among fellow Ignited to get my spark back. Seems I am mistaken though, I don't see any good sport when I look around, well, except one."

"Who is...?" Zenovia asked.

"Shaped creature that prowls around the outer village." His grin was clear in his voice. "I want to kill it, now *that* would be a battle worth the trip out here!"

Phaidros finally managed to push his way back into the conversation. "You're in luck. That is exactly why we want your help."

Dominik laughed, dousing what little confidence Phaidros had gained in one fell swoop. "Ah yes, I remember you! You are the one preventing me from hunting this creature. I wish to kill it by myself, you see."

Phaidros furrowed his brow. "It killed some of the best Ignited that were here in Dasos when there were three together and you want to take it on by yourself?"

"Yes." Dom answered as if it was obvious. "If I am beating all of your best so handily then I think I can take the beast by myself, but am unable to do so until you either fulfill your rite of vengeance or it kills you, or you spend the rest of your time burning away doing nothing. If you are not confident you can kill it then I just need to wait." The zhuk nodded, as if this was the natural solution to his problem.

Zenovia cut in now. "You're willing to wait for a chance to fight this beast yourself? And if we die then oh well? Where's your sense of comradery?"

"Bah," Dom answered, chin lifting. "Every day is a war to live in this world, yes? That is the first of the Exalted Sovereign's teachings. If you wish for respect, you earn it. Your soul being on fire does not mean anything to me until you have proven that it burns hot." He beat his fist against his chest as he said this and leaned over them both again. "Perhaps I could be convinced you both are worthy of hunting the beast with me, in a duel?"

Zenovia's fists clenched in frustration but Phaidros gave it more thought. "Very well," he found himself saying. Dom let out a 'Hah!' of triumph.

Zenovia's gaze snapped to him then back to Dom. "Excuse us for one moment." She then grabbed Phaidros by the shoulder and dragged the two of them away as Dom shrugged. When the two were at the edge of the room, she whispered, "Are you insane, boy?"

"If I can't face him now then I have no chance against the Shaped Beast," Phaidros whispered back.

"You don't right now," Zenovia hissed. "You haven't even been able to hit *me* yet, Phaidros. Don't reach too far before you're ready. Let me fight him and when I've beaten him we can have our third and continue your training without putting you in a hospital bed."

Phaidros narrowed his eyes before he quickly turned back to Dom, "Clearly you are a greater skilled warrior than most. I don't know if I'll be able to defeat you, but surely there is some way I can prove myself?" he said more loudly, though he could feel Zenovia struggling not to strangle him.

Dom lifted his hammer back onto his shoulder. "If you break a single plate off my armor I'll be surprised. I can see your ignited potential, it's like a candle flame. It is so little. If you manage to do this then you will have a chance to kill the Shaped Beast, maybe even more of one since I'm there." He let out a single, punctuated laugh then gestured to Zenovia dismissively. "Go find the Kindlings, tell them another duel is taking place."

"You're not going to take some time to rest or let your armor grow back?" Zenovia offered in a clear attempt to buy time.

Dom scoffed again. "Small Ignited barely cracked it. I am hoping you do better, at least someone other than Sacred Suneater will be worth something out here in this jungle."

Zenovia glared at the two of them. "And what about him?" she said, jerking a thumb towards Phaidros. "Just a single broken plate?"

"Oh no, the beast will not be going easy on him and neither will I. It would be an insult. We will go until one of my plates breaks or the little man is broken on the ground," Dom replied, eagerness barely hidden from his voice.

Zenovia tensed, looking at Phaidros one more time. "Last chance, Phaidros, let me handle this."

Phaidros smiled softly. "Have a little faith, Zenovia, please? I need to do this or else I'm never going to be ready." Zenovia hesitated, but seemed to accept this answer. She nodded one final time then stalked out of the room, expression grim.

"You better get to the waiting room," Dom said to Phaidros. "I look forward to seeing how much that vengeance drives you." Phaidros nodded, taking a deep breath as he stepped out of Dom's waiting room, a pit growing in his stomach. A million doubts had begun to creep into his head like worms burrowing into fresh soil. Was he truly ready? He couldn't imagine getting hit by Dom once and still standing afterwards and he still hadn't managed to land a hit on Zenovia yet. He would have to figure it out quickly, or else he may spend his remaining time to hunt the beast in a hospital bed.

It wasn't a long wait once Phaidros had made it to the other room. Once inside he inspected the blade in his hands, seeing the reflection of the armored warrior staring back at him. It didn't feel like it truly fit him. He had trained plenty, yes, but was he a true warrior? Charon was, his father was, Dom definitely was. Did he deserve to say he stood among them? He reached inside of himself, feeling the warmth of the fire around his soul. It was the single spark of hope he had. To be an Ignited was to look at insurmountable odds and try anyway all for the sake of the experience one might gain from it. However, the line between bravery and arrogant foolishness was often a hazy one at the best of times, as his father told him.

He opened his eyes again, staring at the doors ahead of him as the staff prepared the dueling grounds. The room was too quiet, he thought, as if the weight of the task he was about to undertake should come along with something, anything, to distract him from the company of his thoughts. He took another slow breath in and out as suddenly the doors before him opened.

Phaidros stalked out into the field of rough sand of the dueling ring, Dom walking opposite of him. As he looked at Dom now he saw not a potential ally but an enemy, each step forward narrowing the window of escape for himself against the horror he was about to face. Dom had no grace in his steps; each bootfall felt as if it sent a small tremor through what little hope Phaidros had. However, it was so strange when he realized after the first step out, the next step came easier than the last. The fire within him began to heat up, burning away the doubts as he made it clear to the world that he would not stand down against this threat.

The Kindlings above were announcing the rules of the duel as agreed upon while the two Ignited stared each other down. The countdown began and Dom hoisted his hammer off his shoulder and gripped it in two large gauntlets. Squaring off against the zhuk like this made him seem more like a monster out of some children's fairytale than the proud and honorable visage of an Ignited and Phaidros had to wonder if that was the reflection that Dom's armor chose for him or if it was made like that. Phaidros mimicked him, bringing his sword off his shoulder as he widened his stance, one foot sliding back in the sand and blade pointed towards his opponent. The countdown got to zero.

"Begin!" the announcer shouted. Dom charged at him, bellowing a war cry with the weight and inevitability of an avalanche tearing down a mountain. Phaidros ran the other way.

It was immediately apparent that this was the best decision as a second later the hammer descended on the spot where he just was and hit the sand with a mighty *boom*, causing the rest of the sand in the arena to lift several inches before falling back down. Dom roared after him, "Coward! Face me!" as he lifted his hammer back up, the thrum of the jets of his armor carried him forward in a chase after Phaidros all the way to the wall of the ring.

Phaidros didn't have much time to think, but right now the heat of his potential had become a roaring fire as he tried his best to survive. He didn't have time to look back behind him to see where Dom was, instead he trusted his instincts and at the end of his run leaped up toward the wall, igniting a few jets to spin him around midair so he landed feet first on the wall. The momentum kept him planted there for a precious second before he threw himself back off and over the advancing zhuk. He twisted in the air and swung his blade in an arc down at his opponent, the motion making the blade flash in the sunlight. Dom was at full charge so he couldn't stop himself in time but he did swing his full body around into an upward swing in counter. Phaidros barely missed the hammer hitting him square in the chest while his blade connected to Dom's shoulder, creating a resounding *crack* through the arena. However, the sheer weight of Dom's swing threw Phaidros off balance throughout the rest of his trip back to the ground, limbs flailing and jets flaring to try and make him upright in the air. It failed to do so, sending him into a small tumble before he caught himself, one hand and knee in the sand as he skidded backward, sword held in a tight grip in his free hand.

Phaidros felt a rush of adrenaline fill him as he let out a heavy breath he didn't realize he was holding. He didn't die, he had managed to dodge an attack *and* managed to hit him! If he had the time to be proud he would, only his opponent was already coming after him again.

Dom was unnaturally fast for someone of his size and if it weren't for the enhanced reflexes granted to Phaidros by his ignited soul, he would have already been a bloody stain on the floor of the dueling ring. The zhuk's hammer dropped so the head of it dragged menacingly through the sand as he then picked it up and heaved it in a low arc. Phaidros threw his body upward, the force of the blow causing a gust of wind to blow him backward and just out of reach for Dom's grasping hand. Phaidros felt as if he had just avoided death's own grasp as chitin scraped against chitin.

Still, the young Ignited landed on his back, scrambling backward, jets creating a cloud of dust and sand as another hammer blow missed him by a hair's breadth. This time, Phaidros had anticipated the small jump he and the sand made, activating jets on his legs that spun him upwards and back in a backflip back onto his feet, blade at the ready.

All the while, Dom was laughing. "Run, little man, run! I wonder how much you can do that before I break your leg! Then there will be no more running for you! What will you do then?" He swung his hammer forward again. This time Phaidros braced and threw himself upward with a jet-aided jump, getting a single foot planted on the hammerhead that he sprung off of again in another twisting jump. His sword slammed into Dom's helmet and made it jerk to the side as he passed overhead. He had missed his target of the same plate he had struck earlier and as he landed he found that he barely even stopped the momentum of Dom's strike. The hammer swung around and crashed into the side of him. Time seemed to slow for a moment as the hammer met the initial resistance before sending him flying across the arena in a shower of splintered chitin followed by Phaidros bouncing off of a cracked stone wall and hitting the sand.

Phaidros' vision spun in circles, his suit flaring with messages of destroyed plates and others cracked. He blinked them away, stabbing his sword into the ground as his body quivered and struggled up onto one knee before falling down again. He looked ahead blearily to see Dom stalking over with slow steps, his hammer over his shoulder like an executioner's axe. "You are very brave for stepping into the ring with me," Dom called out. "But you fight like a little gnat biting a tiger. There will be honor for you if you surrender to me now. Your armor will not take too long to repair, but one more hit? And you're out until your time is up."

"I can't," Phaidros wheezed out, finally getting his knees under him and one foot planted on the ground. "Not yet, it's not over yet." He returned to his feet shakily, bringing his sword back up. "Not until I avenge my father and kill that beast."

Dom's head cocked to the side, gaze thoughtful. "You can't avenge your father in a hospital."

"I won't be, because I'm going to beat you."

Dom let out another laugh. "There is the spirit of a true Ignited, perhaps you would have a chance if your sword could pierce my armor." He stepped forward and Phaidros cried out, bringing his sword up and aiming for the center of the spidering cracks along one of Dom's shoulder plates. It hit square, Dom didn't even try to block it and chitin splintered under the impact. It wasn't enough. Dom dropped his hammer, grabbing the blade with his hand and gripping it tightly. He held it in place as he stepped into the strike and grabbed Phaidros by the neck, hoisting him off the floor just like he had the man before. "As it is now? You should give up and leave the hunt to the real Ignited."

Phaidros grunted, choking out a breath as he struggled against the man's grip for a moment. Then with his free hand he threw a punch forward, landing it in the center of Dom's shoulder plate. The hidden stinger activated, the plate in his gauntlet opening and a sharp spike slammed into the armor plate that sent a few more chips flying. Dom barely even registered the hit. "Lots of fight in you, even in the jaws of defeat." Phaidros punched him again, still only leaving another crack and Phaidros with a slowly depleting level of oxygen. "You will end up seeing your father soon with that attitude."

"That may be," Phaidros choked out, a crack following as he punched uselessly at Dom's shoulder. "But if I don't try"—another crack as he punched his shoulder again—"then you would be right, I would not be ignited." His lungs burned but with it he could feel his potential burning brighter. "So no, I won't give up." One more crack. "Not now, not until the deed is done!" He reared his fist back, using the last of his strength, the fire within him raging as he slammed it forward, the spike finally finding purchase and creating a deep fissure in the shoulder plate. Dom blinked, stunned, dropping Phaidros as he stepped back. The motion made the plate fall in two pieces and hit the floor in a cloud of dust.

Silence fell over the arena, all except for Phaidros struggling to catch his breath and coughing. The scattered attendants of the ring all cheered for the young Ignited's victory over an opponent that had been making them all look like children pretending to be ignited. Dom looked at the broken plate in bewilderment before he just began to laugh again. "I suppose I deserve that for underestimating you. You are tenacious, little man." He reached down, grabbing Phaidros by the arm and hoisting it up in the air as if to present a champion as he looked out at the rest of the crowd. "And such tenacity should be celebrated with your head held high! Stop choking."

"Easy for you to say, your grip is intense," Phaidros managed to wheeze out, finally having the strength to look up into the crowd. He found Zenovia, whose fingers were gripping the edge of the Ring so hard he could see small cracks in the stone. There were several Kindling staff members around her, most likely trying to talk her down from jumping into the dueling grounds. When Phaidros could finally breathe normally again he could stand taller than he did before, a muted pride filling his chest. If that last punch didn't land, that would have been it. Everything he was fighting for would have been destroyed before it even had a chance to find its own legs.

"I've had worse," Dom replied dismissively. "Now! With great victory comes great celebration. Surely there is *some* place for revelry here in the city? I haven't had a good enough fight to celebrate yet to know these things."

Phaidros' brow furrowed beneath his helmet; it was just now hitting him how friendly Dom was being. "I—well yes. You were just trying to make me give up a minute ago, why are you so eager to spend time with me now?"

"Eh?" Dom looked confused at the question. "Yes, because you were a runt before who could not break a single plate of my armor." He tapped his chest with his fist. "But now you are a strong warrior able to make even a zhuk clanner like me lose a plate!" he said with excitement. "The flame around your soul burns true now, and that is someone I am willing to fight alongside! Not some green babe." He leaned over, visor looking into his. "I will hunt with you, help you get vengeance for your father—but now it is time for us to drink and eat." He let go of Phaidros' arm and slapped him on the shoulder. "Come! And invite your mother with you. I will not have my feast be denied to me!" he said before beginning to stalk away from the Arena.

"She isn't my mother," Phaidros quickly corrected but still followed after him.

"She sure speaks for you like one." Dom chuckled.

Phaidros shook his head, looking down to the ground where he walked. He looked to his hand gripped around his sword and realized it was shaking. This was his first true victory, yet the thought of losing horrified him. He was so close to that reality today and even then it was a shallow one; he had barely managed to break a single armor plate off of Dominik and he wasn't even shaped. It was in that single step forward that he realized how far the path ahead of him still went and how little time he had to further it along.

A little over three more weeks now, that was his deadline, and he was not sure he would be able to get the vengeance he sought. A chill ran through his spine as he was faced once more with the fact that he may die soon. The levity of the victory was gone and beneath his helmet he looked haunted.

Was he really willing to die for this?

CHAPTER 11

Despair will find you. It is impossible to go through life without feeling it. It will make you wish to hide and cower and give in to its embrace. When the time comes, lash out like a cornered animal, fight with every ounce of your being and drive it back.

-Collected Teachings of the Exalted Sovereign

Dasos as a Holy City of the Exalted Sovereign was specifically one dedicated to warrior Ignited. However, a city cannot stand on the tips of spears. A third branch of Ignited existed beyond warriors and the smiths that armed them, the Artisans: doctors, artists, musicians, diplomats, and craftsmen filled the ranks as there was more than one avenue of improving oneself. The city invited a token number to the city along with any family they may have to keep everything running smoothly.

The most popular among these in Dasos were the chefs, as warriors weren't exactly known for cooking anything other than whatever meat they hunted if they could get away with it. The Feast Halls, as they were known, dotted the city landscape, taller than houses, with bright signs to attract warriors returning from hunts and their families to their tables. The competition, as with all Ignited, was fierce. Where there was competition between chefs, there was delicious food.

The Lion's Share was the choice for tonight. The tables were full, large mugs and glasses were filled with liquors and spirits, and the savory scent of well-seasoned meats filled the warm air. Dom was already three mugs of ale in and he, Zenovia, and Phaidros had only been there for ten minutes.

Outside of his armor, the zhuk was still a mountain beside everyone around him. His skin was pale with a purple tinge to it and his eyes had no pupils and seemed metallic with scintillating colors gleaming off of them depending on how the light hit them. His hair was more like flexible spines which he kept short and bunched up in a small top-knot. From how Zenovia had described the zhuk, Phaidros had expected them to look a lot more bug-like, but despite a few key differences they seemed completely human. A human with weird eyes and antlers on his head and everything else. His uniform was decorated with various metals and he wore fur over his shoulders tied in the front by a heavy chain. Phaidros had remembered seeing him in his igniting ceremony, and thought it strange how quickly they went from strangers to companions. He was one of the most decorated people in the hall, with Zenovia only wearing a necklace of various claws over her uniform and a single, silver badge with an arrow pointing upward pinned just under her left shoulder.

Dom was regaling a story to Zenovia about some campaign he fought in on some far-off world, with Zenovia looking at him as if he wasn't entirely telling the truth but suffering through the story anyway. Phaidros meant to pay more attention but he was lost in his own thoughts, staring down at the foaming drink in front of him, watching as the individual bubbles popped. The fight still bothered him, how easily he had been tossed aside, how the Shaped Beast before them would be even worse. He was going to die and not even the flame that burned within him managed to quell the buzzing swarm of doubts in his head, gnawing and biting at him relentlessly until he felt a weight shove his shoulder.

"You look like you are staring death in the face, little friend," Dom said, grinning widely. "And he is not saying very comforting things. When I see death, I plan to give him a good punch so he knows to give me a good new life when I reincarnate," the zhuk added, looking to Zenovia and hoping to get an amused smile but received none.

Zenovia's attention was on Phaidros, her intense stare softened ever so slightly into one of concern. "What's wrong, Phaidros?" she asked.

Phaidros sighed, not answering immediately as he pulled his drink closer, looking like he was about to take a swig before deciding against it and answered, "I'm just worried is all." The confidence and determination were gone now, muted. "For this hunt." He looked to Dom. "I could barely crack through your armor today and I'm supposed to try and hunt the beast that killed my father in a few weeks. I am no longer feeling confident that this is going to end well," he admitted, shoulders slumped in defeat.

Zenovia and Dom shared a glance before looking back to Phaidros. "So, you want to give up then?" Zenovia asked, tone calm.

"I don't know," Phaidros answered softly before he met her gaze. "I don't know if vengeance is truly so important to me. I'd have to move away from the city, yes, find somewhere else to live and work, but as long as my brother was with me I don't think it would matter all that much," he said. "Yes he's cindered and would have trouble but we would be able to get through it I think. I could just make Suneater douse my potential and walk away. It would be easy and I wouldn't have to follow my father into the grave to do it." He looked to Dom next. "You'd have a much better chance at finishing off the beast than me so I should let you. To continue forward now is suicide."

Both of the other Ignited were silent for a time, Zenovia's frown deeper than before and Dom's smile softened. Zenovia was the first to answer. "Being in the Order isn't for everyone, it is a commitment to live by the teachings of the Exalted Sovereign but more importantly it is a commitment to yourself, to look deep inside of yourself and say that you wish to be better and will take the steps to do so."

Dom then added, "Think of it like this, right now you are faced with a difficult, near impossible challenge ahead of you." Zenovia shot a glare to Dom but Dom continued regardless. "You could turn away from it and find an easier path, many people choose to do this thing, but what do you gain from it? Don't say your life." He quickly jabbed a finger into Phaidros' shoulder before he could retort. "I know you are scared, you have every reason to be, Phaidros, my little friend, but fear is a part of everyday life and I would say the most important part."

"That doesn't sound right," Phaidros retorted, wincing.

"It is!" Dom replied, picking up his ale and taking an audible slurp from it before putting it down and facing Phaidros more directly. "Fear is when we are the most alive. Fear makes the heart pump harder and faster with adrenaline, fear forces you to move away or toward the source." His wide grin returned. "And no matter what decision you make, you learn more about yourself, your limits, what you can and cannot do, fear forces you to change and change is what life is all about."

"So you're telling me I can run from this?" Phaidros asked, confused at the point.

"Hah! I am telling you the opposite. Normal people get the choice to run and hide from fear, Ignited though? An Ignited should seek it out wherever it may be because feeling fear means we are close to something that will make us better." He jabbed a finger at Phaidros' shoulder again. "Like today, you were scared to face me in the ring, yet you did it and came out alive and with a big strong friend, yeah?" He flexed one arm as he looked at Phaidros.

"Yeah...?" Phaidros repeated with uncertainty.

Dom then shifted, lifting a finger. "From what you have told me, this was one week of training and you managed to do this. Before that? You were not even Ignited. You are focusing on the negatives here, little friend. A week ago you were not Ignited, you were afraid but in that moment of fear you chose to take one step forward and become so. In one week you have broken one of my armor plates, something some Ignited with years of training couldn't do, think of what you will be able to do the next week? And the week after that?"

Phaidros opened his mouth to respond and then closed it, thinking. There was some sense to what he said. He was terrified to become

Ignited, he was terrified to face Dom, yet he did both of those things and managed to walk out mostly unscathed. Those were both choices that didn't end with him dying however. He still wasn't sure, a grimace formed on his face as he considered.

Zenovia then spoke. "You did all this so you wouldn't have to leave your brother alone, right? You're trying your best to protect him. That's why you became Ignited and that's why you're considering leaving. Ignore him." She says with a dismissive wave of her hand. Phaidros blinked but Zenovia continued before he could speak, tone heated. "You say you're doing all of this for him, but from everything I've heard, you just don't want to be alone." She pressed her index finger against the table, leaning in. "It is good to have other people to fight for and with, to help inspire you to go beyond wherever you were before, but at the end of the day you need to think about yourself and for yourself. Your brother needs to do the same, you can lean on each other all you want but you also need to be able to stand on your own two feet." She sat back upright, her usual, calm demeanor taking hold again. "So I ask you, without your brother here, without any other people here that would be waiting for you, would you run away?"

Dom seemed to like where this was going, because his grin was wider than ever as he excitedly turned to Phaidros waiting to hear his answer. Phaidros sat stunned, Zenovia's words piercing through him like an arrow. He *was* using his brother as an excuse wasn't he? Some part of him felt ashamed for that. He had talked big at the beginning of this all, saying grand things about avenging their father and making sure he wouldn't leave his brother behind. Yet the second things began to look truly dangerous, he was again using his brother as an excuse so that he could run away? He looked downward. "I…" he began, struggling to find the words. "You're right, Zenovia, I have been rather cowardly in all this haven't I?" He looked to Dom. "And you're also right, I have made a lot of progress in a short time," he said with a small smile before he ran a hand through his hair, gripping and pulling back at it as he struggled through his thoughts. "If I wasn't worried about my brother… I think I would wish to see this through to the end and defeat the beast."

At that, Dom slammed his hand on the table a few times in cheer, nearly knocking the drinks over as he grabbed Phaidros' shoulder and shook him before pushing his way out of his seat to look at the crowd, pointing at Phaidros. "You see this man here? This man is going to kill a Shaped Beast!"

"Why do you have to make a scene?" Zenovia muttered with an exasperated sigh, rubbing at one of her temples.

"A drink! To the Shaped killer!" Dom shouted, raising his mug into the air, the other patrons looked at them in slight confusion, Phaidros seeming the most embarrassed of all, and yet they still raised their mugs and cheered. Dom gulped his drink down in three loud, audible gulps then sat back down besides Phaidros. "Do not worry, little man, you have my protection. Besides, a challenge like this? You're following in the footsteps of the Exalted Sovereign himself."

"Aren't all Ignited in the Order?" Phaidros asked.

"Everyone wants to be the Exalted and Sovereign part, but many people just drop the third part. He who Defies! The first identity he ever got. The Exalted Sovereign who Defies."

Phaidros knew this, but Dom was right in some regard. No one really called him "The Exalted Sovereign who Defies." They just called him "The Exalted Sovereign." Perhaps because it begged the question, what was he defying? Isn't it others who would defy someone who is an Exalted and someone who is a Sovereign? "What do you mean?" he asked.

"You are defying expectations of course! The big Shaped monster is supposed to turn you into a smear on the jungle floor but you will kill it. What else will you do?" He laughed. "This will be exciting to see."

"Besides," Zenovia said with a shrug, "you have the benefit of having knowledge of what you're going up against. The final gift your father could give you." She didn't say that with pride. "We're not going to let it get the better of us this time. Your armor will only take a day or two to regrow the new plates and then we'll be able to continue training."

"In the meantime! I will show you how we train back on Rodina," Dom exclaimed. "Then you will no longer be a little man but a big strong man. Not as big and strong as me, but it will be the second-best thing." He hesitated before correcting himself. "Third-best thing. The women back home are even bigger and stronger."

Zenovia cleared her throat to try and redirect the conversation away from wherever Dom intended on dragging it. "We can talk about training another day. For now you've won a great victory today, Phaidros, you should celebrate it."

"Yes! The Exalted Sovereign would strike us down if we do not celebrate properly, so you are going to need to drink." He pushed Phaidros' mug closer to him. "Drink a lot! Let the future be a problem for tomorrow for one night."

Phaidros smiled at the two of them. His mood now was lighter than it had been but a few minutes prior. Though he realized he hadn't actually even agreed to keep hunting the beast; he had only answered Zenovia's hypothetical situation. Yet now it seemed wrong to bring that up, Dom already calling to the serving bar to start sending over plates of various dishes, half of them Phaidros didn't recognize the name of. Phaidros took a deep breath and finally took a long pull from his drink, washing away his doubts for the moment and allowing himself to finally see today for the victory it was. Dom was right, he had accomplished much in a week and he was curious to see what he could accomplish in the next.

The proceeding feast lasted for hours into the late night. Eventually the alcohol did make Phaidros feel better. Even Zenovia seemed to get nearly as boisterous as Dom was as the night progressed. It ended with Zenovia having to drag Dom out because he was intent on going into the back kitchens because he could not believe that they didn't have "Szeraze" which he insisted was something every chef worth their fire would have.

Phaidros ended up walking alone the rest of the way home. The moment he walked through the front door it felt like a weight settled on his shoulders, exhaustion overcoming him like a wave. Today was a tempest of highs and lows and he was happy to be done with it. He hadn't slept in a few days, so he decided to go easy on himself tonight and give himself some rest. The moment he hit the mattress, he fell asleep.

The next day, Phaidros' armor still hadn't fully repaired itself. He had never seen how the armor repaired itself, since it had never been so badly damaged before. Where all of the plates had been destroyed there were now yellow-white plates forming in their place with the plates that were only cracked turning more of a dark brown. Phaidros did not like the fact that when he poked the yellow-white spots, the armor was squishy. He tried not to think about that as he headed out into the city proper to meet up with Dom and Zenovia. They had agreed last night that they could not train today, but that didn't mean they couldn't strategize—and meet with their smith to see if she had anything to help them yet.

The three stood outside of *Daxia's Hoard* with Phaidros knocking on the door. They were met with silence for about a minute and began to wonder if now was a bad time, when the door opened and Daxia stood there rubbing one eye. "Yeah?"

The second Dom saw her he immediately slid behind Phaidros for protection, muttering in a language Phaidros didn't understand. "You did not tell me she was a longshi!" he said defensively. "Quickly, we must leave before she cinders us all!"

Phaidros blinked, glancing back at Dom. "Are you scared?"

"As you should be!" Dom exclaimed.

Daxia grinned. "He's right, if he isn't careful with how he speaks to me I'm going to burn his potential to a crisp."

Phaidros felt that it was a bit odd that Dom was so scared of Daxia, considering he loomed at least two feet over her. "Can... you really do that?" he ended up asking before he shook his head. "I'm sorry, Daxia, this is Dom, he's our third. Dom, this is Daxia."

"Did you come here to cower at my door or did you actually need something?" Daxia said flatly, ignoring the introduction.

Zenovia finally cut in. "Yeah, remember that request I made back when we got the armor? I wanted to see if you had an update on that."

Her tail swayed thoughtfully behind her as if she were considering shutting the door in her face before she opened the door wider. "You can come in."

Zenovia nodded in thanks, muttering to Phaidros as she passed,

"She can" to answer his earlier question, giving him a look that told Phaidros he should stay on Daxia's good side as she entered the shop. Phaidros followed after with Dom practically glued to his back, trying to keep him between himself and Daxia. As they passed Daxia gave him a fang-filled grin and hissed, which made Dom shrink further and got another snicker out of the dragon. She closed the door behind them and then walked into the workshop part of her shop. There were new projects lingering about including a half-finished set of armor and something that looked like an axe but Phaidros could see a lot of open mechanisms and gears inside that made him wonder what the end product would be.

Her workbench was cluttered with various, half-finished rounds that looked like they were small corkscrews ending in a sharp point. There were several slits in the sides. She grabbed a pistol out of a pile of what Phaidros thought was junk and began to fill up a clip. "I've been working on something and I think I hit a breakthrough," she said after taking a break to yawn. "It won't work on ignited armor really, the plates are too big, but if you're dealing with a big dumb lizard like the reports suggest then it's got lots of smaller scales on it. You can't breach the scales with normal rounds because its shaped body is simply too powerful. So, I give you…" she trailed off as she picked up one bullet and wiggled it in the air triumphantly. "Ripper rounds." Her voice didn't sound nearly as triumphant.

Dom squinted from behind Phaidros. "Seems like a normal armor-piercing round to me."

Daxia beamed. "And that is where you are wrong, my big cowardly friend," Dom glared at her but did not offer an argument.

She pointed the gun at the half-finished armor and Zenovia immediately shouted, "Cover your ears!" All three of them did so as Daxia fired the pistol, the bullet lodging itself into the chitin plate. Dom cursed again, Phaidros was sure it was something about Daxia being crazy. She walked past them all to carefully pluck the bullet from the armor and held it up for all of them to inspect. "When under sufficient speed, scalpel blades stick out of the ends of the bullet. It doesn't mean much for the armor you guys have but for a scaly hide and a glancing shot, it should rip through some scales to give you an opening."

Phaidros had never seen Zenovia look so fascinated by something. She took a step closer, examining the round. "So I can use this to make some weaknesses on the beast for others to exploit. A magazine of this before switching to normal rounds to then target. It's not a direct solution but it is better than what I had before."

Daxia nodded. "Yeah, dealing with Shaped things is difficult. Sometimes they just have an identity that makes them invulnerable and you're just out of luck unless you have an equally powerful identity that is really good at destroying things... it... doesn't have one of those, right?"

Zenovia shook her head. "From what I can tell it has a fear identity."

Daxia nodded sagely. "Well, you shouldn't have a problem then."

"How many of these do you have ready?" Zenovia asked, sounding eager.

"Oh about twelve–" She looked at the round in her hand. "Sorry, eleven. The materials and tech I need for them aren't exactly standard issue, at least, not anymore."

"What do you mean by that?" Phaidros asked.

"Well... they were more common in the second age when everyone was fighting dragons," she said with some reluctance. "Not so common anymore, so no reason to rip scales off of things."

Phaidros saw Dom staring at the rounds with new reverence before asking, "Is there any way to add this thing to a hammer? For curiosity's sake. I do not want to hunt dragons."

"Uh huh," Daxia said, not sounding convinced, "anyways I'm working with a guy down in the market district to get the materials for more. I should have enough for your hunt by the time your time's up. Don't you worry."

Zenovia nodded. "Thank you, Daxia. You've been a great help."

Daxia returned the nod. "I know, you're welcome. Now is there anything else you needed? I was in the middle of a nap."

Zenovia and Dom shook their heads, the latter doing so with more eagerness. "Just looking for the update, thank you."

"Yes let us go now and leave the dragon to rest," Dom said, already moving towards the door and failing to look casual about it. He exited, Zenovia following.

Phaidros followed as well, but lingered at the door before looking back to Daxia. "Hey Daxia?"

Daxia was already fiddling with another one of the bullet casings as she looked back at him over her shoulder. "Yeah?"

Phaidros hesitated but bowed to her. "Thank you for the other day. I was really letting my mind run rampant and you helped set me straight. I managed to pass Zenovia's test and get Dom on our side thanks to you. So—thank you."

Daxia stared before giving a more genuine grin and a two-fingered salute. "Anytime, Phaidros. If you need any words of wisdom that doesn't involve smashing your head against a wall, just let me know."

Phaidros was about to speak again before he heard Dom's voice from the other side of the door. "Phaidros! Are you alright? She is not eating you is she?"

"I'm fine!" he called out, giving Daxia one final bow of his head before slipping out the door. Zenovia was waiting with her arms folded and Dom looked like he was about to charge the door to save his friend.

"Ah! You are safe, this is good. I was worried about you," Dom said with a relieved sigh.

"Daxia's harmless, Dom. You shouldn't be scared of her," Phaidros said with a small chuckle.

"No longshi is harmless," Dom said. "Even one who has become a smith. Several of them have become involved in the war back home." He shook his head, clicking his tongue. "Terrible stories come from the survivors of those battles."

"We do not care from where your blood reigns, only where it is spilled," Zenovia reminded Dom, sounding a little impatient. "She's in the Order, so she's one of us, so you can't keep treating her like she's the Shaped Beast. Besides, you being scared of her after the pep talk you gave Phaidros yesterday is just embarrassing."

Dom stood up taller after that. "It is only right to be scared! Some challenges are too much for Ignited—maybe when we are Shaped there is a chance."

Zenovia rolled her eyes. "Right, anyways, this is our one rest day so we should make a plan for what we do going forward."

"More duels!" Dom immediately suggested.

"How about a hunt," Phaidros offered, both of them looked at him. "We're going to be hunting a Shaped Beast, surely there's more jobs that Suneater can give us right? It'd give us a chance to figure out how to work together."

Zenovia raised a brow. "Good idea, Phaidros."

Phaidros beamed a little; Dom, meanwhile, stroked his chin in thought. "Hm, it will have to be a good hunt. I say we take multiple, all at once! To really challenge us."

Zenovia nodded thoughtfully. "Alright, let's go see Suneater and see what we can grab." With the group all in agreement they set off towards the temple.

CHAPTER 12

Bonds will strain and bend, but you must hold fast. Separated
we are but hills, united we are an unscalable mountain.

-COLLECTED TEACHINGS OF THE EXALTED SOVEREIGN

T HE "COMMISSION BOARD" was a holographic display right in
front of the temple. Here listings for hunts remained scrawled
across the screen. There were all manner of listings that had
various hunting party request and sizes: protecting chefs as they looked
for ingredients out in the jungle, two Ignited requested; arresting poachers of the native wildlife, three Ignited requested; Hunt an invasive
behemoth that was traversing into this continent, fifty Ignited requested,
transportation provided. The board was updated live with rites of vengeance and other notably important commissions displayed across the
top. From what Phaidros had been told, the Order of the Ignited worked
similarly in the galaxy at large, getting requests for assistance and aid
from organizations, governments, and from within the Order itself.

It was usually crowded here in the morning but by the time Phaidros
and his companions had made it there it was clear enough where they
didn't need to shove their way past anyone to get any jobs. However

it did mean that the more challenging ones were most likely already taken. "Alright let's see here," Dom said, squinting at the board, Phaidros couldn't help but notice how he was staring at the behemoth one, as if considering if the three of them could handle that. He let out an internal sigh of relief as Dom looked away from it. "Bah, nothing worthy of the burn here," he said with a huff.

"That's good, we should worry about something easy just to see how we work together," Zenovia suggested.

Dom waved the thought off dismissively. "Back on Rodina if what you went up against didn't have a chance to kill you then it wasn't worth Ignited time."

Zenovia narrowed her eyes, "Didn't you say you were in a civil war? Wouldn't every commission have a chance to kill you?"

Dom grinned though Phaidros noticed the faintest strain to it thanks to his enhanced vision. "It did. The best ones were when those eh, what do you call them, Defiant Ones? Were involved."

"The Children of Defiance," Zenovia corrected.

"Yes, yes those ones." Dom nodded. "They and some dragons decided to stick their greedy little noses into things and it gave us plenty of challenging Ignited to fight." He points to the board. "That is what we need! Ignited opponents, they are always good for the potential, yes? What about this one, a big jaguar vulture is coming close to becoming shaped!"

Zenovia shook her head, "I don't need another surprise and for this one to end up shaped by the time we get to it like the last beast was. What about this one? A herd of Barkbiter Saurus are endangering the ecosystem to the west of the Razor River."

Dom scoffed. "You want us hunting *herbivores*? What is the worst they could do?"

That sparked an argument and Phaidros watched as his two trainers got too distracted bickering with one another to pay attention to the board. He shifted in place, not sure what to do but he glanced at the board, ignoring them for the moment as he scanned what was available. Nothing seemed to jump at him, but he needed to stop the verbal firestorm that was slowly growing next to him. "Hey! What about this one?" he called out.

They both turned to glare at him instead and he regretted getting their attention for a single moment as they both said, "What?" In unison.

"It says a colony of Chorus Apes has a new matriarch to the south and they've been interrupting other commissions in the area and that they're Ignited, would that work?"

"Chorus Apes?" Zenovia questioned for a moment, before humming thoughtfully. "I don't know, Phaidros, hive minds might be too difficult for a first mission."

"Did you say Hive Mind?" Dom immediately pushed Phaidros, gently, away from the board so he could get a better look. Phaidros had not seen a more determined look on a man's face before he poked his finger through the holographic display and stared at Phaidros. "We are doing this one."

That reaction piqued Phaidros' curiosity and he smiled a little. "Alright, let's do that one." He looked to Zenovia, a hint of pleading in his gaze.

Zenovia mulled it over, arms folded. "I'm not sold on it but…" She looked to Phaidros then sighed as she glanced away. "Alright, alright. You should have a say in your own training I suppose."

Phaidros beamed and Dom let out a cry of victory, "Yes!" The three accepted the commission on the board, information on it being transferred to their datapads and their armor when they returned to them. With the matter settled, the three split ways, Phaidros eager to see how the three of them stacked up against this new challenge.

The group set out the next morning at first light and began heading south outside of Gate Six. The area of jungle the Chorus Apes were situated in contained a species of trees that were about twice as tall as the ones near Dasos, and all of them were Ignited. Phaidros was never certain on how trees could ignite, but if Suneater had once been a tree and made it to an Ideal, then clearly he was missing something. The fact they were Ignited meant that they were no longer going to be dealing with a docile jungle around them; it would fight back if it saw them as weak. "So how do you fight a hive mind?" Phaidros had asked as they were traversing the jungle at a bounding run. With the armor and their ignited souls, it might as well have been a nice morning jog that they could keep up all day.

"That'd be a great question for Dom," Zenovia said, glancing over to the zhuk. "The nazeko are all capable of tapping into one, it's what helped them carve out their place in the galaxy."

Dom was uncharacteristically silent for a long moment. "Tear off the head and the body will not know what to do with itself," he replied, a hint of venom in his tone. Phaidros noticed he seemed even more intense today than he did when the two of them fought. Dom was more than eager to fight these apes and the curiosity ate at him but he pushed that aside for now. "So we just need to kill the matriarch?"

"Yes," Zenovia answered. "The rest of the apes won't make it easy, however if we approach this with caution and coordination then it should be simple enough."

Dom grunted at that and Zenovia and Phaidros had begun to think of how to tackle the situation as the jungle slowly changed around them.

The trees extended further into the sky, the jungle around them growing darker as each tree struggled to get as much sun as possible with their wide leaves. Phaidros couldn't help but notice how each of those leaves were covered in spines and when a bird had made the mistake of swooping in too close to one, it snapped it up inside of one leaf and did not let go. He made an effort not to imagine himself getting snapped up next. The trees themselves swayed in an invisible current, their bark creaking with each bend, their branches stretching out far and wide in a tangled web. "We're getting close," Zenovia began, switching to their internal communications which made her voice sound like a series of clicking and chattering mandibles to anyone not on their frequency. "Listen closely, Phaidros, and you'll be able to hear them, your suit will pick them up after you've spotted them. It'll have to be what you rely on since you still can't use life sense."

Phaidros nodded and listened to the jungle around him. Between the usual buzz of insects and chirping birds there was a distinct howl of an ape echoing in the distance. Another answered it soon after. "I hear them," he answered, drawing his sword off his back as the group stopped their dash through the jungle and began moving with more caution, weapons ready.

"They will do all they can to protect their matriarch, you'll find her where the most apes are," Dom said, eyes up towards the trees. "They most likely already know we're here. They will begin to surround us soon."

"Then I am getting to a higher vantage point," Zenovia said, then immediately set off towards a tree, scaling its trunk with ease before kicking off to one of the branches. Phaidros could hear more howls echoing through the jungle, noticing more and more how they began to come from all directions, Dom was already jogging up ahead, hammer at the ready. Phaidros and Zenovia had tried to come up with a plan beforehand, but they did not have too much knowledge of the colony, so they would need to see how it worked first… which meant that someone had to be bait. That bait, obviously, was Phaidros. "Just keep yourself ready, Phaidros, Dom and I will keep you from any real danger."

Dom grunted his assent. Phaidros didn't know where Zenovia was anymore, but her assurance was enough to make him feel a little more at ease. The howls were loud now, surrounding them completely as Phaidros scanned the trees, looking for any signs of their quarry amidst the ever-shifting jungle.

He spotted it after it howled at him, its brown fur making it blend with the warm tones and colors of the trees that surrounded it. It was as he expected, a large ape high up in the trees, one strong hand gripping the wide branch beneath and the other one carrying a stone. Phaidros' armor outlined the creature the second he saw it, then the other two dozen that he had not managed to spot a second after. He brought up his sword in a defensive posture. "Yeah, they're all here," he said with some wariness.

"I got sight," Zenovia replied. "Dom, can you–"

Dom had switched to open communications as he shouted into the open air, "Hello my furry friends!"

"Dom, what are you doing?" Zenovia hissed.

"You will be showing me to your matriarch now! And I will free you all! This is a promise."

Phaidros looked to Dom with an incredulous look as the apes began to howl, stomping their hands and feet on the trees above them in a raucous chorus with one another. He saw Dom's head swivel around before he peered off into the distance. "There you are…" he said with malicious excitement before the jets in his armor roared to life and he rocketed off into the distance, devastating whatever plantlife might be between him and where he was going.

The apes acted immediately, half of them hurling their rocks at him and Phaidros and some of them leaping off the trees after Dom. An unfortunate one managed to land right into the way of his hammer and was left a mess of bone and viscera against one of the great trees with a swing that might as well have been Dom swatting a fly and he disappeared into the underbrush.

Phaidros was by himself, his training kicking in as his sword flashed through the air, swatting away some of the stones that were raining down towards him. Gunshots followed soon after and he saw several outlines fade to nothing as apes fell from the trees in a lifeless heap. Zenovia was stringing out curse after curse into their internal communications, aimed at Dom, but the zhuk didn't seem to register it in the slightest.

"Zenovia! New plan?" he asked, sword cleaving through one ape that had tried to jump down onto him. He was surprised at how easy it was, this was his first time fighting something that wasn't in Ignited armor. It gave him a new appreciation for the smiths and also the suit that protected him. Some stones rained down from him but they might as well have been rain drops. This also had the unfortunate effect of covering him in ape blood, coating his visor in the stuff but a filter change in his visor corrected all of the colors. He didn't want to give that setting any more thought than he had to.

"Chase after Dom, we can't get separated," she said. "Move ahead, I got you covered, get up into tree level if you can."

"Right!" Phaidros called out and moved to follow her instructions. More apes descended upon him but a regular, pointed rhythm of gunfire made any that were an actual threat to Phaidros drop to the ground in a bloody heap. What he thought were dozens were actually hundreds and Dom's path had been clearly marked by the destruction left in his wake. Phaidros began to wonder what Dom meant by 'freeing' them. He tried to follow after him but apes were beginning to flood the jungle floor in front of him, forcing him to divert up a tree with more hot on his tail. With a quick pivot Phaidros leapt off towards a tree, feet planting and scraping against the bark before he kicked off to grab one branch. An ape landed right above him but Zenovia landed a shot right between the eyes that sent it falling backwards. With the newly made free space, Phaidros pulled himself up atop the branch and took a moment to survey the situation.

It was here that Phaidros could see why Zenovia had called them a hive mind. His suit began to highlight more he hadn't seen before, with Zenovia being a single green highlight in a sea of red. They moved as if they were one organism, a horde of the creatures moving forward and retreating as if they were part of a sentient, amorphous blob. One that was beginning to completely encircle Zenovia. "Zenovia!"

"I see them." She raised her rifle, firing a shot that sent three in a line tumbling to their deaths in the jungle below. In the same second she pulled the trigger she twisted around, jets flaring to life as she kicked the skull of another ape and sent it spiraling off the branch before she completed her turn and sent off another volley that downed more. Phaidros had to force himself not to stare in awe as she made each motion seem effortless and calculated like a choreographed dance. It was different to watch her now that he wasn't training directly with her. To see how years of Ignited training and experience could blend together in one awe-inspiring display of skill and discipline. He hoped that he could become like that someday. Though if he wanted to get there, he needed to stop the trees from trying to eat him.

While he was distracted, several leaves of the tree he was perched on had been slowly creeping up on him, spined leaves ready to snap shut. He made a run for it right as they snapped, sword arcing around him and cutting through giant sections of leaf. There was more resistance than he expected, with a rip like he was cutting through thick, threaded tarp. Vines snapped after him seconds later and his quickened reactions made him cut away several more before he tried to run. Apes had gathered on the other side of the branch but kept back from him, making him have to choose his opponent. He was about to choose the apes when, mid step, another vine whipped around his ankle and hoisted him into the air foot first. A leaf three times his size then snapped him up, pinning him between spines that locked him into place. He struggled against its grip before he activated the jets in his armor, the heat burning the leaves until it caught fire and was forced to let him go. As graceful as a fish on land, Phaidros fell back to the ground with flailing limbs.

Dom's voice finally crackled through the team's internal communication. "Hah! I have found the Matriarch!"

"Dom!" Phaidros shouted as he had to fight off a bunch of apes that swarmed and beat on him with heavy fists. "We're surrounded back here and need help!"

"Do not worry, little friend, it will be over soon, just give me two minutes with this oversized monkey. You should see it, it is three times my size!"

"I would love to see it!" Phaidros shouted as he finally managed to get one of the apes off of him with the help of the stinger in his gauntlet. "But you left us behind!"

"Eh? You both are fine, though there are a lot of apes around here now that I see that. Must be even more than there!"

"Dom!" Zenovia bellowed in fury.

"Fine fine, watch this." Nothing happened for another painstaking thirty seconds as Phaidros and Zenovia were struggling not to be dragged to the ground and beaten to a pulp, but all of the sudden all of the apes howled out in an ominous, pained cry in perfect unison. The weight of their voices made the leaves of the trees shake and a moment later the apes began to all run off into the same direction save for a token few. "That got their attention," Dom laughed over the comms.

"What did you do?" Phaidros asked, watching the apes go while cutting down the few that tried to distract him.

"I gave the matriarch a new limp. You better hurry, friends, otherwise it will be me who is monkey food instead!"

Zenovia landed besides Phaidros, loading a new clip into her rifle. She switched away from their private channel to speak openly, "If they don't, I'm going to kill him instead, are you alright?"

Phaidros nodded. "Yeah, so much for the plan, huh?" He said, trying to lighten the mood and began to run in the direction Dom went.

"If this is how Dom is going to behave when we fight the Shaped Beast he's going to get us killed. We don't need a bull charging blindly ahead, we need someone who will work with us, no matter how good he is," Zenovia grumbled as she followed after him.

Phaidros frowned, not that Zenovia could see it and the two chased after the fleeing apes, clearing through any that had tried to delay them.

When they had reached Dom, the zhuk was laughing as if he was having the time of his life as apes swarmed him. Each swing of his hammer sent waves of them flying through the air and blowing the rest back from the sheer weight of his swings. The jungle was littered with corpses that the trees were eagerly snapping up, starting to see the apes as prey. "Hello! I am glad you managed to show up, the Matriarch is escaping, but it will be difficult with a crushed knee haha! Are you both happy now?"

Zenovia muttered, "Yeah, that's it, I'm going to let him die." Phaidros nudged her shoulder and gestured towards the Matriarch that was limping away, the smaller apes covering her retreat. The Matriarch was a large ape as wide as the tree trunks that surrounded them and hands that were as big as Phaidros was tall. Her legs were much shorter than her arm and as she moved on all fours Phaidros could see the clear limp. "Let's just get this over with," Zenovia said with a sigh and leapt up and off towards one of the trees to give chase from above.

Phaidros looked to Dom. "We're going after it, can you keep the apes off of us?"

"What do you think I'm doing? That thing is more scared of me than you! Go, little friend, and give that thing a good stab for me, yes?"

Phaidros nodded and without any further delay chased after the Matriarch. It wasn't hard with her crippled leg but the apes began to switch targets whenever he got close. That was, until Dom noticed and began carving a bloody path towards it again, which would send all of the smaller apes back after him. Zenovia kept Phaidros' path clear until the Matriarch saw she had no choice but to stand and fight against him. Internally, Phaidros felt like this moment could have been the entire hunt if there was better coordination, but that was a thought to share after the fight was over.

The ape howled in anger at Phaidros, drumming her fists against the ground in an effort to intimidate him. He was intimidated, but he did not back down. He readied his blade and charged the Matriarch. The ape swung at him with one of her massive hands, hand outstretched to try and backhand him into a stain against the tree. He kicked backwards, narrowly avoiding the first swipe as the second hand came down to try and crush him from above. It slammed into the earth where he just was and he twisted around and stabbed his sword through the back of her hand and into the dirt beneath. She howled again and Zenovia took the opportunity to unload a few rounds into her exposed chest. The bullets pierced her hide, but she was a large enough beast that she wouldn't go down like the others did. Still, Zenovia managed to make the Matriarch bleed from her chest.

Despite their efforts however, they could not get in close for the kill. All it would take was one good crushing squeeze from her hand and Phaidros was as good as dead. Every few swipes or snaps at Phaidros he'd narrowly dodge before Zenovia and Phaidros would strike back and prevent her from getting the upper hand. It wasn't until Dom had come barreling towards them that they had an opening. Perhaps he had just gotten bored of crushing small apes. Stragglers came after him but he just bowled through them as if they weren't there. "Phaidros, after me!"

Phaidros had barely any time to react as the Matriarch reached out to grab Dom. Dom dropped his hammer and put his hands out to both sides, stopping the beast in her tracks with a roar of effort, his plates beginning to crack and the metallic plate beneath beginning to groan from the strain. Phaidros acted immediately, leaping up and using Dom's wide shoulder plates as a stepping stone to vault over and into the Matriarch, pulling his blade back and stabbing her down into the breached hide that Zenovia had created earlier. The sword sank deep, cracking through the already damaged ribs and into the heart as the beast reared back and then fell to the earth with one final cry of pain before she stilled. Around them the rest of the Chorus Apes stopped in their tracks, their howling now much more chaotic before they began to scatter into the jungle. No more Ignited matriarch made the tree leaves and vines descend upon them in a rabid feeding frenzy as they tried to escape.

Dom rolled his shoulders as he stood up straight, flexing his gauntlets as if to shake off a numb limb. Phaidros was atop the creature, still feeling adrenaline pump through him as the fire within him raged with new life. They did it? A small surge of pride added to the warmth of the fire as he pulled himself to his feet and turned to see Zenovia whistling for Dom's attention so she could punch him.

The blow connected, Dom's head jerking to the side but the rest of him not budging an inch. "What was that back there? Was that your attempt to be cute? We could have died," she growled.

Dom slowly turned his head back, a small spiderweb of cracked chitin on his faceplate now. "You didn't and we killed the Matriarch, this is a success, yes?"

"You agreed to join this team if Phaidros cracked your plate, he did, you're supposed to be working *with* us, not just charging into danger and leaving us to deal with our problems."

Dom waved it off and Phaidros saw Zenovia's hand twitch as if she was fighting back the urge to strangle him. "Ah but strategy worked! I got the apes off of you, it is all good, right, Phaidros?"

Phaidros felt both of their gazes on him again. He looked between them both and sighed, "I mean yeah we killed the Matriarch but we were in serious trouble back there." Zenovia was about to speak up again but

Phaidros continued, "Towards the end there though, with you keeping the Apes busy and letting us make openings was good though. We need more of that, not... the beginning of all this." He gestured where they came from. "We managed to salvage it in the end, yeah, but... we need you not to run off on us, Dom. You may think you can handle it all but let us work with you."

Dom seemed to shift in place and Phaidros' words seemed to have better luck than Zenovia's. "Forgive me, little friend. I was very excited to kill the Matriarch and free small apes from the hive mind."

"Good job freeing you did," Zenovia snapped, gesturing to the picture of carnage behind them all with a bloody red adding to the warm tones of the jungle in a sinister way. They had carved through brutally, perhaps more brutal than what was necessary if they had approached this better. "They're all dead now and the trees are snapping up what remains of the colony."

Dom looked behind him, then at his discarded hammer. He reached up, scratching the back of his helmet in silent contemplation. "I suppose this is true," he eventually said, voice quieter than Phaidros had been used to hearing from him. There were no more arguments from him.

"Let's just go home," Zenovia said with a sigh, holstering her rifle over her shoulder as she stalked back in the direction of Dasos.

Phaidros hopped off the Matriarch and started after Zenovia, though he stopped to look back at Dom when he didn't hear footsteps following him. Dom was still where he stood before, looking down at the broken corpses that surrounded him. Phaidros couldn't see his expression through his helmet but the zhuk seemed frozen. Phaidros felt a creeping feeling of worry before he told Zenovia to wait and walked over to Dom. He placed a hand on his shoulder, "Hey, are you alright?" he asked in genuine concern.

His voice seemed to break whatever trance Dom was in because his antlered helmet shook side to side. "Hm? Oh, yes. It is nothing, little friend." His tone was distracted, but it quickly recovered to the same joyful tone Phaidros was more familiar with. "Zenovia is right, yes? We should be going home, today is a tremendous victory! We will need more missions to train and keep us busy until we face the beast." He nodded, picking up his hammer and striding past Phaidros as if the previous moment hadn't happened at all.

Phaidros watched him with growing concern as he walked away. Everyone who had come to Dasos did so because they were at a point where they were struggling to keep their flames lit. What made them come here? Dom said it was all a vacation to him, but after that display, how he spoke in the Lion's Share and at the board, he wasn't sure whether or not that was accurate. What about Zenovia for that matter? He wished he had more time to ask them, but with their time shrinking by the second, he knew it would have to wait. With a sigh, he followed after them for what was sure to be a quiet walk home.

CHAPTER 13

Through salvation, they will find peace and you will be the shepherd that takes them from their uncaring and cruel god.

-BOOK OF THE FATHER, FIRST PAGE

C HARON STOOD AT the bank of the river, staring within. The rushing water did not give him sight at what lay beneath, though it did give him a murky mirror to see himself. His uniform was covered in dirt and a beard had begun to grow out without a razor to shave with. The most notable change, however, was how his eyes had changed from a pure sapphire blue to a blue-green ocean. He hardly had paid it any mind and with a quick switch to his soul sight the world darkened around him save for schools of glowing orbs of white swimming beneath the surface of the water. He lifted a branch in his hand, the other sliding across the surface while transferring vitae into it. The branch smoothed into a sharp point, the branches folding into the rest of the wood like clay. He let go of the branch and it continued to float in mid-air. Then with a flick of his wrist downwards the makeshift spear stabbed through the water and retreated back with a jerk of his hand with a wriggling fish at the end of it. He could have just sapped its vitae and pulled it out of the water himself, but he learned on the first day that the fish tasted absolutely disgusting if he did that.

A fire was already waiting behind him and with another gesture the spear floated over beside it. He walked over, finishing off the fish and spearing through with a makeshift spit, letting it sit over the fire and begin to cook. Around him, the once vibrant jungle had been cleared away and a makeshift shelter had been set up nearby made out of solid wood. It turned out, being able to manipulate dead matter was great for construction. When he initially had come out here, he was sure he would have to set up some makeshift tent out of tree leaves, but vitaemancy had practically eliminated any problems he thought he might have while he was out here. He was sure that by the end of the month, he'd be able to return to Phaidros with his head held high. With a content sigh he sat down by the fire in a makeshift chair, watching the fish cook. Beside him, his knife remained planted into the ground containing Exaltation. Charon watched the fire idly before thinking aloud, "I need armor if I'm going to fight."

It is dangerous for you to return to the city as you are. Suneater will notice.

The knife rumbled beside him. "I know," Charon said with another sigh, "So, what I'm thinking is that there's a cave system nearby that stretches down to the ruin layer. So I can get some of the chitin off of the insects there and make armor off of that."

The knife rumbled again in thoughtful contemplation before Exaltation spoke.

They who skitter in the dark could be of assistance, but to keep the armor going you would need to constantly feed it vitae and it wouldn't provide you the physical benefits that the Ignited have in their armor because of the powered systems beneath the chitin. You would have armor that regrew itself and that you could mold, nothing more.

Charon mused on the idea for a little longer. That didn't sound completely useless, but if it was going to require even more vitae, he wasn't sure how viable it was for his short-term goals. If he was careful with how he stole vitae from the jungle around him, it could work though. If the monster had attacked the city however... He stopped the thought before it continued, shaking his head. "Well I can't just go in there in my uniform, one wrong step and it'll tear me to pieces."

You do not need armor when the jungle around you is yours to command. Let it tear you to pieces after it has cleaved through legions of your puppets.

There they went on about the reanimation again. Even after a week, Charon didn't feel comfortable using the power, it had too many moral implications behind it that he would rather not think about. The other powers were useful enough but Exaltation did make a point, it was tremendously useful—if it wouldn't make Suneater banish him on the spot or worse. Would that be worth it? If it meant he got to save his brother? The fish had finished cooking and he pulled it off the fire, idly twirling the ends of the stick in his hands in thought. His brow furrowed, Phaidros surely would be saying that he was doing all of this for Charon, but was Charon doing all of this for Phaidros? He wasn't entirely convinced. Cindering had ruined his life and he was already beginning to see how his brother treated him differently, the same way everyone else had treated him. He didn't want to save them for their sake, he wanted to save them because then he'd prove to them that even while cindered he was still stronger than any of them and they should feel ashamed for looking down on him all this time. He took a single bite of the fish before pausing as the trees nearby rustled.

Someone approaches.

This was all the warning Charon got before an armored figure came stalking out of the edge of the jungle. They were alone, but Charon knew that the Ignited here on Dasos rarely traveled alone. He pushed himself to his feet, fish discarded. His thoughts raced, the stolen vitae helping keep them from lagging behind. Two clicks from the armored figure confirmed Charon's theory, there were more Ignited nearby. With a flex of his will he switched to his soul sight, seeing the ball of light in front of him burn and seeing two more burning light motes scattered in the jungle out of immediate sight. He kept his eyes locked on the armored figure. The ridges of the armor were somewhat familiar to him; the last time he had seen it was when it was dark, they were one of the Ignited that had initially questioned him about the "meteor" that fell a week ago.

They switched to open communications, their tinny voice calling out to Charon. "You are far from Dasos, cindered one." They looked around at the clearing and the dead trees—and then at the small shack that sat proudly behind Charon. "Is there someone else here with you?"

Charon was giving himself a thousand different curses in his head. Of course he would be found out, of course the Ignited would have inevitably found him here especially after boldly making a campfire in the middle of the jungle. This was bound to happen but Charon was hoping he'd have at least another week. He began to speak, hoping he could somehow make this situation better. "No, it's just me. I am out here training."

Charon assumed then that the Ignited was making a quick life sense of the area, finding that he was correct. "It would be safer for you to train under the guidance of Suneater and reigniting your soul, out here you risk falling prey to the Shaped Beast your brother is supposed to be killing." He did a double take as his gaze stared right at Charon's chest. "Your potential..." he began, voice trailing off.

Charon seized the opportunity. "I've managed to grow some back out here by forcing myself into the dangers of the jungle."

The Ignited considered in silence before he looked back at the house again. "And you built a house in the meantime, in less than a week. You are quite the crafter, cindered one." Charon tensed, these lines of questions were not working out in his favor. He couldn't just say he had been working on it for far longer, it was abundantly clear beforehand how much he struggled to even walk. "And you stood up rather quickly when you saw me approach and I haven't even seen your cane," the Ignited continued, stepping further into the clearing. "So please, tell me more of this training you've taken part in that has allowed you to recover so quickly."

"What does it matter to you?" Charon said, his heart beating faster.

"Suneater gave me a commission to find the falling star, just as before. When my party and I could not find it the initial night, they said to look out for suspicious, wilting foliage and beasts. Then I come into the clearing here now and see that a good nine hundred square feet of jungle has been cleared by one, lone Cindered. One who also managed to build a house in the same time and has new potential lingering around their soul. I could see how someone with a devour identity might be able to recreate this but you? No. You may see why I am suspicious."

Charon set his jaw. Off to the side, his knife rumbled.

Do not let them take the book.

The subtle movement was noticed by the Ignited, whose enhanced vision and his suit systems most likely showed him the knife as it vibrated from the power of Exaltation's voice. They stepped over to the knife. "Stay there," they commanded and they knelt down and pulled the knife from the ground, inspecting it. Charon tried desperately not to inch his way towards the house and his mind couldn't help but point out how now the Ignited was between him and the river. All it would take was one good surge of his power and the man would be sent into the flowing water. The fish were voracious enough to probably distract him for a good few seconds—but then there were the other two waiting in the jungle. The Ignited looked back to him from the knife after finding nothing of interest. "So, where is it?"

"It?" Charon asked.

"Don't play stupid with me," the Ignited hissed, pointing the knife at him. He then idly flipped it in his hands as he stood upright again. "Something fell from the sky and you took it with you that night. That can be the only explanation for all of this." He gestured with the knife around the two of them, pointing out the dead foliage. "Nothing close to winter on this world to make them start dying, it is not in season for the sapper locusts to emerge for another two years and there are no Shaped on the planet with an identity that could do such a thing save for the Suneater themselves. This on top of the suspicious house that's behind you. So please do not continue to waste my time, or this friendly chat will start to become a lot less friendly." A click from his helmet followed and his two companions made themselves known, one, a drasil from what Charon could tell based on the bark-like ridges on their armor, perched atop a tree with an arrow nocked in an intricate-looking bow and the other resting a twin headed axe atop their shoulder, etchings in their armor marking them as someone from ikaroa heritage.

They were trying to intimidate him. He knew one wrong twitch would end very badly for him. The leader could probably lodge that knife into his throat before he could finish saying "burn to ash," and thus he tried, carefully, to de-escalate the situation. "There is no need for that, I am Cindered, you all could break me a hundred different ways and I'd be powerless to stop it."

He heard clicks coming from one of the other Ignited and the leader stepped in close, looming over him. They flipped the knife over and held it out to him hilt first. "You are still our duty to protect, cindered one, though that might mean saving you from yourself and whatever danger has Suneater scouring the jungle for you. Where is it?" he asked again, more insistent this time.

Charon did not shrink before him, despite every fiber of his being wishing to cower like a shamed pup. There was no way out of this, he realized and defeat slowly creeped into his mind. His shoulders slumped and a frown crept onto him. His teal eyes looked up to meet the visor of the looming Ignited. "What will happen to me?"

"That is up to the Suneater to decide, but I am sure the punishment will be based on the severity of what you're hiding from us."

Charon hesitated, opening his mouth once before closing it and pondering further. "It's… in the house, in my bag under the cot."

What are you doing?

His knife rumbled, but he kept a firm grip on it. Even when Exaltation seemed bewildered they still sounded like they were exalting some God. There were some clicks shared between the party before the ikaroa stalked over past the two to head into his makeshift house while the archer remained behind with their arrow nocked but not drawn. Charon hung his head.

Think about what you're doing, Charon, what you are giving up and what you are returning to should you allow Suneater to take the book. You will be Cindered once more, barely alive, barely dead. Your brother will keep moving ahead while you are stuck in purgatory; do you truly believe that he will not look at you the same way these three look at you now?

The knife began to rumble a little too much that a small tone emanated from it. Charon dropped the knife before the others took it as a threat. Exaltation's words made him tense further.

Life will move on without you, your brother moving to greater deeds beyond this world with you being left behind, alone, forever a stain on the legacy of the Ignited and your father.

Charon's fists clenched and the leader of the Ignited glanced down to the knife still vibrating on the ground. Phaidros wouldn't leave him, no matter what happened he knew he wouldn't be left behind... right? He thought back to the last time he spoke to Phaidros. He had told Charon that he couldn't wait for him. This was only the beginning... and possibly end of Phaidros' journey. If he succeeded, how many more times would Charon have to hear 'I can't wait for you', or would his failure to catch up be what led to Phaidros' death? No one else could help him. No one else would help him. It had to be Charon. It had to be.

You have read all but the rituals, Charon, use your power and you will be able to defeat three faltering Ignited on this backwater world.

A few clicks came from inside the house and the leader looked from the knife to the house.

Charon took in a deep breath and drank the vitae around him. It started with the trees just beyond the perimeter, the fish in the river, and then swept inwards towards the three ignited presences around him. The feeling of the ignited vitae mingling with his own stolen felt like hot irons against his chest and he screamed in pain. The two Ignited he could see suddenly stumbled as if struck with sudden breathlessness. Charon could not drain them completely, but now he surged with vitae. He had cried out in pain so they wouldn't immediately suspect him, which gave him one second of opportunity which he intended to make use of. He drew his hand back as he stumbled in mirror of them. In that motion he poured his vitae into the earth beneath him, feeling it as an extension of himself before he thrust his hand forward. A single pillar of earth shot from the ground and slammed into the Ignited across from him and he heard the crack of plates as the man was sent sailing through the air. The leader tried to activate his jets but couldn't reorient himself before he hit the water with a splash.

There was no turning back now. Charon had been Ignited before and he knew how these teams would fight in coordinated strikes. Charon had caught his footing and was already wheeling his arm towards the archer as they drew back an arrow. His vitae flowed into the arrow itself right as it fired. Behind him the axeman came crashing through the wall of his house. The arrow flew but with a duck and quick flex of his will, the arrow curved and slammed into the approaching Ignited's neck between the plates with the force of a bullet hammered into an armor's weak spot. The force of the impact knocked them off course and made the axe swing barely miss Charon. The wind shear that followed knocked him off his feet anyways but the second he hit the ground he pushed out more vitae and made the section of earth beneath him shoot up into the air and launch him skyward. He reached out for the spear he had made earlier and it flew towards him before he caught it in the air and hung by it. Vitaemancy was truly incredible, he thought, but now was not the time to revel in victory that hadn't happened yet.

He still had plenty of vitae but the Ignited below were regrouping. The ikaroa was pulling the arrow from their neck with the archer running up to try and assist them while the leader managed to throw themselves out of the river into a run. They still had the book. An idea formed in his head as he pulled himself atop the hovering branch and balanced upon it on his feet. It felt odd, as if he was standing on top of a second pair of hands. Once he caught his bearings he willed the branch down low, careful of his balance before he swooped down into a dive, riding the spear like a board as he swung around the edge of the clearing, extending his will as he passed, the ground around them raised, walling off the group from escape. He could hear panicked clicking coming from the three and he had better sight of what the leader had been going for, his knife. They reached it just as the archer was preparing to take another shot. They didn't learn did they?

Still, with explosive force two projectiles were launched at him but he had already filled them with his vitae and yanked them to either side. They were too fast for him to fully swing them back into the Ignited and it still had some weight as if he were physically pulling at them. The motion made him nearly fall from his spear. He caught himself and with a roar of effort threw his hands forwards. The rising ground trailing behind him sped past him in dangerous spike formations and forced the Ignited to dash to either side and isolate their fallen comrade. Charon jumped off the spear, making it fly up into his grip as he charged at the Ignited struggling to get back to his feet. With a swift motion, he lodged the spear into the space the arrow had gone earlier and poured more vitae into the spear. The branch hardened and thinned as he willed it to become denser then shoved the power forward into the point. There was a creak of metal and chitin straining against the wood before a sickening crack was heard. There was no scream, no defiant cry, just silence as the ikaroa's soul floated away as if it were a weightless feather.

Charon let go of the spear and scrambled for the book; the man had it in the messenger bag still and tried to pull the whole bag off of him in his panic. A mistake and one that had two Ignited now standing on the spiny wall of earth he had created. "Get away from him!" the leader bellowed and descended upon him. Charon threw himself backwards just in time to miss the kick that cratered the earth where he just was. He willed the earth around them to twist and try and spear through the leader but with a well-aimed punch it crunched through the much thinner earth. The archer had learned their lesson and was moving to flank him. The element of surprise was gone. Options were running out and he was about to be surrounded. This was going to be the end unless—he gestured behind the leader and his vitae poured into the corpse of the ikaroa.

He now saw through two sets of eyes as theirs snapped open. He could see the heads-up display of the armor flashing vital warnings but ignored them as with his new puppet, he pulled himself to his feet. Once more he was surprised at how easy it was to use this power, eerily so, as if being in two separate bodies were as easy as being in one. Charon had spent a lot of vitae, he could pull more but it would cause another surge of pain and that might not get him the same opportunity the last attempt had. He threw himself to the floor as attacks came from both sides, making both Ignited have to dodge each other to avoid cracking each other's armor. Which was perfect, because it made the archer come straight into the path of the axe that was swinging for their shoulder. A startled series of clicks resonated out of the archer, Charon could only imagine what they must be thinking seeing the dead body of their friend attacking them. He tried not to let the thought get to him as he scrambled past towards the axe-wielding corpse who swung again. With the walls on either side of them, it gave the archer very little room to maneuver. They tried to leap over the wall to escape but Charon ordered a full charge and the axeman came crashing into them and made them hit the dirt with a heavy thud. They already had their axe over their head, and Charon willed them to drop it into the archer's head.

The leader would not let their companion die and came swooping in, bringing up both arms in a cross to block. The axe cracked and shattered the plates beneath it, biting into the metal beneath as sparks flew from the impact. Charon was safe for the moment, so once more he took a deep, painful breath, stealing more vitae from the two living Ignited. The pain that followed made him drop to his knees, but he could see it still affected his victims, making them shiver. It gave him the fuel needed to keep the puppet going and with another quick flex of his will, the immediate escape backwards closed. The metal creaked further as the axeman put all of their dead weight into their axe. The leader then dropped their guard, letting the axe slam into their chestplate as he reared back a punch and slammed it into the axeman's head, then another, and another in quick, blurring succession.

The puppet seemed completely uncaring of the damage even as it broke through chitin and steel to smash into its face as it brought its axe back again and swung it into the same spot, cleaving through chitin and steel to plant the axe straight into his heart and drop him on the ground. Another soul joined the others beginning to float into the air with the archer following suit seconds after.

Charon was heaving breath in and out as he stared out of two sets of eyes. Even with its face bashed in, he still seemed to be able to see clearly. He pulled his vitae back from the axeman and they unceremoniously slumped to the floor. Silence followed and Charon could hear nothing else but his own breath and his own beating heart. Trembling hands gripped at his head as he slowly curled in on himself. He killed them. He killed them all. These were not annoying bugs, fish, or trees. These were Ignited, people he had lived with for most of his life and he killed them all so he didn't have to go back to being Cindered again. Not only did he kill them, he used their corpses to kill each other. What would Phaidros think of him now? He couldn't face him now. Not after this.

His thoughts swirled down and down into the depths of horror as the weight of what just happened sank in. Tears stained the corners of his eyes and left clean streaks down his otherwise dirtied face. He had forgotten the knife that contained Exaltation, there was no way to find that now without scouring the jungle, but he needed to hear a voice, any voice, that would save him from his own thoughts. He crawled over to the river, makeshift spear in hand, and pricked his thumb, letting the blood drop into the water. Exaltation's visage appeared a moment later, as if they were standing behind him in a reality beyond his own.

You are still alive, child. We were worried for you.

The surface of the water rippled as Exaltation spoke. Charon wasn't sure why, but the pressure in his chest went away and he felt relieved. "Yeah, I'm alive," he replied softly.

And they are dead. We are sorry that it turned out this way, child. We are sure it is difficult to have to do such things to those who were once your allies.

"I... don't know what to do," Charon said. "They won't forgive this, they won't forgive me. I hated them for how they treated me, but I... I know I had to kill them or else they'd know but..."

Do not linger on what has happened. Your path has been set, child, and you have chosen the Father's teachings over your God's and look at the results..

Charon glanced over his shoulder at the twisted landscape that had once been a dead clearing of jungle. It... was truly incredible, so much so that he could hardly believe he was the cause of all of it.

We are proud of you, Charon. Despite your Cindering, you managed to defeat three armored Ignited. That is something even your God would praise if he were not a hypocritical and cruel creature.

Exaltation's words offered some comfort, even as he continued to cry. He didn't know how much he needed to hear those words, and it made it easier for him to come to terms with what he had to do. Exaltation was right, he managed to defeat three Ignited as a *Cindered.* If the Exalted Sovereign did not recognize that then was he truly a god worth worshiping? The sadness in his heart gave way to bitterness but he shook away the thought. "I need to help my brother still, I can't go back now but surely there must be a way."

If you return now, your power will be discovered and Suneater will not allow you a chance to leave. You will have to choose carefully a time to give assistance.

"It'll have to be the time of the hunt, I'll have to keep a close eye on the jungle and the Shaped Beast's territory. I'll have to keep track of communications in the city as well." He slowly glanced over to the three corpses, more importantly, their helmets. "I might have an idea…"

Chapter 14

When bravery fails you, look to your companions
and be reminded that you are not alone.

-Collected Teachings of the Exalted Sovereign

P HAIDROS STOOD ARMOR clad in a large elevator shaft while the lift slowly carried him and his companions downwards into the earth. Dom stood beside him, hammer on one shoulder as he looked up to the last wink of natural light that shrunk further and further above. Every twenty feet or so they would pass some fluorescent lighting that kept the shaft lit, with the metal cage that was the elevator also having lights set up in the corner. They had to be at least two hundred feet below and he still saw tree roots, though those were slowly starting to fade into solid rock. "I have a bad feeling about this, Phaidros," Zenovia chimed in from the side, hands busying themselves on putting a hefty-looking suppressor on the end of her rifle, though her attention was on their fourth, Daxia. The longshi was currently lounging inside of a large cart that was hovering beside the three. It took up most of the free space on the wide platform and inside were several chests that Daxia had told him contained 'important tools' and didn't explain anything further.

"Bah," Dom said, looking to the other Ignited, "it is a good thing to see the ruin layer! To see the Teyhozkin is an honor, to meet one in battle even more so."

"Phaidros still needs to learn life sense," Zenovia countered. "That'll make the ruins especially dangerous."

"Nothing like training under pressure, eh? Little friend?" Dom gave Phaidros a playful shove on the shoulder.

Phaidros wasn't sure whether or not he was going to regret being trapped in a cave with Dom and Zenovia for however long they took. When they had returned back home the other day, the three immediately went their separate ways. Phaidros had used all of his spare time to work on agility training in his armor until the next morning. The three of them met and went on another commission, Dom and Zenovia argued on how to tackle the problem again and the same result happened, near death for all parties. This happened again the third day, then the fourth. On the fifth day however, while the two were bickering, Phaidros continued to look at the board right as a new commission had popped up for diving into the ruin layer to retrieve more chitin for the smiths to use. When he had suggested this to the group, he had never seen Dom look so excited and then so crushed when he learned that Daxia was going to be there too. Zenovia was wary, but had been trying to let Phaidros take some of the reins away from her in training and thus agreed reluctantly. It was a show of trust that Phaidros was thankful for, he just wished that she and Dom didn't feel the need to disagree on everything. He thought Daxia might help in this situation, but when he looked at her in the cart it looked like she was taking a nap.

"They aren't Ignited, Zenovia, can they really be that dangerous?" Phaidros offered. He could feel her frown through her helmet.

"They aren't stories to scare children for no reason," she said with a sigh, "They aren't just big bugs, they're... something more. It is hard to explain."

"In old times," Dom cut in, "my people used to think they were our gods. This was way before our time now, back in the second age."

That answer caused a flood of new questions to fill Phaidros' head but he subdued the urge to ask all of them at once and instead asked a more urgent question. "What should I expect?"

Daxia finally decided to join the conversation from the cart, so she *was* awake. "They're completely silent. Even when they're moving across loose rubble, they just don't cause any sound. So keep your eyes peeled and your night vision filters on."

"If you see your reflection, or anyone else you have seen recently, it might just be them oh and do not get too frightened or else it will just get bigger," Dom added.

"If one runs from you, let it run, you do not want to accidentally be led into a nest of the things," Zenovia added further. Phaidros was starting to wonder if Zenovia was right about this being a bad idea.

"Okay…" Phaidros began warily. "Any helpful tips on how to deal with them?"

"They try to avoid light and fire. The trick here is going to be to isolate one of them so I can grab all the chitin while making sure we don't get ambushed by more," Daxia said, finally opening one glowing ember eye to look at Phaidros, the look seeming way more sinister than she probably intended. "So watch my back."

Dom nodded. "And it is just like hitting Ignited armor, the plates will still crack if you hit them hard enough."

That put some ease to Phaidros' fears. "Is there a reason why we don't bring them up to the surface?"

Daxia shrugged. "Despite all the children's tales, they can't exist on the surface. People have tried but they just fade into smoke the second they even leave the ruin layer."

"Okay, one more question… Why is having life sense so crucial to this?" Phaidros asked.

"Because life sense shows you the true nature and soul of what you're looking at. Most Ignited are seen as like a star burning white hot, shapeless until they become shaped. The Teyhozkin do not look like that in life sense, they look like giant centipedes or spiders or anything else you can imagine skittering around in the dark—hence the usual reference to them as such."

Phaidros nodded, taking a deep breath. "How much longer?"

"We should be hitting the ruins any moment," Daxia said and, as if on cue, the mine shaft opened up into a vast cavern, three of the walls disappearing around them. The lights atop the cage swivelled outwards, bathing the area they were descending into with light. Phaidros now saw what the others were talking about by 'ruin layer.' Here, thousands of feet beneath the surface, Phaidros saw the shape and impressions of a crumbled city, weathered with time and preserved beneath the stone of the world. If he squinted hard enough, he could make out individual buildings that were now smashed and crumpled together. Perfect rectangles of open space dotted the landscape, windows, Phaidros assumed, each a portal into an infinite abyss of darkness. A second glance made Phaidros realize that buildings were stretching from the ceiling as well, as if a city had been folded in upon itself and shoved into a cave haphazardly, the natural formations of rock crushing all in its way as it was placed.

The lift reached the cavern floor with a dull thud, the cage lifting in front of them so they may enter the lost city before them. It was quiet, eerily quiet. Phaidros had grown up to the white noise of the ever-moving and screaming jungle around him or the sound of city life in Dasos. Here there were no birds chirping, bugs buzzing, trees groaning, vines snapping. There was only a lonely, eternal silence. Zenovia clicked on a flashlight attached to her rifle and was the first to step out of the lift. "I'll take point," she said, her voice echoing throughout the cavern.

Dom quickly moved up beside her, jerking a thumb to himself. "I think it will be best if I take point. If anyone comes close I'll crush them." He lifted his hammer for emphasis.

Zenovia only sighed in response. "I need you close to Phaidros and Daxia since he can't use life sense. If one of those bugs slips past all of us you'll be the last line of defense."

Dom grunted his disagreement. "Which is why we need your keen eye to make sure no one slips behind us, yes? You leave the front to Phaidros and me."

Phaidros sighed, already they were at it. He spoke up a bit louder than he intended. "I'll take the lead, that way you both can watch my back. Zenovia, can you stick with the cart to make sure nothing gets to Daxia?"

Both of them looked at Phaidros, tension in the air before Dom grumbled and stepped in behind Phaidros while Zenovia sighed, "Alright, Phaidros, just be careful where you step." Phaidros looked to Daxia to see her appraisal of the situation but all he could see from her was a furrowed brow and her tail flicking behind her in what he could only assume was annoyance. With the matter settled, Phaidros led their way out into the ruins, sword in his hands, night vision on and head on a swivel for any of the Teyhozkin. The hovering cart followed behind him, with Zenovia standing beside Daxia who returned to lounging and Dom behind the cart. When they stepped up to the ruins proper, they looked even more massive than from the elevator. The windows were big enough that he could stand on Dom's shoulders and still have room before they hit the top of it.

He wasn't sure what he was looking for, but it had been less than five minutes before he was beginning to see things. He'd sweep his head across an open window they were about to pass and swear he saw tinted eyes glowing in the dark through his visor before they scattered away. Without any sound to follow, he wasn't sure if he was hallucinating or if he actually spotted them. When he called out the sighting to the others, Zenovia or Dom would check, then follow with 'clear,' before they moved on. Time passed and they had to walk through one of the ruined buildings to continue exploring the cavern, the inside of it was a featureless, slate grey room tilted on its axis with hints of plaster and marks on the walls. On one side of the room was a staircase stretching up further with another trailing downward under the surface to who knows where. At the other end of the room was another wide window or door frame, Phaidros wasn't sure at this point, and the group passed through and were in the open cavern again. Around them was what looked like a courtyard with clearly marked pathways and entrances into buildings that surrounded the main square. "Contact," Zenovia said over their internal comms, switching off her light as she gestured ahead. Up on a small building, pressed against the sheer wall was a large silhouette with too many legs. It had been curled up in a circle on the wall and when Phaidros tried to squint to get a better look at it, he noticed that at the end of those legs were not the usual pointed legs of an insect but the hands and feet one might expect on a human. Its back was covered in layers of armored chitin, with two feelers lazily waving about in the air. The thing looked like it could make the armor of two dozen Ignited at least from its sheer size. He didn't notice any mandibles or pincers or stingers, so he didn't see anything immediately dangerous. "We need to get it to engage without scurrying off."

"I can handle that," Dom said, carefully stepping to the front of the formation.

"Dom," Zenovia said with annoyance.

Dom looked back at her with disdain clear through the helmet covering his face, waiting for her to continue.

"There has to be a better way," Zenovia said, her tone growing more impatient and once more the two descended into bickering.

"You guys…" Daxia hissed as quiet as she could while still making her voice heard, "are clicking too much."

Phaidros had practically tuned out their voices as he stared up at the creature warily, the clicks of their armor reaching a fever pitch that was beginning to echo throughout the cavern. The insect's head turned and lifted towards them, and instead of the face of a centipede or a spider like Phaidros expected, he saw *his* face. No, that was just him seeing things, it turned back into something more befitting of an insect. It peeled itself off the wall silently then faded into a vague silhouette and then reappeared on the floor as if it had just landed from a fall. There was a slight tremor from the impact but otherwise it made no sound. Phaidros looked back behind him to his arguing companions and Daxia, then behind them to see that another insect was fading in and out of sight from the building they just came from and skittering down the wall.

"We're surrounded!" Phaidros finally managed to shout over the noise and turned to face the insect coming straight for him.

When he completed his turn though he did not see the centipede-like creature from before, instead it was his father barreling towards him with two blades shimmering in the dark from an unknown light source. Phaidros brought up his sword just in time to parry the blow as it went for his midsection. The blades clashed soundlessly and Phaidros was forced from his feet. He stared up in horror at the visage of his father, no not his father, the bloody corpse of his father left to die alone in the wilderness. Zaharias' mouth moved but no voice came from it, a single bloodshot eye staring down at him with indignation as he reared up for another strike. Phaidros was paralyzed, the past week and a half of emotions shoved down deep inside bursting forth just as a flood of light blanketed the cave. The insect returned where his father had once been, though it wore his face with large mandibles gnashing and bite marks lining his features. It scurried off into the dark and he heard Dom swinging his hammer behind him just before there was another flood of light, followed by silence.

Phaidros' heart pounded in his chest. He wasn't ready for this, he wasn't ready, in a few weeks he'd die just like his father did. His body was shaking, and the air that filled his lungs never seemed to be enough as his breathing quickened. A hand went for his arm to pull him to his feet, muffled voices ringing through his ears before he finally recognized them as Dom's, they were in open communications now.

"Phaidros? Are you alright?"

Phaidros jerked away, scrambling to his feet. His final tie to sanity snapped. "No! No, I'm not alright. I just got attacked by my dead father. You and Zenovia are supposed to be helping but when I'm not scream-ing at you both to stop fighting for five seconds you're back at it again. I'm going to die, I'm going to die down here," he spat in both accusation and panic, voice echoing through the cavern while his gaze snapped between Dom and Zenovia who were both trying to avoid eye contact.

He was about to say more when Daxia cut in, in her hands looked to be a giant flood lamp. "Phaidros, you need to calm down or this'll get worse."

Phaidros bit back the urge to throw or break something in frustration. "Oh it'll get worse? How can it possibly get worse?" His head was starting to feel light, as if those words stole the last of his precious oxygen, and all around him he swore he saw twinkling eyes traveling through the dark. They were surrounding him now, he knew it, this was going to be his end. "I can't– I can't." He backed up away from the others, one hand clutching at his helmet as if it was the thing suffocating him. That was, until his boot hit a section of stone that crumbled beneath him. In an eyeblink he reached out to grab the edge of the stone but that too crumbled and Phaidros fell into the abyss. When he looked up towards the hole he saw Dom carefully peering over the edge of the rapidly shrinking hole before he hit the ground with a crunch of chitin. He had landed square on his back in a new room, though it didn't look to be the one that the staircase from before led down into. The new room was massive, with empty frameworks hanging against a wall, counters sectioning off one corner with a line of stone blocks separating one portion of the room from the wider space. On the opposite side, the floor indented into two deep pits that extended to either side and into domed tunnels. The crater he now lay in was right beside it, stonework cracking beneath him as he stared up at the ceiling above.

He lay there for a long moment. The panic rose in swells, he was about to scream before he heard a voice crackle in from his helmet, "Do not worry, friend, I am coming for you!"

"Wait, Dom, we have to stay with–" Zenovia tried to cut in before a silhouette of black chitin fell from above. Phaidros snapped out of his trance to throw himself out of the crater, the call to act becoming a clarion call through the chaos of his anxious mind. Dom came crashing down where he had once been lying feet first. The man staggered, fractures crawling up the legs of his armor.

Phaidros stared, unsure of what to say before his mind settled on, "Dom, what are you doing here?" Phaidros asked, exhausted.

"You said your dead father attacked you, yes? I was not about to let you have to face more of those things alone." A moment of hesitation followed before he added, "… and this is not the first time you have been upset with me since I have joined your hunt. I wish to make amends."

Phaidros wanted to be angry, he felt it rise in his chest but he forced it back down with a sigh. "You're trying your best, Dom, but after we're out of here? I can't have you and Zenovia butting heads anymore. Don't do it for her sake or your own, but my sake, please? You respect me because I beat your challenge, respect my wish for this."

Dom stared at him in silence before nodding. "I will try," he answered, finally.

Zenovia spoke over their comm channel, "You both alive down there?"

Phaidros looked up, seeing Zenovia peering down now alongside Daxia. "Yeah, we're alive, I don't see a way of getting up easily without clawing our way back out the roof but that just might make more of it crumble away. Is there any way to bring the cart down?"

Daxia's voice joined the channel; she must have had some sort of external setup for it. "Not unless you want it in pieces and to make an even bigger crater. You made a lot of noise going down, so you're gonna have some friends heading your way." That made Phaidros' stomach lurch, but she continued talking, "We'll make our way down to you, just stay put."

Zenovia spoke up next, "Just try to stay calm, Phaidros, we won't be long."

Dom and Phaidros exchanged glances and even though helmets hid their expressions, Phaidros hoped Dom could see the fear in his eyes, begging him to save him from the uncertainty that surrounded them. Dom gestured down. "They will be coming soon, if you want to see them for what they are, now is the time to learn life sense." He turned his head. "Here they come now."

From all entrances apart from the roof, they came. Dozens crawled out, fading in and out mid-motion and when Phaidros looked at them, he saw a myriad of images take the space where their forms were. He saw his father, a corpse dragging itself along the wall, another the same man but in his armor crawling on all fours, a young man with determined eyes and gnashing fangs. He saw himself both young and impossibly old, a warrior, a cowering animal. He saw the beast of his nightmares loom higher and higher like an impossible shadow with teal eyes burning like two globes of all-consuming fire.

"Phaidros! Close your eyes and focus," Dom shouted, the urgency in his voice compelling him to obey. Silence followed before a hammer crashed against nothing. "Listen to nothing else but the sound of my voice. What you see is not what is before you."

Phaidros could still see the images burned into his mind, "I can't," he said, voice strained as he could imagine those silent creatures swarming around him now. His father's death, his brother's disappearance, the stress of the impossible task that lay before him, how could he focus on anything else?

"You must!" Dom exclaimed, Phaidros could hear the wind pick up and the earth tremble from the weight and strength of Dom's blows, but no crunch of chitin or indignant hisses of insects ever followed. "If you do not, I will have to face these things alone and I will die. I do not know about you, but I have plans much bigger than a funeral here."

"I don't know how!" Phaidros shouted back, his hands tightening into fists as he struggled to find some connection, any connection.

"You do not need to know how! It is not a skill learned in a textbook but a feeling." Phaidros heard Dom stomp by to the other side of him and another tremor followed. "Feel the fire in your soul, it is this light that makes all that is dark and horrifying flee before it, but it is not the only flame in this world. You are not alone in the dark, feel the heat of my fire, Phaidros!" Another quick series of steps past him followed by a rush of wind, echoed through the chamber. "It is the guiding light that will help you see."

Phaidros took deep, trembling breaths. Maybe he had a point, to try and connect with all life was hard, but if he could connect to just one other then perhaps it would be easier. He reached within himself, focusing on the warm heat of his burning potential, it centered him. The feeling was still unnatural to him and depending on his mood it was either a fire that made each step more certain than the last or it was a horrifying reminder of his impending doom. He tried to focus on the former, letting the warmth wash over him.

A star lay within him. Without sight he could still see it. A mote of light, surrounded by white fire that flickered upwards soundlessly. The flame looked... weak, sputtering as if an unknown wind threatened to snuff it from existence at any moment. This was him, all that he was condensed down into a single, finite expression. A weak fire. Yet, even the weakest fire still fought back the darkness. And just like in the night sky where stars shone upon the world, his light was not the only one, even if the others felt so distant. With one final, deep breath, he tried to search for those other stars.

Nothing happened at first, just the cold, empty void of uncertainty, but out there, in the dark, he felt the faint whisper of heat somewhere else. A fire similar to his own, alone in the darkness. Did it struggle like he did? Did it feel the same fear that he did whenever he stumbled? He focused on that heat, breath calming, and when he felt like he was ready he opened his eyes.

The darkness surrounded him but there, clear as day, he saw a glowing white star burning defiantly. The flames around it licked at the open air. The flame itself was thinner than he expected, forming a small layer around the pure light of the soul it surrounded. The longer Phaidros stared at it though as the soul danced through the darkness, the layer of flame seemed to grow larger. Was that Dom's potential? The fire grew thicker and fuller by the second yet there was an oddness to the flame. It looked like the tongues of fire were... scared? To burn their full intensity, the flames muted by choice. He tried to search for more flames and he could see two more above and in the distance moving quickly through the ruins, Zenovia and Daxia he was sure. The former's flame was much like his own. A weak fire surrounded it, the flames like fingers desperately reaching out for life as potential slowly burned away. The latter seemed to glow more than burn with the tame flames meant to create where once there was only destruction. These were his companions, his friends, and seeing their light meant he was not alone in the darkness, not anymore. With more confidence, he tried to feel all else around him… and then he saw them.

Dozens of insects close to his original first impressions. Some were shaped more like spiders, others more like centipedes. There were no more images of him or his father or other people he knew, only what they were. Phaidros wondered why he could see Daxia's and Zenovia's flames through the walls but not them, but there was most likely no answer that anyone knew. What he did know was that Dom had been keeping them off of him and it was time that Phaidros helped him.

He rose to his feet, focusing on the warmth around him as he gripped his blade in both hands and kicked off to strike at one of the Teyhozkin that was about to flank Dom. The blow connected, cracking the chitin and sending it skidding off course. "Did you find your flame, friend?" Dom asked, a grin audible in his voice.

"I did," Phaidros said with more relief than he was expecting. "I'm ready to fight."

Dom laughed. "Good, good! My armor plates could use the break."

"I'll watch your back, Zenovia and Daxia are on their way."

"And I will watch yours! Let us get to killing gods, yes?"

Phaidros felt excitement well within him and the two set to work. Back to back in a twisting circle they struck and lashed out at the insects that came for them. They were strong, but Phaidros had nothing to back into but Dom and vice versa. They held their ground as horrors beneath the world assailed them from all sides. Two fires dancing in tune to one another. Two fires creating hope where there was none. Two fires that grew in heat and intensity in defiance to the world that sought to snuff them out.

Time passed, Phaidros wasn't sure how much, but light flooded the cave followed by gunshots. The remaining insects scattered into the tunnels and everywhere else they could find. Phaidros lifted his head to see that he was standing on a pile of dead Teyhozkin alongside Dom, panting heavily. Armor plates were broken and shattered, the exposed metal skeleton beneath showing through in a few areas. Smoke drifted from the corpses beneath their feet.

Zenovia came running over as soon as she was sure the room was clear and Daxia hopped out of her cart to follow after. "Ash and cinders, you two, you look like you've been through hell. How are you both alive?"

Dom fell back off his feet to sit down on the pile. "You do not need to worry, Zenovia, Phaidros can life sense now for sure. Though we are not shaped, so maybe this was less impressive than I thought." He huffed, kicking the chitin of one of the corpses. "I was sure we had the moment."

Daxia waved her hands. "Hey, you three, have your moment off of the chitin, I gotta get to collecting before the bodies disappear." Dom shot back up and hopped off the pile alongside Phaidros and Daxia called the cart over to her. She pulled out a large tool that was meant to separate shells from the creature beneath without breaking it.

Zenovia was there to greet them at the base. "I'm surprised you're both not dead."

Phaidros looked at Zenovia and she hesitated before adding, "...but I'm glad you're not and, thank you, Dom, for saving Phaidros."

Dom waved his hand dismissively. "I was just going to get us both killed, it was Phaidros who rescued me." Phaidros looked at him next and he lifted up a hand to scratch at his scarred helmet. "...but I am sorry that I jumped without thinking, Zenovia."

Zenovia hesitated before replying, "It's fine, you got the job done."

Phaidros let out an internal sigh of relief. "Going forward, I'd like to call the shots. Both of you kept arguing because you thought your way is best, so we're going to do it my way instead."

Zenovia looked like she was about to protest but then stopped. "Just take advice as you need it, you're still young."

Phaidros nodded. "You both can give your suggestions, but I'll make the final call. It's my hunt, my say."

Dom hummed before nodding his assent. "You have done well for such a new spark, yes? You are brimming with potential! I will follow your words, little friend."

Phaidros smiled. "Thank you both."

They both nodded in reply. "What's our next move then, oh fearless leader?" Dom asked.

"Set up a perimeter around Daxia while she works, then let's get out of here."

Both agreed wordlessly and moved into positions. Over the next few hours, Daxia painstakingly pulled away plate after plate of chitin from what beasts she could, however the bodies decayed at a rapid rate. The insects returned every once in a while but a quick flash of lights and strikes from the Ignited sent them skittering back into the dark. She was only able to get about three Teyhozkin worth of plates before she dropped her tools back into her cart. "Alright, that's about all I'll be able to safely grab. Good job, folks, aside from the almost dying part. Though I guess that's what warrior Ignited are supposed to do."

"We're ready to head out then?" Phaidros asked.

"Yeah, I'll keep the lights on, battery should be good till we get back if you all watch the other angles.

"How long have we been out?"

"Oh about a day or so, half of it was you and Dom fighting them off."

Phaidros could hardly believe that, but felt a small swell of pride that the two had managed to last so long. Perhaps they had more of a chance against the Shaped Beast than he thought. He switched back to life sense once more, seeing the fires within them all. He was not alone, as long as they were here he would not have to face the future by himself. With more confidence in his heart and a feeling of control over his destiny and the future ahead, Phaidros led the way out of the caves with the others to head back up to the elevator. When the light of the new day shined on them once more, Phaidros felt as if he could take on the world.

CHAPTER 15

United our valor is known, it is not enough to find allies willing to stand with you. You must learn as much about your friends as you do your enemies and then their strengths will become your own.

-COLLECTED TEACHINGS OF THE EXALTED SOVEREIGN

PHAIDROS' NEWFOUND CONFIDENCE, unfortunately, had to wait for his armor to grow back. Which meant more down time. He was tired enough after their mission into the ruin layer to finally get some sleep, but once the new day rose he found himself not sure what he was going to do himself. A knock on the door interrupted him in the middle of his breakfast and he answered the door to see Zenovia standing there in uniform, arms folded. Phaidros blinked in surprise. "Zenovia?"

The older Ignited squinted at him. "What? Am I not allowed to come visit you?"

Phaidros quickly threw up his hands defensively. "No not at all! It's just unexpected is all. Is Dom not with you?" He looked around for the large zhuk but saw him nowhere to be seen.

Zenovia continued to squint before letting out an exasperated sigh.

"No, I just wanted to talk to you. Want to take a trip up to the wall? It's only been a few weeks since the start of... everything, but now that we are *forced* to wait, I think it might be good for us."

Phaidros paused—even on a down day he might have tried at least to run laps around the city or pick up some new skill just to keep his potential healthy—but he slowly nodded. "Yeah, I can do that."

"Great," Zenovia said, a hint of gruff awkwardness in her tone like internally she was struggling with something. "Hurry on then, we're wasting sunshine." Phaidros quickly finished up his remaining meal and went after her. Together, the two made their way to the edge of the city and took a lift up to the top of the wall.

The Wall of Dasos itself was from an earlier age, an age filled with dragons and a resistance fighting to overthrow them. It sat tall enough to overlook all of the warm tones that made up the leaves of the ever-shifting jungle on the outside. Parapets lined it, once filled with gun emplacements that have long since been removed in the ascension of the Exalted Sovereign. Now all it was was a separating line between civilization and the jungle beyond it, only used for events or to look out at the jungle or for people to race alongside it.

When the two reached the top, Zenovia took a seat down along the edge of the jungle side, looking out beyond. The wind carried a cooling breeze to combat the oppressive heat of the sun. Phaidros sat beside her, also looking out. The jungle was deadly, but there was beauty in its danger. From here the trees looked as if they were all swaying to an invisible ocean current beyond the city edge. Silence hung in the air as the two sat, with Phaidros unsure of what to say.

Thankfully, Zenovia broke that silence. "We've been through a lot already, haven't we?" she said. "Nearly three weeks now, it's moved like a blur."

Phaidros nodded. "Yeah..."

That wasn't much to work with, Phaidros knew, but he still wasn't sure where Zenovia was going with this. She seemed to struggle with something for a moment longer before continuing her thought. "We've been through a lot and I have seen you grow and change so quickly it's startling and... at the beginning of it all, I didn't believe in you," she admitted, Phaidros remained quiet; he remembered how they argued the first week. "I've seen fresh-faced Ignited newly sparked and in over their heads walk straight into battle and die when they see what kind of horrors are out there, Phaidros. Yeah, everyone out in the galaxy talks about how peaceful things are now, but the Ignited, us, the warriors, we don't get to live in it. We see the worst the galaxy has to offer and we have to push onwards." She then looked over to him, blue eyes intense. "I thought you were going to give up, or die, or worse, but... that was unfair of me."

Phaidros looked confused. "Why are you saying this now? We still haven't killed the Shaped Beast yet."

She huffed, "I'm saying this because I am trying to say I'm sorry, Phaidros, because you lost your father and actually tried to do something about it and all you got was my distrust and anger at my own failure lashing out at you."

Phaidros nodded slowly, trying to summon up the words to say what he felt. "I wasn't exactly making it easy," he finally admitted, "and... it was wrong of me to blame you for him dying, but I have to ask... if he cared so much, why did it have to be him?" There was a strain in his voice that wasn't there before,

Zenovia frowned, looking down, hands clutching the wall. "Your father cared about you more than you could ever know. I've been on Dasos for a long time, Phaidros," she said with a small sigh, "I remember when all three of you arrived, when you were barely even a child. Everything he did he did for you and Charon, so that you all could stay on Dasos under the Ignited's protection... but Za was sometimes too empathetic for his own good. His family grew to beyond you and Charon, he wanted to protect the people outside the gate, he wanted to protect Theseus and... he wanted to protect me." She had her own strain now, but she had much more control of it than he did at the moment. "I don't think he could have lived with himself... knowing that he lived when Theseus and I died. I barely know how I am."

Silence lingered again, Phaidros struggling to keep calm, but he had to ask then. "Why do you do this then, Zenovia? How do you keep going?"

She seemed surprised by the question, before her expression turned somber. "I wish I had an answer, Phaidros. You'll find many of the Ignited that are here will say the same. When you've fought for so long, you lose sight of why you took your first steps, you stop trying to look after a while. You put yourself into a routine that is... hard... to escape from. I fight because it is all I have known," she said, strain growing more present in her voice, "and why I have been stuck on this planet for decades because I can't find myself anymore."

Phaidros had never heard her sound so distraught, it was uncanny, but... it was nice to know that he wasn't alone in his fears. He remembered them all there in the ruin layer, their fires burning together, no longer alone. That meant she didn't need to be either. He lifted a hand up to place on her shoulder, "Then—after this mission, after we hunt the Shaped Beast, I'll help you." She blinked in confusion, looking at him with some surprise while he looked as determined as ever. "It is the least I can do for how you've helped me, Zenovia. I know you didn't do the best job of it at the start, but you're trying your best, I know you are. We all are. When this is all over, we're going to work on you next, I bet Dom would help too."

Zenovia scoffed at the mention of Dom but sighed. "How did *I* end up being the one being comforted?" she admitted with a small, subdued laugh before returning her attention to the Jungle. "Just... try not to end up like your father, okay?" she asked sincerely.

"I have you beside me, so I know that won't happen," Phaidros said with a small grin. She looked back at him with disdainful disbelief. "Okay sorry was that too much?"

She just shook her head. "Thank you, Phaidros, I wanted to come up here to try and make amends but somehow you are the one who ended up comforting me at the end of all this."

"It's the least I could do," Phaidros said, still smiling. Silence lingered once more before Phaidros finally asked, "You said Father came to Dasos for my and Charon's sake... but why did you come here initially?"

She frowned. "I don't know if I'm ready to talk about that yet," she admitted, running a hand through her hair. "We're doing better than we were before, but not that good. Just... know that when I mean fighting is all I've known, I mean it."

Phaidros nodded, accepting that answer for now and didn't want to push. "I won't pry, just know that... I really do appreciate what you've done for me in this short time. You're saving my life bit by bit, I'm going to repay you someday."

Zenovia half smiled. "Let's kill the Shaped Beast first, hm?" She then stood up, looking down to Phaidros. "Keep up the good work, kid. You're doing great and I can't wait to see where you go."

Phaidros smiled in return. "Thank you again, Zenovia, I won't let you down." Her smile turned into the first full one he'd seen out of her and without a word she began to walk away, leaving Phaidros alone atop the wall. He felt as if some weight he had been holding had been lifted off of him now. One he didn't know he was carrying. Any lingering resentment he had towards Zenovia was gone. With their moment shared, he felt like he could truly focus on what lay ahead of him, killing the Shaped Beast.

CHAPTER 16

*Weakness is as temporary as one's will to overcome it. Those who are strong
have a duty to protect the weak until they too can find their strength.*

-COLLECTED TEACHINGS OF THE EXALTED SOVEREIGN

4 Days Later

SINCE THEIR FORAY into the ruin layer, training had gotten a lot
smoother. Dom and Zenovia no longer competed for leadership
and Phaidros stepped up to take charge. He still relied heavily
on their advice, but whatever judgment call he made was the final say.
The missions that followed had gone with little problems and the three
were working together as a much better cohesive unit. A lot of the fears
Phaidros had were beginning to fade away, with each new day bringing
new confidence with it that they were getting closer and closer to a
chance at victory over the Shaped Beast.

The image of a horrible monster appeared in his mind; he had not
seen the beast yet but Zenovia had described it to him. It was eerily
similar to the shape of the silhouette he saw in the ruins. He didn't want
to give the reason for that any more thought than he had to; it was the
one, final opposition in his way. One of the few, final uncertainties left
in his life. The other was Charon, he had not heard a single word from

his brother, he would rather not think that he was dead out in the jungle just like their father, but each passing day of silence ate at the edges of his confidence. He tried not to let it distract him from his training.

The three were out in the jungle, armor clad as they went through drills against invisible enemies, moving among one another with the fluidity of water, practicing being able to move as if they were a single entity as opposed to three separate Ignited. It was said that the greatest of the Ignited could move like the nazeko, in perfect cohesion with one another as if their minds were linked and souls bonded in the dancing fire of their ignited potential. Phaidros could see the three of them getting to that point one day, but not before the end of their month time frame. Yet they were improving.

That was until, in each of their visors, an icon appeared below their own. A sun with stiff branches of light rays being overwhelmed by a set of sharp teeth. Suneater. "The beast has come. Your time to act is now."

All three Ignited paused, sharing looks before Phaidros spoke up. "We still have several weeks, Sacred Suneater, why the urgency?"

"It is striking out at those who linger beyond the wall. It must have been recovering from whatever wounds the previous hunters did to it, but it is back now." The words brought the fear Phaidros had been doing so well to hide back to his forethoughts. "Your rite of vengeance is still being honored, but I am mobilizing the Ignited to evacuate who they can. They will be instructed not to harm your beast, but it will be placing them in danger and should another Ignited fall due to your inaction…"

Zenovia continued where Suneater was trailing off. "Then the rite of vengeance is forfeit. If we're going to do this, Phaidros, now is the time."

"No. You're right," Phaidros answered, so quickly that he even surprised himself. "We don't need to kill it yet, just chase it off to buy us more time. We can do that, right?"

"Hah! And here I thought we were going to have to do boring training for another two weeks. This beast is considerate to come to us instead of making us waste the efforts trying to hunt it." Dom laughed, the jets of his armor already activating as he began to sprint back towards the city, Zenovia and Phaidros following after.

Within the jungle, Charon sat in a den dug underneath the jungle soil beneath a tree. He wore ignited armor that belonged to a dead Ignited, one of the three that had hunted him nearly a week ago now. Their bodies were still nearby, without heads that is. He needed those to tap into communications with the city. The desecration of his once comrades was numb on him by now. They were dead, he was alive, and if he was to keep being alive he needed to use what was left. The jungle did not care about such things, why should he? The Ignited never cared for him once he had cindered. Exaltation had been his only companion for two weeks now, his only comfort. There was little else for the book to teach Charon and he had to subsist through carefully plotted hunts in the jungle where his origin point could not be spotted. Nothing was a challenge for him; if any defied him, it withered and died and its vitae was used to fuel him onward.

Beside him on a makeshift table was one of the helmets of the three Ignited, the other two in various points in the forest just within range of each other, and more importantly, the third being just within range of the city's communication. It took some creativity to get the trackers out, while still making the suits be able to interact with one another, but being able to access the internal commands by simply reanimating the body made it much easier to get them out. He had wanted to keep track of city-wide communications, which kept anyone tuned in updated on notable hunts by fellow Ignited and updates to the commission board. The Shaped Beast would be one such hunt that was kept track of, so he tuned in every day to listen for it so he knew when it would be time.

He pushed his vitae into the head within the helmet, his vision suddenly seeing two perspectives. He activated short-ranged communication with another head and helmet deeper in the jungle, which was relaying the communications from the third after a brief moment of static.

"The merchant quarter is being attacked by the Shaped Beast," a clinical voice recited. "By order of Sacred Suneater all warrior Ignited who are nearby are to assist with due haste. Do not engage the Shaped Beast. I repeat, do not engage the Shaped Beast." Charon sat there in stunned silence. It was happening already? No, it was too soon, Phaidros could never be ready by now but knowing him he would surely try to fight it anyway. He needed to be there with him. Charon shoved himself from his chair, one hand reaching to the side with an open palm as a spear flew into his hands. It was the spear that he had used to kill the other Ignited, though he had learned since then that he could make it denser and denser if he poured more physical material into it and smoothed it out with vitae, thus turning what was once a wooden stick, into a staff or spear worthy of an Ignited.

You are in a hurry.

Exaltation called out from his knife lodged into one of the walls, he had found it after his previous fight had ended. Charon stopped in his tracks to look at the object. "Phaidros is in danger. He needs me," Charon answered, grabbing his shoulder bag and tossing that over his shoulder with the book inside.

You are not ready,

Exaltation answered, making Charon hesitate.

If you reveal yourself now, the Ideal will be made aware. When they are, you will be taken and the book along with it. All of the power you have gained will be for nothing. Let your brother fight the beast.

Charon hesitated further. Perhaps Exaltation was right and he was acting too rashly. His mind was in a panic, no longer lagging like it had done weeks prior. The only reason he learned vitaemancy in the first place was so he could stand tall alongside Phaidros and avenge their father together. That was in the beginning though, before he had left to hide in the jungle, before he killed other Ignited to keep his secret. If he went now, he would surely be caught. Could he risk that, if it meant he could save his brother? Would Phaidros understand? Phaidros would do the same for him, wouldn't he? *I can't wait for you, brother.* That is what Phaidros had told him. "I'm not going to make him face this alone," Charon had eventually said, though it came out with more strain than he intended.

We can do nothing to stop you, child. If you must save your brother, then do so. We hope your faith in him is not misplaced and he will help you when the wolves begin to circle you.

Charon was already hurrying for the entrance. "I will do whatever it takes to make sure Phaidros and I make it out alive."

Death is not the end, Charon. If you must, ascend.

"No," Charon quickly replied. "We'll talk more later. I need to leave." The sacrament made no more protests as he stepped out into the jungle. With one deep breath vitae filled him and he pushed it into the spear and made it float horizontally. He hopped atop it, then willed it forward, shooting in the direction of Dasos and pulling more vitae as he went.

It was his time to prove himself.

⁓

The Merchant's District was chaotic. Blood ran through the streets, large gashes tore through the concrete structures and stalls. Screams echoed throughout as people ran for the wall or ran to their ships. The Shaped Beast brought fear everywhere it went; with how many bodies it left behind, it was clear that it was doing this not out of some predatory sense of hunger but to bask in the fear of its prey.

Phaidros, Dom, and Zenovia had arrived. They did not need to look hard to find the beast, as one looked into the potential of all around them and they could see it burning like a bonfire nearby. Where the rest of their souls looked like a small, white star with a flame surrounding it, the beast looked like a set of shining eyes peering through tall grass, burning with ferocious intensity.

They heard the creature soon after, a high-pitched keening echoing through the air. Zenovia froze for a moment, memories flashing back of the last time she faced the creature. Dom nudged her with his shoulder. "No time to waste, we need to move!" The three ran through the city streets, passing mangled corpses and torn-up buildings along the way. Phaidros had never seen such destruction before and they were heading towards the cause of all of it. A brief flash of guilt speared through him as they ran. He had met some of these people only briefly when he went here with Daxia. Now they were dead, because he wasn't ready fast enough, because *he* had to be the one to kill the beast and prevent all other Ignited from trying. He tried not to let that disturb him too much as they continued on.

The beast stood towering over its prey, some poor family of four who had become paralyzed in fear like a bird stunned by a snake's gaze. In front of them was Daxia, clutching something to her chest as she stared in wide-eyed fear and defiance up at the beast. Smoke gathered at the corners of her mouth but no fire came. The Shaped Beast had reached the heart of the merchant's square, splintered woods and scattered bodies filled what was once a bustling center of commerce. It stalked towards them without rush, long tail swaying contentedly behind it as it raised its sword-like talons into the air. The people below stood in horror, clutching to one another for dear life as they stared death in the eyes.

They were so distracted they didn't hear the sound of the oncoming avalanche that was Dom. The Ignited roared across the square, hammer in both hands. He was a little more than half the size of the beast but still when his shoulder slammed into the creature it stumbled to the side. The hammer blow that followed soon after slammed into the beast's stomach and sent it crashing backwards through a few stalls. "Beast!" Dom bellowed. "I have been waiting to meet you for some time now! Do not die easily or I will be sorely disappointed!"

Phaidros quickly rushed to Daxia and the family. "Daxia? What are you doing here?" She was still shaken and a quick repeat of her name got her attention.

"I was uh, helping with the evacuation but it came after us faster than I thought." She shoved what she was holding into his chest. "I brought the ripper rounds, make sure Zenovia gets them." Behind them, the beast reared back angrily, its tail helping keep it steady on two legs as it brought its weight down onto Dom before three rounds crashed into the side of its head.

Zenovia stood nearby on a rooftop where she got a clear view of the beast. It turned its gaze to her briefly, a look of recollection in its single remaining eye. It remembered her but otherwise the bullets seemed to only annoy it. It knew who the real threat was, at least for now. "We need your help, Phaidros!" she reminded him.

Phaidros glanced down to the magazine of bullets in his hand then to her. "Thank you, I will, you should leave with the others."

"No promises, I'm shaking like a leaf right now but I'm going to stick by in case you guys need some emergency repairs." Phaidros didn't have time to protest; the family had run away as soon as the Ignited showed up and Daxia fled away from immediate harm. Now he turned his attention towards the beast.

Its gaze turned back to Dom just in time, as the Ignited was using the time gained during the distraction to charge forward. He twisted around to gain momentum as his hammer came swinging around. It braced, one large hand coming up just in time to not only block the hammer but catch it. Dust blew around the two engaged fighters, the momentum making the beast slide a foot in the dirt before coming to a stop as the two wrestled for control of the hammer.

Phaidros was not about to let his companions do all the work however. With the family rescued and no other innocents in the square it was just them and the beast now. The jets in his legs roared to life as he ran towards the creature from the flank. Its tail rose before lashing out at him. He ducked backward beneath it into a slide before popping back up into a run and sprung to its back. His blade wheeled through the air in a deadly arc before biting into its scaled hide.

The creature roared in frustration at the gnats swarming around it as it braced both its feet, then firmed its grip on the hammer head before forcing it down. It looked Dom in the eyes and opened its maw to try and bite at him. The move forced the Ignited to let go of his hammer and back up.

"Phaidros!" Zenovia called out and Phaidros leapt from its back just in time to have its tail not wrap around his waist and only end up grabbing him by the ankle, holding him upside down.

"Zenovia!" Phaidros called in reply, holding the magazine of ripper rounds and launching it at her in a quick pitch. She caught it with one hand, the other already unloading her current magazine onto the ground and slamming the new one into place to take aim.

The beast turned, ready to skewer Phaidros. This time Zenovia was ready, shots rang into its tail, the barbed edges of the ripper rounds deploying just before impact and doing just as Daxia described. The rounds ripped through the scales of the tail and exposed vulnerable flesh beneath. More importantly, it freed its grip on Phaidros. The young Ignited spun in the air, jets in his armor righting him mid-air as he swung his sword over the new opening. The motion severed the thin end of the tail completely off, a small spray of blood and roar following before he landed. "Thank you!" he shouted over the comms, turning to face the beast and seeing it was staring right at him.

He froze. It was one thing to talk about fighting that which killed his father but another to see the razor-sharp talons and teeth and the horns and that look of anger in its eye, the other looking as if it had been gouged out. Even the fight with Dom had not prepared him. "Focus, little friend!" Dom shouted over the comms.

The words brought him back to reality right as the beast charged at him on all fours in a pounce, mouth open. His eyes widened, all of his training going out the window as he ran away, a single talon catching the edge of his foot before a well-placed shot knocked the hand while tearing a gash into its hide. The creature raced after him, the instincts of a predator had taken hold and now it was locked on Phaidros.

Zenovia poured fire into the creature as it sped after the young

Ignited, blasting at claws and maws that got too close to him and tearing away more scales. "I made some openings for you, Phaidros, you need to act!" she shouted.

They were right and he knew it; with a deep breath he steered the beast and him towards a wall. He leapt forward, jets carrying him upwards before he planted both feet upon the wall. With a quick twist he spun around right as he activated the stinger in his right arm. The spike speared through an opening Zenovia had made in its jaw. The force made the beast's top half reel back while the bottom slammed through the wall as it fell flat on its back. Phaidros' stinger retracted and he landed in a roll on the other side of it now.

"That is how an Ignited does it!" Dom shouted.

Blood trickled from the puncture in its face, the creature testing its jaw as it flipped itself back onto all fours, more shots ringing against its head. Then the sound was heard again, a deafening keen that made all three Ignited freeze in place as the beast's Shaped powers began to worm its way into their mind, filling all thoughts with nothing but with deep seated, primal fear. They had been expecting this, Zenovia had told Phaidros about it, but to truly experience it was another matter entirely. Suddenly Phaidros was no longer a brave Ignited but a scared little boy staring down the monster of his nightmares. His frame trembled as the beast rose again, stalking forward and dragging its claws against the floor before swinging wide for Phaidros, intent on cutting him to ribbons.

He couldn't move. He stared death in the face, at least he could go to his father knowing he didn't close his eyes before the end. Then a weight shoved him forward as Dom braced and the hand smacked him in the side of his armor. Plates cracked and shattered for a brief moment before Dom was sent spiraling into another building further down the square. "Dom!" Phaidros shouted. He looked to the icon on his helmet's display to see Dom as orange, showing his armor's integrity had been severely breached, but his soul and his potential were still holding on.

Phaidros grit his teeth, Dom had managed to save him from that blow, but he was still in serious danger. The creature loomed over him as he hurried back to his feet before Zenovia had found her wits to keep firing at him. This time a shot managed to crack through one of its horns before a second split it in two. That got its attention and it forgot Phaidros for a moment before Zenovia activated her jets and started to lead it away. "Check on Dom!" she shouted over the comms.

Phaidros did not argue, running to the cloud of dust and pile of rubble to see Dom forcing himself to sit upright. The entire left side of his armor was now splintered with chunks of chitin falling to dust. Phaidros could see exposed metal beneath with some tears even through that where the blow landed. Dom grunted, "That thing has an arm."

"Are you alright?" Phaidros asked, worried.

"I will survive, Phaidros, can't feel my arm but that's better than you being dead. I'll catch up to you both. Do not leave Zenovia with that thing." Phaidros nodded then began to run off before Dom called from behind, "And Phaidros. Remember what I said. When you feel that fear, there is only one thing for an Ignited to do. When all your thoughts fail you, run straight at it. It will be better than just sitting there and being sliced meat."

Phaidros hesitated, then nodded and ran off. With no one watching Dom now he unceremoniously slumped back against the ground. "Ow," the young Ignited heard uttered from behind him as he ran after Zenovia.

The two had left his sight, but now that he had learned how to use his life sense, all it took was one brief flex of his will to be able to find them. He saw a white burning star running from a burning set of eyes amidst tendrils of shadowy light. The star stopped and three gunshots followed accompanied by a pained roar afterwards. The star then leaped up in a zig zag motion upwards, she was heading towards a roof. "Where are you, Phaidros? I can't keep this thing distracted forever!"

Phaidros leapt up on the roof opposite of her, the creature in the alley between the two of them. "Here," he answered just before both of them stumbled from the buildings beneath them being crushed by the creature's strength. The sudden holes in the wall made the tops start to crumble as Zenovia ran over and leaped to Phaidros' building. The beast came up the new pile of rubble to charge at them.

Phaidros surged forward, blade whistling through the air to slam into its wrist as it tried to grab Zenovia and pull her into the new cloud of dust. The beast retreated its hand before they both jumped off the side of the building that was still standing. The beast came crashing through seconds later. Phaidros turned to face it, sword swinging through the air in sweeping parries of its claws, giving Zenovia time to retreat further before she spun around to start laying covering fire into the creature so it couldn't crush Phaidros but after six more shots the rifle clicked. "I'm out of ripper rounds, work with what you got," Zenovia said quickly.

Sparks flew through the air as its claws raked over his sword, each swing forcing Phaidros to give ground, forcing him nearly off his feet from the force of it and nearly taking the hope of a victory along with it. Hope was sputtering out yet he clung to it for dear life. It could not end here. He would not go quietly, this was about revenge at the beginning yes, but now it was about the others. He needed to help his team, his friends, to make sure they made it out of this alive.

Hopes alone could not stop a beast like this however, not while he was only Ignited and not Shaped. The creature got a final good swipe in and it knocked the sword from his hands. Zenovia was in the middle of reloading her weapon, cursing under her breath. Phaidros looked at his sword flying through the air and then at the beast. His eyes widened. For the second time today he swore he was going to die.

"Phaidros!" a familiar voice called, unhindered by a helmet. A blur of speed followed before Charon appeared, flying through the air with both feet planted on a spear. Phaidros couldn't get over his bewilderment before Charon leaped from the spear just as it collided with some exposed flesh on the beast's neck. He sailed through the air before landing in a skid on the other side, facing the beast which had staggered back, grabbing the spear in its neck and ripping it out.

"Charon, what are you *doing* here?" Phaidros said, switching to open communications, eyes wide with awe.

"Saving your life," Charon replied. Phaidros was in pure disbelief of what had just happened and immediately switched his life sense back on to see his brother's soul. He saw that it was overloaded with unlit potential, a teal tint to what was supposed to be pure white. He wasn't sure how that was possible but now was not the time to ask these questions. Charon was here and that meant someone else for him to protect. Phaidros ran for his sword.

The beast roared in anger and caught a bullet in its open mouth which caused it to sputter blood. Zenovia let out a sigh of relief. That's when the keening started again. Phaidros had just grabbed his sword, turning around to his brother and Zenovia. As Ignited, the two had some resistance to the creature's power, but Charon was not ignited. His brother stood there, trembling like a leaf in his armor. The creature rounded on him, claws flexed. Phaidros felt his feet carrying him forward before his mind was even realizing what he was doing. The whole world seemed muffled as he threw himself forward with everything he had. The creature's claw raised, Phaidros wasn't going to make it, it was too late. "Charon, no!" he cried.

Charon thrust his hands forward, crying out in panic. Then both he and the creature suddenly reeled back in pain. Phaidros skid to a stop as the creature swiped at the air in front of him. Charon threw his hands out again and the screaming resumed. Phaidros then switched his perception back to their souls. Where before the flames of the Shaped Beast licked at the souls of all nearby, now there was a line of light between Charon's soul and the beast's and he could see the ignited potential of the beast draining.

"Ash and cinders," Zenovia said in muttered awe, lowering her rifle briefly. Phaidros even saw Dom running back over with Daxia—or was it away from? No, with. His hammer was over his shoulder and Daxia had some tool in her hand that looked like a blow torch. Both stopped to see what was going on.

Charon's screams continued, his hands remaining locked in front of him like someone's hand forcibly pressed to a burning surface. The creature writhed in agony before finally it turned around, tail sweeping to slam into Charon, severing the connection while he tumbled through the streets. The creature wheezed, tail lashing in rage, spittle drooling from its maw from exhaustion but it was too angry to care.

Phaidros was torn from his stupor. "Distract it. Distract it now!" he called, before he rushed the creature and Zenovia began firing at it again with Dom now trying his best to help without dying in the process.

⮞

Off to the side, Charon's vision came and left in waves of blurry nothingness as all attention on him had been forgotten. He was in pain, indescribable pain, but his soul brimmed with vitae. The three Ignited were doing their best, but they could not stop the beast, it did not seem to even think of running away. Charon needed to do something, anything. His gaze drifted to one of the bodies left in the street, some ra man Charon had never met. Even if he couldn't immediately move, he could still help…

⮞

Blades cut portions of scales free and hammers smashed others, but with every blow they made, the creature paid them in kind. They were all so distracted, they didn't see the merchant running into the fray, going for the creature's legs and grasping desperately at it.

"Cinders, what is that person doing, get them out of there!" Phaidros cried.

The creature was distracted by them for a brief moment before its tail snaked around and whipped at the person, splitting them in two from the force. Yet the torso continued to move. It was then that Phaidros had noticed something familiar. It was the man that Daxia had bought her coffee from, yet now his eyes were a distinct, bold teal color.

He quickly looked around himself, seeing the other corpses begin to get to their feet on shaky limbs, all distinct. "The bodies, they're getting up," he said shakily.

"Can look later, busy dying!" Dom warned. Yet Phaidros needed to know. His perception switched back to seeing the potential of his surroundings. In each of these bodies he saw a small, teal droplet of energy, potential he guessed, in the center and a network of lines that all extended to one origin point. Charon.

Charon was still sitting yet moving his trembling hands about in strange gestures. The previously dead civilians all began to rush the beast in a suicidal charge. The beast took the bait, striking at all around it. This gave Dom an opening and he brought his hammer down on what was left of its tail, crushing it and making it fall limp to the floor. He barely registered the newly moving corpses; there was a fight going on, that was all that mattered to the zhuk.

Phaidros stared in silent awe before the creature began to keen again. Yet despite its effects on normal people, the walking corpses went on as if there was nothing wrong. Phaidros saw bodies severed and cut to pieces before their bodies became like clay, reforming again and rushing up to the creature anew. A whole crowd was now climbing and amassing on it and weighing it down in the process. Phaidros finally shook his head and joined the action again as the creature tried to claw the bodies from it before slamming itself on the ground and rolling trying to get them off of it. Phaidros went for one of its arms, finding a gap amidst all the bodies and slamming his sword down on its wrist. It struggled, but Dom soon followed suit and Zenovia ran up to it to begin trying to fire rounds down its gullet.

None of them noticed as the bodies' hands started to shift into bone-like claws and spears as they repeatedly stabbed at the beast. All was chaos and screams. Then the creature writhed in one final death throe before falling still. All of the Ignited watched as its ignited potential snuffed out in an implosion before the Shaped soul drifted away towards the heavens.

All was silent save for the labored breathing of all the Ignited. Then they all slowly turned to Charon. Now that he had a chance to truly look at his brother, he could see how his eyes had been the exact same teal color as all the corpses.

"Charon…" Phaidros began, surprised to feel a small tremble in his voice. "What have you done?"

CHAPTER 17

*Complacency leads to stagnation. Never become complacent
in life, always seek more. Ambition will guide you to
your true self. Stagnation only leads to death.*

-Collected Teachings of the Exalted Sovereign

3 Months Ago

THE CROWD ROARED as Charon twisted through the air, narrowly avoiding an axe aiming right where his chest was a moment ago. The movement was graceful, elegant, limbs sweeping out and trailed by the fire of his armor's jets that brought him to the other side of his opponent. It had almost been two years since he became the champion of The Ring. He had been undefeated since. Every opponent that met him met the same fate and each time he would be met with a roaring applause as he not only bested them, he made a show of it.

He did not press the newfound advantage he had with his technique. He allowed his opponent, Cora was her name, to turn back toward him. She had been a newer arrival to Dasos and quickly made a name for herself in the ring. Which was how this match came to be; she wished to see the champion in action. She had disappointed Charon, like all the others. She came at him again, axe swinging in quick horizontal and vertical chops. Charon danced just out of her reach once, twice, and on the third swing at him he ducked low, leg spinning around and kicking up dust as he knocked the feet out from under Cora and leapt back. He turned to the crowd, arms outstretched and grinned wide. It was all too easy.

The cheers of the crowd rang around him again, swelling him with pride that had long since replaced the warm flame of his potential inside of him. He turned back to his opponent as she got back to her feet, brandishing her war axe again and growling in frustration. Charon felt he had played with her enough, it was time to end it. The engines on his limbs burned hot while he prepared to launch himself towards her. He knew the exact angle he was going to jump and leapt in an explosive cloud of sand. He sailed through the air, body twisting once more as he extended a leg to deliver a powerful kick.

Then he felt a stabbing pain in his heart, no, not stabbing, burning. The sudden panic in his lungs made him swing too fast, giving Cora time to parry the strike as he landed behind her in a stumble. He quickly turned back toward her; when did it get so hard to breathe? His suit display was trying to inform him of her movements but it was all starting to make him feel nauseous. She did not give him a reprieve to try and recover; she was on him in a moment, axe slamming against him and cracking his armor before the impact itself sent him slamming against the dirt. The audience cheered in surprise at the champion getting knocked down. He tried to shove himself back up, do anything, yet all he could feel was the growing heat within him. It was not the comfortable flames of his potential within providing him with confidence. The flames were hungry with their food supply dwindling by the second, they struck at all that was left for them to burn, his soul.

Charon screamed. Not the scream of a warrior facing his death head on, but the scream of a man on fire with no water to douse him. Cora hesitated in her next attack as she switched her perceptions at the same time as the Ignited in the audience. They saw what little remained for the fire to burn and the edges of his soul begin to blacken. One man leapt from the high wall in the crowd to run to Charon. His father, Zaharias. "Charon!" he cried, yet Charon could not muster up a response. He could feel the flames in every fiber of his being, burning, searing, purging all that he was and all that he would ever become. Kindlings arrived seconds after his father did, Cora backing up as they did so, expression hidden under her helmet. Charon writhed on the ground in painful agony as the crowd was shocked into silence.

"We need to bring him to Suneater," a Kindling had said to his father who was trying to keep Charon from thrashing about.

"Then don't just stand there, help me!" Zaharias barked back. The Kindlings moved around Charon but were finding some trouble because of his armor. They managed to hold him down long enough to deactivate his armor and pull him out of it. The screams were unfiltered now, filling The Ring and never ending until the Kindlings managed to get him onto a stretcher and escort him out of the arena in haste with Zaharias following.

Phaidros was waiting for them outside, a terrified expression on his face as he saw the pain in his brother's features, the scratching screams from his throat, and the tears streaming from his eyes. He looked to his father for some sign that everything was going to be okay but Zaharias did not spare him a glance. Phaidros followed after them all, disturbed but wanting to be there for his brother.

Charon's screams did not cease. Yet by the time they reached the temple they had become raspy croaks, the intensity still there yet the sound that came out did not match the severity at which Charon squirmed against his bindings. Two of the Kindlings had ushered Phaidros away before the rest entered. The Ideal was perched atop the root of the great tree, though was already moving down to meet them halfway across the temple grounds. Suneater did not need to ask what had happened. They simply gestured for the others to step back as they approached Charon, kneeling down besides the stretcher. Zaharias stood nearby and watched the Ideal work.

Suneater's hands went to Charon's chest. "He is cindering," they said. "You are privileged to be in my city. As otherwise the Exalted Sovereign is only known to intervene just before the point of them becoming a complete invalid." Zaharias' eyes widened.

Through Charon's muted cries, Suneater spoke. It was not a language that Charon recognized, yet it seemed to be working because Charon's screams died out and were replaced with whimpers. His breathing was labored, his eyes blinked back open but they were unfocused and flicking around as if searching for something.

"I… I can't see." Charon forced the words out, struggling to make his voice audible to the others.

"It will take some time and effort for your sight to recover," Suneater said, louder than they were speaking before. "As will everything else. Yet with time and patience, you will heal."

Zaharias looked at Suneater, body tense. "How long?" he asked.

"Years, decades on average," Suneater mused.

"Decades?" Zaharias said, horrified.

"Such is the nature of cindering. Since you have so little potential to work with, it will take much more to bring it back to normal levels. We could ignite him again and the process would speed up, however, he would have to be able to handle and work through the pain." They looked down at Charon who was barely registering the conversation.

Zaharias's brow furrowed in concern before he knelt down beside Charon. "Oh my son," he said, tone strained. "I had warned you about becoming complacent." He shook his head. "Look at what you've done to yourself, Charon." His son finally looked up at him, seeming confused as if he hadn't even realized his father was there until just now.

"Father…?" he asked weakly.

Zaharias couldn't look him in the eye. "Perhaps this is my fault. I should have pushed him harder. Now he's…" He trailed off. "Please, I need a moment." Suneater bowed their head before returning their attention to Charon and giving further instructions to the Kindlings.

"Father? Is that you? Where are you going?" Charon croaked.

Zaharias walked outside of the temple where Phaidros waited with fear written in his eyes.

"Will Charon be alright?" Phaidros asked his father meekly.

"He will live," Zaharias said, tone solemn. "We will assist him as best we can… but whether he rises from the flames as the phoenix or becomes lost to the ashes is up to him. Run home, Phaidros. I will return with your brother when we are ready."

Phaidros opened his mouth to protest but quickly shut it. "Yes, Father." With a haunted expression, he left to go return home.

Zaharias sighed and looked back towards the temple entrance. Finally, after some hesitation he entered the temple again to look after his son. The son that had just ruined his own life.

CHAPTER 18

One cannot be expected only to succeed. Failure brings with it scars and lessons that should be cherished. Do not look down upon those who fail then, only offer them a hand so that they may try again once more.

-COLLECTED TEACHINGS OF THE EXALTED SOVEREIGN

CHARON SAT, BREATH heavy, seeing through dozens of different pairs of eyes all at once that were all connected to him. It took concentration to focus purely on his own set of eyes, only to see that his brother and his two companions were staring at him. With great effort he pushed himself to his feet; the bodies stood idly by without his commands. His brother was speaking to him but he didn't quite register the words. He felt as if he was floating and sound was muffled as his teal eyes locked onto the bodies that were under his control.

"Charon!" Phaidros called, finally snapping the older brother's attention to him. Charon didn't respond still; he knew what Phaidros was asking about. He wished it hadn't been revealed like this but under that creature's power he had panicked and couldn't think of any other solution than to use it.

The large zhuk was poking one of the corpses, which barely registered he was there. "Hello? I am talking to you, little human. How did your hands become swords? I am very curious."

Zenovia was just staring in silence, whatever thoughts she may have were hidden beneath her visor, but there was a cold intensity behind it that made Charon uncomfortable.

"I…" Charon began, not sure how to explain what he had done. "I saved you," he eventually settled on. "All of you."

"We had it under control," the zhuk interrupted. They certainly didn't, but Charon was still too dazed to argue.

"How did you get the bodies to move?" Zenovia asked, tone curt.

Charon hesitated, he could tell them everything, but it wouldn't make anything better. There was only one thing he could do, tell the truth and hope that Phaidros would see reason to side with him. "Remember what I told you? I had found a way to fight alongside you." He gestured around them all to the shuffling corpses. "This was it."

"Charon… look at what you've done to them," Phaidros said, horror present in his voice as he gestured to the twisted configurations that were forced upon them by Charon.

Charon opened his mouth to speak and then closed it again, he placed a hand atop his bag that held the book and took a step back. The corpses around him all began to shuffle towards him lazily. Before long they stood with Charon and turned to face the Ignited. "It doesn't matter," he eventually said. "I helped you all and I wasn't even ignited. You should all be thanking me," he said, an anxious laugh leaving him as he spoke. He looked to his brother. "I told you, I told you I would be ready when the time comes and I was. If I wasn't here, you would have died. Now you're alive, we all won, against a Shaped Beast at that. What does it matter how I did it?"

More figures began to approach now, Ignited, of all different shapes and sizes clad in dark chitin armor, who had seen that the creature had been slain from the distance and came to check up on the would-be heroes. They were in their private channels because Charon could hear the clicking coming from all of their helmets. Phaidros only spared them a glance before taking a step towards Charon. "You did and I'm thankful for that, Charon... but this?" He gestured to the corpses surrounding him. "It... it isn't right. It isn't natural. Why don't you release whatever hold you have on them all and we can speak to Suneater about what happened? They'll want to hear about this."

That made Charon's eyes widen and he took a step back, the horde around him beginning to shift restlessly. "I... I can't. Suneater will try to take it all away. I know they will. Then I'll just be Cindered again," he explained, a frightened tremble in his voice.

Up above, everyone noticed the sound of groaning branches as the giant tree that shifted above them all began to sway, side to side. Moments later all of the Ignited with their visors on saw the sigil of the Suneater in their display. "All Ignited. You must seize Charon at once. Subdue him, he must be brought in for questioning."

Charon watched as all gazes turned toward him. A few already began to move toward him but Phaidros quickly ran forward, putting himself between the Ignited and Charon. Dom moved to his side by instinct but Zenovia stayed where she was. "Wait! Sacred Suneater, just let me talk to him. I'll get him to come peacefully, there is no need," Phaidros begged.

"No," Suneater replied. "Every moment he is free is a danger to us all. Seize him."

The Ignited began to move in again and Charon backed up and away toward the jungle, placing the horde between him and the Ignited. He looked around frantically before spotting the corpse of the Shaped Beast.

Phaidros had leveled his sword, Dom following suit with his hammer. Zenovia sighed. "Step aside, you two, this is for his own good. Whatever is going on the Suneater will make sure nothing bad happens to..." She hesitated as she glanced off to the side and watched as the Shaped Beast twitched and groaned before slowly pushing itself to its feet. Its single eye burning a bright teal color. It let out a wet-sounding hiss, blood drooling from its mouth and it made even the Ignited begin to back away.

"Charon, wait," Phaidros pleaded. "What are you doing?"

Charon saw now through the eye of the beast, but this would not be enough. He was going to need more. He looked up to the soul of the beast still floating away into the sky and reached for it. The soul flew right back towards him like a bullet before coming to a sudden halt and hovered around him. With his other hand he willed his spear back into his hand. "I can't go back. I won't let you," he said, bitterness in his tone. "I worked hard for all of this, just like the Exalted Sovereign wanted and because you all find it distasteful you wish to tear it away from me?" he yelled, anger rising in his weak voice. The horde and beast begin to growl. "No. I'm done being the bad omen of what you shouldn't be or shouldn't become." He grimaced, stepping further away. "Phaidros, don't let them take me, I don't want to go back to how I was." All Phaidros did was stare at him, wordlessly. He didn't need to see his eyes to know how Phaidros looked at him, with that same look of pity that all the others gave him. Hope dwindled, he had his reanimated and the shaped soul, but he could not stop all of Dasos. So he did the only thing he could do—he ran, all of the bodies following after him.

"After him, now!" Suneater's voice called over the comms. The Ignited began to move, brandishing weapons.

"I call forth the rite of vengeance!" Phaidros quickly spat into the comms, voice panicked. All of the Ignited froze.

Zenovia finally approached, teeth clenched as she spoke. "Idiot boy, what are you doing?"

Phaidros continued quickly. "My brother has forsaken the city and left it in danger as you said. I have a right to be able to fix this personally in the eyes of the Exalted Sovereign himself."

Dom put himself between Zenovia and Phaidros. "He has a point. This is a matter to be settled between family before it comes to the rest of us," he said over the comms.

Silence followed and like an angry shuddering of leaves, Suneater spoke. "Phaidros, you are to report to the temple at once. All other Ignited, you are to remain mobilized. Clear the Merchant's District." The Ignited quietly did as directed and Phaidros let out a small sigh of relief.

Dom turned to Phaidros. "You will not have to speak to the Ideal alone, Phaidros, we are a hunting party and as agreed I will see this through to the end."

"But the beast is dead," Phaidros said in confusion.

"I believe we saw different things, as I saw it get right back up again and walk off with your brother." Phaidros could hear the grin behind Dom's voice. "Not often do we get a second chance to take on a challenge such as that. Besides, I want vengeance for my armor." He tapped the destroyed sections of it, where chitin was already beginning to slowly fill back in with glistening white ever so slowly.

Zenovia frowned. "You've made a mistake here, Phaidros, but if I can honor your father's memory by keeping you safe then I will," she said with a nod. "I just wish you didn't let Charon off like that. We should have captured him *then* plead for Suneater's mercy."

Phaidros sighed. "I just need a chance to talk to him one on one, this is my chance to do that. Otherwise who knows what Charon could have done or what they would have done to him." The other two nodded. "Well, let's not keep Suneater waiting then. I have a feeling the time table for this rite will not be nearly as forgiving as the last one was. "

The three re-entered the city. Dom, despite his injuries, was insistent on seeing this all through to the end. He was the only one who truly got hurt during the fight which in itself was a miracle and if he hadn't then Phaidros would be dead for sure. The three made their way up to the stone temple at the base of the great tree where Suneater awaited them... or at least, the avatar of them was. The tree itself *was* the Ideal, but the person that stood before it was just an extension. Phaidros knew that, but without life sense he had never really thought much about it. Phaidros got a strange sense of dread when he looked into its potential and saw a similar ball of fire without a soul connecting it to the soul of the tree, which shone large and brilliantly like a small sun. It had the same shape as Suneater's sigil, stiff branches of fire surrounding teeth devouring a sun. The fire within the person was white, as all ignited potential was, but after seeing what Charon had done he wasn't so sure its origins were so honorable.

Suneater spoke before they even reached the great root that it stood upon. "Just what are you thinking? Calling a Rite of Vengeance now of all times. Every moment that Charon is left to his own devices he endangers us all even further. To fight a Shaped Beast is one thing, but you now tread the grounds where the dead walk, beings beyond the touch of the Exalted Sovereign."

Phaidros reached up to his helmet and pulled it off to look into Suneater's glowing eyes. "He's my brother, Suneater," he said with far more confidence than he felt. "I'm not going to just sit idly by and let the Ignited descend upon him like a pack of hungry wolves."

"Your brother," Suneater repeated, tone picking up like a windstorm, "will invite ruin upon us all if it saves his pride."

Zenovia spoke up next. "You know what is going on here, Suneater. Phaidros will be facing his brother alone and he will need to know what he is going up against lest he die."

"I am considering letting that happen as punishment for the stunt you pulled in the Merchant's District." Suneater bit back before steadying themselves, taking a deep breath that sounded like a gust of wind. "Forgive me, the power that Charon used is ancient. I have remained watchful for it for eons, always knowing one day I would see it again, but its masters are patient beings. All it takes is one lapse of guard for it to slip through."

"But what is it?" Phaidros repeated, more insistent this time.

Suneater sighed. "Vitaemancy, power over life and with it, death," they answered. "It hails from the Amaranthine Planes, in lands where there are no stars and dead roam the lands eternal. This is not 'Memory' or where souls go to reincarnate. It is something else, something far more sinister. You need only look up at the sky to see it, to one as young as you all you might not even notice, but having lived as long as I have... I have seen the stars in the sky wink out one by one, each another world claimed by them.

"As to why you have never heard of it? For your own good," Suneater explained. "Charon must have received one of their books. Its power is great and mighty. It does not require the sacrifice of one's self that potential does. One barely even needs to understand the power they wield to use it, to the book's very design. If the public were to know of this ancient power, many would wish to seek it out, ignorant or uncaring of its cost."

"And what is the cost?" Dom asked. "So far I am only hearing positives."

"Slavery," Suneater answered. "Oh it is a chain that extends far or a cage where you never even notice the bars. Yet by using it, you put yourself in his power. The power is borrowed and he may claim it at any time and you along with it. With potential, your power is your own, with no one being able to take it from you save yourself and your own actions. Yet such is life."

Phaidros' eyes widened as he stepped forward. "Then my brother is in danger?"

"Are you not listening, boy?" Suneater hissed. "We're all in danger. You saw what it did to the Shaped Beast. It burned him yes, as if he had touched the metaphysical flame himself, yet now he hides away in the jungle, sapping the life from all around him and most likely growing an army. Not to mention the Shaped Soul he has now claimed, a soul that he may be able to bond to himself to gain the creature's power." Suneater pointed at him. "And now he has the time to do so, thanks to you. I plead with you to revoke your rite of vengeance and allow us to descend upon him now before he grows more powerful."

It felt odd that an Ideal was pleading to him for anything, but the rite of vengeance was something sacred. The Order of the Ignited was a religion and organization that prized self-improvement above all, to deny anyone a chance to do so was nothing short of sacrilege in the eyes of the Exalted Sovereign. "No," Phaidros answered, shaking his head and speaking before Suneater could cut him off. "Doing so will only make it worse. If I go, there is still a chance to save him. The Exalted Sovereign tells us to not look down on those who have failed, only reach out a hand so that they may try and get up again. I will not deny my brother that chance."

Now Suneater's voice turned pitying. "He does not want to get up, he wants to bury himself where no one can look."

"Then I will pull him out," Phaidros answered, determined.

Suneater sighed again. A moment of silence passed through the room before they finally replied. "You have till the sun sets tomorrow to bring your brother back, dead or alive."

Phaidros let out a sigh of relief, bowing his head. "Thank you, Sacred Suneater. I will not fail."

"You cannot," Suneater replied. "And due to the severity of the task at hand, I will offer you assistance, so that should the worst come to pass and I am right, you will have a fighting chance." They reached out a hand. "Your sword, give it to me."

Phaidros hesitated, surprised by the offer before he stepped forward, taking his sword and offering it to Suneater. The Ideal slipped from the branch gracefully before gently taking the sword by the hilt in one hand while the other gently rested upon the blade.

They turned away from Phaidros and stepped back up onto the root before taking a knee and lifted the sword, head bowed. "All living beings have potential, we are able to grow and change as our life continues, what we do with it is how we shape the form it will take. An object is nothing without the hand that holds it. Thus, we determine the potential of every tool at our disposal. For a Shaped and beyond? This is literal."

A single branch curled its way down from the tree and into the room as it touched the blade. The length of steel burst into an ethereal fire that bathed the room in the light of life. "And so, I imbue your blade with a piece of me and my potential. From now on, your sword will **devour** all that stands in your way."

The three Ignited stood in awe of the flame in front of them. "A shaped weapon..." Dom muttered under his breath. "The greatest gift a Shaped can bestow, a piece of themselves upon another. You are truly blessed, little friend. I could only dream to one day hold such a fine tool in my hands."

They couldn't see what was happening, but soon the flame began to die and the branch retreated. Suneater turned, the last essence of flame lapping at the air as the Ideal held the sword aloft. Where before the blade was straight edged and simple, now near the hilt were teeth like serrations with the blade hooking elegantly one way like a sharpened fang. They descended from the root to hold the sword back out to Phaidros by the hilt, "use it well. For all of our sakes. If you die, your brother will not be able to use it unless he is Ignited, so be at peace knowing that."

Phaidros gently took it by the hilt, feeling the heat of his soul extend to the blade in his hand as if it were an extension of him. When he switched to his life sense, he saw the weapon too as a length of fire with the silhouette of gnashing fangs in the flames. He then looked to Suneater and bowed deeply. "Thank you, Sacred Suneater. I am undeserving of such a gift."

"If you succeed, you do deserve it," Suneater answered. "The Ignited do not idly give gifts to those who do otherwise."

Phaidros nodded, then looked to the others apologetically. "...I am sorry, you two, but this something I have to do alone."

Both Zenovia and Dom flinched at that, Zenovia speaking up first. "You cannot be serious."

"I just made a big deal about killing that beast a second time," Dom complained.

Phaidros shook his head. "I cannot have you die for my rite this time. This is between me and my brother." He looked down. "You both will be needed in the defense should I fail and Dom will need time for his armor to recover and..." He looked up just in time to see Zenovia's fist crash into his visor.

It connected with a crack, making Phaidros reel back as Zenovia followed through with the punch, finger raised as Phaidros caught himself. "Nice try, boy. I had to leave your father to his fate once and he died. I'm not going to do that to you too. You can tell us to stay behind all you want but I'll just follow you anyway, rite be damned."

Phaidros then looked to Dom, who shrugged. "I would punch you too but you need your helmet. I will not be going for your brother, I will be going for the beast. It is a good compromise, you see," he said with a sagely nod.

"But your armor—" Phaidros tried to reason.

"Bah, the armor makes me protected but slow. A good hammer is all I need—and maybe pick up some drasil fruit from the medical bay."

Phaidros then looked to Suneater for help and they offered none. They didn't want him to go alone either, and three was still traditional for the rites anyway. If Phaidros continued to argue Suneater would simply shrug their shoulders.

Dom rounded Phaidros and slipped an arm over his shoulder. "You're stuck with us, little friend. I am sorry to say. It is best you choose only the easy battles because if you thought fighting the Shaped Beast was hard, hah! You will be wishing that I let you die back in that fight."

Zenovia nodded in agreement. "Whatever your brother has in store for us… we'll be ready, but we'll leave him to you. It'll be all on you to get him to stand down… please try to do that before those monsters of his kill us."

Phaidros looked at them all in disbelief for a moment before he sighed in defeat. "Alright, you both can come with me."

"We know," they said in unison, pointedly.

"…and thank you both, for standing with me through this," Phaidros said. "It is nice to know that I am not alone here."

Dom laughed. "You are Ignited! You are never alone." He pushed off of Phaidros' shoulders as he began to make his way out of the temple. "Now come! We should not keep your brother waiting! From everything I have heard he is an impatient man."

Phaidros smiled at that, looking to Zenovia once and nodding, this time with more confidence, then the two followed after Dom.

"Be careful, Ignited," Suneater called after them. "For the powers of death will tear you asunder otherwise and we will have three more enemies we will need to contend with."

Phaidros looked over his shoulder towards Suneater, hesitating, then nodding before continuing on. It would not come to that, he would talk his brother down and he would lead him home. Charon had saved his life today, Phaidros would do the same for him.

CHAPTER 19

*Cast aside doubt. Cast aside fear. For where you will soon
tread, your steps will carry the weight of legions.*

-BOOK OF THE FATHER, FIRST PAGE

CHARON PACED ABOUT deep in the jungle. Death surrounded
him on all sides. The vibrant colors of the jungle had all been
muted to the brown corpses of trees and grass. He had reanimated some of them into vaguely humanoid shapes, an army of trees
standing amidst the people he took with him and the stolen, Shaped
Beast. It wasn't Shaped anymore, but it would serve a similar purpose all
the same. Its soul still orbited him, he had to keep some concentration
on it at all times lest it floated back to wherever this soul would go when
it died.

Embedded in a nearby tree was his knife. As he looked into its reflection he could see Exaltation there. "They're going to come for me, I
know it. I don't know why they haven't done so already but they are
planning something." He spoke quickly, tone edging on panicked as he
paced about.

You have read the section on soulbinding, yes?

the sacrament asked.

"Yes, however, I don't see how I can stop an army by myself with one shaped soul," Charon said.

You do not need to stop an army yourself. With but one shaped soul, you have given yourself an opportunity that most people do not. You can bind it to yourself to become one with the beast, to gain all of its memories, experiences, and power. You and it will no longer be separate, but as one.

Charon hesitated, looking to the soul and willing it to float in front of him. An imprint of eyes stared back at him. "If they come at me in a swarm then I don't see how it will help."

They will be trying to take you alive at first. Their mercy will be their weakness and two souls will become more and more until you are unstoppable.

The direction of the conversation had just hit Charon and he paused. "Kill them… Phaidros will come after me, I know he will, that means…"

You will have to slay your brother. If you don't, then you will be dragged back before the Ideal again. Your power will be stripped from you. You will become Cindered again, a cripple in a world of strength.

Charon frowned deeply, suddenly feeling heavy and numb all at once. All of the paths before him seemed to be closing in around him, threatening to drown him in the abyss of uncertainty. He could not go back, no matter how much he wished he could turn back the hands of time, there would be no doing so. The only options left ahead of him were to keep walking or fall back into the cindering pit of despair. "There is no turning back, is there?" he asked, already sure of the answer, but wishing to give the final whisper of hope one last chance.

Not anymore, child. You no longer walk the path of life but death. Do not be afraid though. It is as the father says in his book. Death is not the end, it is a new beginning. Should you be cunning enough in the coming hours, you will have your freedom and more.

Charon lowered his head, contemplative, the last seed of hope withering away like the jungle around him. He took a deep breath. "So it is, then." He lifted both hands, cradling it in both hands, then with a flex of his will, pushed it into his chest. He did... something, he wasn't sure what, but both his cindered soul and the soul of the shape molded together like wet clay. He wasn't sure what he was about to expect, but there was a moment of nothing, then within his mind there was another presence, one familiar to him, fearsome, brutal. The beast looked at the world through Charon's eyes and for a moment, the two shared disbelief.

Then the fight began.

Charon's body lurched forward, then back writhing against invisible binds as Charon tried to rein in the beast's control. It was agonizing, a dual-voiced cry echoing through the jungle. A flood of memories washed over Charon's mind, as where once there were two, there was now one.

He was not Charon anymore, he was one of the many reptiles that called the jungle home. A runt of its litter. Memories flashed as he competed for the resources of the jungle, every day a fight for survival. Years passed and it had been cornered by poachers seeking its hide. It was scared; if it were stronger then these things would not have singled it out. If it were fearsome then it would no longer need to hide in the shadows of hateful trees, if it were terrifying then these poachers would not be hunting it. With nowhere left to run it lashed out and ignited the moment it bit off the poacher's hand. Newfound strength surged through its limbs, a feeling Charon was all too familiar with, and it tore the poachers to pieces and feasted on an earned kill.

More time passed and it had grown stronger, bigger, faster, more cunning. It desired to no longer live in fear, to be the most dangerous predator in the jungle, to be feared, to no longer have to hide and scavenge; it wanted the entire jungle to kneel before it in terror. It had begun to carve itself a territory and harass the denizens of the city of sentients nearby.

More memories flashed before him and it stood triumphant over a great tiger, head cast triumphantly into the air as it roared. It saw a pair of eyes above it, then its whole being became subsumed by fire. Charon heard the Exalted Sovereign's voice for the first time since he had ignited, "You seek that which you are. You have been terrified of the world around you since the day you hatched, and now wish to be the object of that fear to all that would harm you. Become Shaped, and become fear itself." When it walked from the flames, it stood on two powerful legs and its form grew twice in size. Three Ignited came to face it, two of them died.

Charon relived the memories of facing against his own father as the Shaped Beast, then how the beast feasted upon him after. He should have felt revulsion, but with the beast now a part of him, it felt good to triumph over a worthy opponent. They had to spend several weeks licking their wounds after their victory but when they were ready they returned to the Merchant's District, not to harass, but to murder. Charon saw the beast face down against the Ignited who lived to tell the tale of their glory and against the two others, his brother and the zhuk then Charon himself.

He was not alone in this sharing of memories, as Charon became the beast, the beast became Charon. It saw a human child in a family. His father was not around much and he was often left alone with his mother, Rhea. Rhea... her name was almost lost to Charon, it had been so long since...

Fire. Fire and brimstone surrounded them, a world that was once peaceful caught in a savage conflict. The skies above warped under the fury of great metal beasts in the sky launching fire at one another. Rubble and ruin filled young Charon's vision, drowned out through the sounds of battle and gunfire. Iron collossi strode through the devastation with reality itself warping to the tune of unseen warriors. He was saved by his father and stolen away from the battle, both him and his newborn baby brother.

The beast felt young Charon's fear of a new, strange world unlike the one he had been brought from. His father was now always present, their mother dead and gone in the ashes of their once home. Love that was once distant was now here in how the father taught him how to fight, tucked him into bed, and shared stories of times long past to him in the night till the boy fell asleep.

The boy was now a man; he did not struggle to ignite like the beast had, he had done so amidst a crowd of others, a sword held overhead and the eyes of Life upon him in a great ritual. It relived his rise in the Arena, dueling against other powerful Ignited. It relived him cindering and the horrible pain that came with it and the shame of being the weakest among the pack of a strong. A runt, like the beast was. A runt that sought power, basked in the glory of it, like the beast had.

They were the same, the two realized in the same moment. They wanted the same thing, to be the apex among the strong, no matter what it cost, to make up for how the world treated them while they were weak.

Now he stood—no, they stood, staring down at a pair of hands that were half familiar to them. They felt compelled to speak a language they had never known before. "What are we?" two voices called out in chorus from their shared throat, one edged in a growl and one Charon's own.

You have bound your souls together. Where once there were two lives and experiences, they are now one to be shared. You give the beast all of your vitaemantic powers and the beast gives you all of its shaped power and natural might. You will find it is much easier to control more reanimated bodies with two minds working in concert with one another as well.

Charon and the beast looked up towards the knife that held Exaltation. "Then when they come for us, will we be able to stop them?" This question was more the beast's than Charon's.

Yes and should you find any of their souls worthy, you may take them as well once you defeat them. Do keep in mind that a willing sentient soul will be much easier to bond with than an unwilling one. Self-loathing is often an effect of doing so. You will also notice, by binding yourselves together, that your once cracked and cindered soul is now filled. This will, cost you only some of the shaped soul's natural power to do so but you will no longer need to keep drinking from the jungle to keep yourself sustained. Drink deeply, children, and see yourselves victorious in the coming battle.

The beast and Charon grinned with delight. Once more they would be the most fearsome thing in the jungle. They didn't need to be afraid of their brother coming for him, they would stop him—and maybe even bind him to themselves. Then they would never be without him again, it would take some convincing sure, but they were sure they could do it. They took a deep breath, and all around them withered and died, then they pushed all of the stolen potential out into the wilds around them. Swathes of the jungle groaned in a simultaneous movement as the jungle itself was forced back to life.

When the Ignited came, they would be ready for them.

CHAPTER 20

*Strength alone does not make a person better. It is what they do with
their strength that makes them who they are. Do not seek the most
dangerous and most challenging prey to challenge your might. Seek
out challenges of character, so that you may learn who you truly are.*

-Collected Teachings of the Exalted Sovereign

I T WAS NOT hard to catch Charon's trail. Dozens of small footsteps
and one set of large that left behind snapped twigs and branches
made it clear to know where the runaway was going. Wherever it
went, a trail of death followed. The vibrant color of the jungle was gone
as they traveled, replaced only with shriveled trees and dead animals in
its wake.

Phaidros, Zenovia, and Dom moved at an easy pace, conserving
their energy in case there was a fight ahead. They had stopped by the
medbay to pick up some drasil fruit, a fruit made by the drasil that was
like eating pure potential. It did not fill your own potential, but when
eaten it smoothed away physical injuries. If you weren't cindered, that
is. If you were cindered, the fruit turned to ash in your hands. With
it, Dom was walking normally and in pace with the others. Daxia had

made what quick repairs she could before they left, wishing them luck on their journey.

They had been walking since they left the city and night was upon them. The moon was in the sky and stars were peeking through the trees in a brilliant display, the smoke clouds of the galaxy's edge billowing behind them. Phaidros had thought back to what Suneater had said about how the powers they were dealing with snuffed out the stars one by one. When he looked up, the stars seemed so vast and countless, it made him wonder what the sky must have looked like back then.

"We should make camp," Zenovia said, breaking the current silence between them all.

"We do not have time to waste," Dom replied.

"If the worst comes to happen and we have to fight Charon, we should be in top shape. Your armor is still growing back."

"Yes but we will be giving him that much more time to prepare. Is this really a wise idea?" Both of the Ignited looked to Phaidros to decide.

"Zenovia is right. We need your armor as repaired as possible," Phaidros reasoned, making Dom scoff but then sigh, which was as much agreement as they'd get out of him.

The three made a fire pit and easily found logs to sit upon as they rested around the crackling fire, their helmets off and faces exposed. Dom was the first to break the silence. "Little friend, I know we are going into this without much of a plan, do you really think you can get through to Charon? We should think about how we are going to do this."

Phaidros was busy looking at the fire, blade resting over his knees. He glanced at Dom, "I have to. I won't hunt my brother, I have managed to calm him down before and I will just have to hope that I will be able to do so again."

"You have so much hope and belief in your brother, but he just desecrated several dozen corpses and the jungle itself," Zenovia tried to reason.

"He is scared and he has been tricked by the book, as Suneater explained. There is still redemption for him, I know it," Phaidros said. "It is in the teachings of the Exalted Sovereign."

Dom hummed at that. "It is, yes. However, you also need to be aware that the person you are offering your hand to might just as well try to bite the hand that is picking it up and with that in mind." He looked to Zenovia. "We both think that we should be prepared in case this goes wrong."

Phaidros sighed. "What are you suggesting?"

"I think I should be posted farther away from the group where I can get a clean shot on Charon." She lifted a finger, cutting off Phaidros before he could interject. "Just in case," she clarified. "It would also give me a good vantage point to be able to spot any tricks he might have up his sleeve should he try to lure us into an ambush."

"And I will be close, like a bodyguard," Dom said, grinning as he pounded his fist into his open palm. "It will intimidate him into listening to you."

"I don't want to intimidate him, Dom," Phaidros said in exasperation. "I think if I can get past all of his... guards... then you should stay behind. I don't want him to think this is a hunt, I need him to know I'm there with good intentions." That made Dom grumble but Phaidros soon added, "You'll still be close by and if things go badly you'll get plenty of obstacles to smash through on your way to get to me."

"Alright alright, at least I will be able to get some frustration vented out this trip," Dom said with a nod.

"This isn't a game, Dom, this is even more serious than the Shaped Beast," Zenovia snapped.

"All of life is a game, just some people take it more seriously than others," Dom replied with a dismissive wave of his hand.

Phaidros sighed. "Oh leave him alone, Zenovia. I think Dom has earned a bad joke or two. He's saved my life now."

"And I haven't?" Zenovia huffed.

"You have, but you're not the one making bad jokes," Phaidros said with a small grin. That managed to get a smirk out of Zenovia, which was a small victory in itself.

"You should be," Dom criticized, pointing at them both. "Your life could be over by tomorrow, you should be enjoying your potentially short life every day some monster doesn't manage to skewer you," he said with a grin. "Face death with a smile on your face and in your heart. Otherwise you give the enemy a satisfaction they do not deserve."

"That is why you're smiling all the time?" Phaidros asked.

"Yes! There is no point in improving yourself each and every day if you are stuck dour and sad all the time. Be merry, enjoy life! You only get one. Or maybe two if Charon gets his hands on you." That one made Phaidros frown and in turn made Dom's grin turn apologetic. "I am sorry that was a bit too far."

"No, it's fine, I'm just nervous about tomorrow," Phaidros said. "Sorry to ruin the mood."

"The mood was hardly ruined," Zenovia assured. "This kind of talk is good before a big mission. Dom is right, somewhat, about the need for levity in times like this. It reminds us what we are fighting for, not just for the improvement of one's self, but for life, and all of the joys that come with it. Allow yourself this moment to relax, it'll make sure you're focused in the trial ahead."

Phaidros nodded slowly, eyes turning back to the fire. He did feel a smile come to his face, somber, contemplative. "Thank you both again," Phaidros said softly. "For coming with me on this journey. I would not be here without you both."

Dom nudged Phaidros' shoulder with his elbow. "Think nothing of it, little friend. We are all in this together."

Zenovia nodded. "Of course. Though we should get to sleep soon. I'll stay up longer to keep watch. Dom, I'll wake you up halfway through the night so you can have the second." The zhuk didn't complain, only nodded. Phaidros was about to protest against not keeping watch but decided against it. He was going to be the most important part of this tomorrow; he assumed they meant to give him as much chance to rest as possible.

The night passed without event or harassment by any creatures of the jungle. The usual ambiance, the buzzing insects, chirping birds, and rustling bushes were all gone. A heavy silence took its place, tension filling the air. The world knew something was about to happen to it and the trees sat as stiff as boards even in the distance beyond the trail of death the group had made camp in.

Dom had awoken Phaidros at the first sign of light. The group prepared themselves for another march. It wasn't long before they could see exactly where they needed to go. When they all used life sense to scout ahead, they saw an ocean of teal droplets of potential ahead of them. A patch of color amidst the usual blanket of white lights of the souls that filled the jungle.

Phaidros looked to Zenovia and nodded. She unholstered her rifle and ran off out of sight while Dom stayed at Phaidros' side. The two continued on, weapons at the ready as they scanned the dead jungle around them.

"Are you ready for this, little friend?" Dom asked.

"As ready as I'll ever be," Phaidros answered. After another few moments the trees in front of them sprung into motion, the two immediately entering a fighting stance as they pulled their roots out of the ground like makeshift feet, looming over the two Ignited. "Wait!" Phaidros called out. "I wish to speak to Charon! It's Phaidros." He wasn't even sure if the trees could hear or understand him, but they did stop when he spoke. They swayed lazily side to side, the groan of wood accompanying it as one of its branches bent towards him, the tip of it creakily pointing at Phaidros before it slowly turned and began to stomp off. When Phaidros didn't immediately follow, it stopped and waited.

Phaidros glanced to Dom, sharing a silent nod, before he followed after the tree, testing the grip of his sword in his hand. He was led past the other tree that watched Dom. When he switched perceptions again he saw teal droplets everywhere, like rain frozen in the air that touched every tree he could see. He switched to private communications and spoke to the group. "Zenovia."

"I know. I see it all. Nothing has stopped me yet. Maybe they're just focused on you," she replied, voice soft.

"We can hope," Phaidros answered back.

"I am not liking this," Dom said. "Be careful."

Phaidros didn't respond, looking around him warily. After a few minutes of walking he was brought into a clearing, Charon pacing within it with a book in his hand, teeth gnawing at one of his gauntleted fingers. To one side of him was the once Shaped Beast, most of its wounds still visible. He could still feel its power urging him to cower, though it now radiated from Charon instead. Behind him were the people he had raised from the dead. Each of them had their limbs twisted into sharp bone weapons. It was a sea of expressionless, teal eyes staring at Phaidros that made his stomach churn. "Charon," Phaidros began, "are you alright?" He reached up to take off his helmet, so he could look his brother in the eye.

Charon looked up from the book to him, lips a thin line, suspicion in his bright, teal eyes. "You didn't come alone," two voices replied. "You are lucky we were able to see through these creations or else things would have gone bad quickly."

The change in Charon's voice made Phaidros pause. There was something unnatural to it, like a lizard attempting to speak in time with Charon's words. When he looked into Charon's soul, he saw it had changed, the cracks were gone and he could see an imprint of eyes glaring at him from within what should have been a featureless, glowing white ball. Now was not the time to bring that up, however, he needed to get Charon talking. "I am sorry, I tried but they were worried about what might happen if I came alone," Phaidros reasoned. "I had called the Rite of Vengeance so that the others didn't follow you on your way out here. I wanted to make sure we had a chance to talk about... well, everything that has happened."

Charon frowned, hesitating, his eyes flicked this way and that as he mumbled to himself before turning towards him fully now. "We should thank you then. We were... not certain what the outcome of such an attack would be but we know it most likely would have ended in violence." He shook his head. "We do not want that, though we realize with how things are there is no way for me to return to Dasos. The Suneater will chase us to the ends of this world until we are dead."

Phaidros blinked, then frowned. "I... I only have a day to bring you and the book back, Charon, before the entire Ignited garrison of Dasos will be hunting for you."

Charon paused, digesting the information. His hand gripped the book tightly. "We see..." he muttered softly. His head lowered, then glanced to a knife stuck into a tree. Phaidros noticed how it vibrated.

There will be no hiding,

Exaltation said from his knife, though only Charon could hear him. Charon glanced to it briefly. "Why don't you come with us then, Phaidros?" Charon asked, taking a step toward his brother. "We can leave together. You don't need to be in the Order to be an Ignited and we would not have to go back to being Cindered," he said, a smile forming. "We can help one another and if the Ignited come after us we can fend them off. We can already build an army... all we would need is your help to give it a true fighting chance."

"So you can continue this... necromancy?" Phaidros asked, gesturing to the corpses behind him that now walked. "You're killing the entire jungle everywhere you walk, Charon, those people have families that would want to bury them. You're speaking in two voices now and I can see the imprint of the Shaped Beast's soul on yours. Suneater told me what that book is." Phaidros pointed to the book in Charon's hand. "Whatever comes from that book cannot be trusted, Charon, it'll turn you into a slave."

Charon let out a huff of amusement. "Is that so? Suneater would also see that we become Ignited again and fight through pain and suffering to cure our cindered soul. We did not have to go through any of that to be where we are now with this." He lifted the book. "And now we can even become Shaped. All of this jungle once thought of us as prey and now?" He gestured around to the dead trees that surrounded him. "Now we are the master of it all. Life can no longer look down on us because it is rightfully terrified of us."

"Is that all that really matters, Charon?" Phaidros asked, tone pleading. "What others think of you? I thought as long as we were both together we would be able to make life worth it. I can still help you. You just have to let me. Please just come back with me."

You believe that Suneater will let you live with this power? They will be terrified of you if they leave you as you are. No, the Ideal will devour all of your vitae until you are cindered once more.

Charon looked between Phaidros and the knife, brow furrowed. "Is the book talking to you?" Phaidros asked. "It is lying to you, Charon. Whatever it's saying, you can't listen to it. Suneater told me about how that book is used to destroy entire worlds. The power you are using will be used against you when it no longer needs you."

Lies spread by the tyranny of life. We would make you one of us. A god among men, powerful to make even the Ideals quake in fear of your coming. The Father loves all of his children and that is why he gives his power freely. We speak the truth. They are afraid because we are an antithesis of who they are, but an opposite does not immediately mean it is evil. You must trust us, Charon.

Charon grimaced. There was turmoil in his eyes as he clutched the book tighter. "We can't go back, Phaidros," he said, voice trembling. "It is far too late for that. We did not deserve to be punished by life how we were. Leave Dasos, do not wait for us."

Phaidros looked panicked as he took a few hurried steps forward. "No! I won't leave without you, Charon. You have to listen to me."

"We love you, Phaidros," Charon said, regret dripping from his voice. "But you must go. You don't understand what it was like, the pain, the struggle to even live, while everyone around you looks at you like you're a sick dog that someone should have just put down years ago."

Phaidros approached him further, reaching out for him. "Please, Charon, don't do this, I—"

Charon lifted a hand and Phaidros felt a sting of pain and something tug at him from within; the feeling made him stumble back with a cry of pain and made Charon flinch as well. Phaidros' eyes widened in shock, tears staining the corner of his eyes. "Go!" Charon shouted, the horde around him growing restless.

"No, wait. Don't do this, Charon–" The sound of wood shattering broke through the silence of the jungle, followed by a roar. Dom had heard Phaidros cry out and had immediately begun to fight. More trees brought themselves to life to stop the zhuk. "Dom, stand down! I'm not done talking," Phaidros shouted but the sounds of groaning trees grew more numerous.

"It's too late. There's no going back now," Charon said, shaking his head, eyes wide. "We need to get away. We need more time to prepare and if you will not leave…" Realization dawned on his features as he found a solution to his problem. "Then you must come with us."

Phaidros now looked horrified, leveling his sword before him. The fire within him raged violently as he did so. "Charon, please, do not make me do this."

"Please don't resist, Phaidros. It will make this a lot easier for us both. You'll barely even notice." He raised a hand again in a vague gesture and Phaidros felt pain swell in his chest again. Phaidros cried out in pain, the sound echoing throughout the jungle. Another followed it a second later, a gunshot. A corpse threw itself in front of Charon, the bullet blasting through the body but giving him the split second he needed to rear back, one hand raised in a swatting motion. A cut formed on his cheek, the bullet barely missing its mark, as the swarm surrounded him protectively. A moment later, the sound of groaning wood came from the direction that the shot came from followed soon by the sounds of more gunfire. Zenovia had been engaged.

The pain cut out immediately and Phaidros raised his blade, his emotions in turmoil as the fire within urged him to action. "Charon!" he cried in frightened anguish before he threw himself forward. He needed to get to him, get the book away from him, do *something* to turn this all around. He took his sword in both hands and charged the bodies that blocked him from his brother and swept it horizontally in a wide arc. The strength of the blow cleaved the front line of corpses in two. Before, they would have simply reknit themselves like they did against the beast, however as Phaidros switched his perception to his life sense, he saw that the droplets within were drawn after the sword, swirling around and into the flame of the blade, purifying it and making Phaidros' own potential swell.

Normally he would be horrified, but he needed to act. He stepped forward again, bodies falling around him as he cleaved through the second line, four more bodies falling around him.

That was when he heard the roar and with his enhanced reflexes, forced himself to the side as the Shaped Beast came barreling towards him with the same speed it had in life. It swiped at the air where Phaidros was a second ago as Charon called out to him. "If you don't stop we'll kill them," he said, voice high in panic. "We'll kill them all." The beast continued after Phaidros as he said this, claws swiping as Phaidros parried each strike while retreating.

It was at that moment that Phaidros realized that his brother was gone. How long had that been the case? Back when he first cindered? When he got the book? Or only now. Phaidros felt his heart crack before anger seeped in through the new openings. "I'm sorry, Charon. For that reason alone I need to stop you."

The fire within roared to new heights as the beast brought both claws down on him again. Phaidros no longer backed away but instead roared in fury as his blade collided with the talons, catching them and holding them steady. He was surrounded though, human corpses shuffling towards them with bone weapons sharpened and ready to pierce through his armor.

Then a large figure in broken armor came rushing into the clearing and bellowing a war cry, jets roaring behind him as he leaped up and crashed his body into the side of the Shaped Beast. Dom and the beast went barreling through the clearing before landing in a tumble. "Thought you could just cheat death and walk away from me, huh? Not today!" he cried before bringing his hammer to bear and slamming it into the creature's skull. It cracked, then shattered before its clawed hands shoved it off of him, the wound beginning to knit itself back to its previous state. "I got this one, Phaidros! You have company."

Phaidros turned to face the crowd, a dangerous sweep of his sword catching two that got too close. Then he heard the sound of creaking wood behind him, the trees that were chasing Dom had caught up, branches and vines already snapping to grab hold of Phaidros. Bullets then rang through the air, severing each of the reaching branches. "Stay focused, Phaidros," Zenovia called out, flipping into the clearing away from a tree that was just about to try and grab at her as she fired a few more shots into the crowd. Unlike with the Shaped Beast, the bullets ripped through, creating holes and staggering the bodies before they began to reform. "Charon is yours. Just get to him before we get surrounded."

He did not need another invitation. He rushed forward towards Charon who was creating more distance between the two of them, the undead horde swarming towards him. Phaidros charged them head on, blade arcing through the air in whistling arcs that flashed silver in the morning light. He severed one head before he ducked a sword hand looking to decapitate him. With a twist of his body he swept his blade around in an elegant arc and cleaved through all around him. He rose, slamming his boot into the body before him, making it crash into the body behind it before he skewered them both, twisted the blade and swept it free as he carved a path toward Charon.

Charon did not sit idly by any longer however. His minions were already closing in and now he could make use of his other powers he had yet to show. He lifted his hand and the shards of dead grass, splintered wood and the earth itself rose into the air twisting and molding itself into shards of bone. They suddenly launched themselves in a rain of sharp blades over the clearing. Phaidros brought his gauntlet up to block it, some of the shards sticking into his armor with a few cuts snaking through to his helmetless head. The others should be fine, at least that's what he thought until he heard a grunt of pain from Dom. His armor hadn't fully healed and one of the shards managed to break through.

Phaidros needed to move faster. He cleaved and swept through the bodies until the trees were suddenly in his way. These two had been twisted into more humanoid shapes with thick trunk-like arms that swung at him. His reactions brought his sword up just in time for the first blow and the moment the sword bit into its bark it made the reanimated tree go stiff. Phaidros ducked under the second, feeling the wind brush across his cheek before he yanked the sword free and twisted into another strike. This one hit the tree mid trunk and the shaped power of the blade drank freely of the potential within. Both suddenly went limp and suddenly there was nothing between him and Charon. He raised his sword as he charged his brother.

Charon didn't even budge before suddenly all three of the Ignited felt an overwhelming wave of fear wash over them. Phaidros was locked into place. Dom was forced back off his feet, the Shaped Beast's claws pinning his hammer down to the side as its maw opened in threat. Zenovia was grabbed by tree vines with a wooden fist ready to squash her like a bug. "Charon! Stop!" he called out, anger boiling at the back of his throat intermingling with the fear that came at him in waves. "This is between you and me!"

"If they had their way they'd take us back. We will not let that happen. You have tried to play the hero this whole time, standing up for me as if we could not do so ourselves, for our father's memory. Now's your time to prove that you are. Drop your sword and we will spare them, for now."

Phaidros felt fresh tears on his cheeks. How could this monster have once been his brother? He grimaced, why was the fear so much stronger now? He tried to take a step forward but dropped to one knee, mind screaming at him to cower before him. No, he could not give in, not now. Charon was just outside of his reach. He looked to either side, seeing Dom struggling with one hand on his hammer and Zenovia struggling against her restraints. They had both come here for him and now they were going to be at the mercy of his monster because of him. He didn't believe that they would be kept alive for long, not if the Ignited were going to keep hunting Charon after this. It was happening again, Phaidros was going to lose them both. He couldn't do that, it had only been a short time, but Dom and Zenovia had already done so much for them. They took a boy barely able to defend himself and helped turn him into an Ignited worthy of his father's legacy, saving his life on multiple occasions. Even when Phaidros was angry with them, even when he didn't believe in himself, they always followed him, believed in him, saved him. Now it was his time to save them. He needed to get up, not for his sake, but for theirs. He would *not* let his friends die, without them, he would be nothing, and without them he would become nothing again. "I can't," Phaidros said weakly, "I can't do that."

Charon's eyes shut halfway. "Then they will–"

Phaidros roared as he tore himself upwards, sword arm extended. Charon's reactions were enhanced with the Shaped's soul, but with so little distance between them Phaidros had gotten what he wanted, a small cut on Charon's cheek. "Free yourselves!" Phaidros bellowed to his companions as he felt another surge of potential flowing straight from Charon. The connection between him and his constructs wavered and Dom shoved the Shaped Beast back and slammed his hammer in an upward arc into its jaw, sending it reeling. Zenovia managed to pry herself free from the tree, twisting away from it and landing nearby Dom. "Good cindering work, Phaidros! Keep up the pressure! We'll keep them off your back."

That left him and Charon, with no one in between them. Phaidros felt his potential roar like a bonfire within him and a presence watching him, but there would be no distractions now. Fear bled away into rage as he threw himself at Charon with renewed vigor.

This time his brother was ready, ducking backwards and relying on the strength and speed the Shaped soul gave him to do so, carrying him backwards. Then suddenly beneath him, the ground shot up in a pillar and Charon rode it upwards before it shunted him into the air and out of range of Phaidros. He twisted through the air with grace that reminded Phaidros of when Charon was Ignited and let the book float off somewhere where it wouldn't get in the way of his hands. Phaidros was already on the move though, leaping up onto the earth and using it as a stepping board to chase after him, jets roaring to life to carry him the extra distance. Charon threw his hand towards Phaidros and one of the tree branches from nearby shot out towards him. The rest of the tree began to thin as if it were being compressed and forced down a high-pressure container. Phaidros struck it midair but the movement put him right next to Charon without his sword ready. Charon was already wheeling through the air and his kick connected to Phaidros' shoulder. Phaidros shot back down to the ground into a tumble. A wall immediately shot out of the ground and he slammed into it, more spines quickly following and slamming into his armor, cracking plate after plate before a final one shot for Phaidros' head, as Charon finally landed opposite of him.

Phaidros bellowed another war cry as he desperately swept his sword upwards in time, breaking several spikes in the process to cut off the killing blow from reaching him. The earth turned to dust and Phaidros blasted off towards Charon, who sneered. "We were the greatest champion of The Ring when we were ignited before. We were the most fearsome predator this jungle had. You think you can beat us now that we're bound?" Phaidros lashed out at Charon in a series of swipes and stabs as Charon ducked and weaved with a dancer's grace. Each strike and dodge came quicker than the last, the wind whipping around the two of them as Phaidros tried desperately to land a blow. Phaidros backed Charon up to a tree but the latter just kicked back onto it and over Phaidros. In the same motion he'd reanimate more of the land around Phaidros to keep him occupied before landing and charging in for a kick. The maneuver succeeded and Phaidros slammed against the wood, blood gushing from a now broken nose. He spun around just in time to block another spear of earth from running him through. "You can't win on your own."

Phaidros spat out excess blood, grinning through a swollen eye as he went after Charon again, though his movements were starting to get worse. "I'm not alone, Charon," he said, "Maybe you forced yourself to be, but I didn't. I am not alone now and I never will be." He just had to believe his friends heard that. He ran in to strike at Charon again.

The others!

Exaltation cried, but it was too late, Charon threw his hands forward and in that same moment, a shot rang through the air.

Zenovia had been helping Dom fight off the horde while Phaidros fought Charon, but she was always keeping an eye out on how the fight was going, letting Phaidros deal with what he could. When Phaidros started going off about not being alone though? That was the signal she needed. She had hidden her intentions well and when Phaidros surged forward, she had lined up her shot and fired.

The shot went clean through Charon's skull; all of his connections sputtered as potential had to seep back to heal Charon's wounds but it did what it needed to do. Phaidros cleaved through the broken earth and threw his fist to the man's chest; the stinger within shot out and shattered the breast plate. Charon stumbled back, eyes wide as Phaidros descended upon him, blade raised before it pierced straight through his heart and exited out the back of his chest. Charon stared in disbelief at his brother, a silent moment shared between the two of them before the necromancer coughed up blood. His legs trembled and his gauntlets scratched up against Phaidros' armor, trying to push him away. Phaidros felt fresh, hot tears run down his cheeks.

"I'm sorry, brother," Phaidros choked. "We both should have just left Dasos when we had the chance." Charon tried to answer but couldn't quite muster the energy as the sword rapidly drained him of his potential. Tears welled up in his teal eyes, the color slowly fading back to blue as they both collapsed to their knees, Phaidros cradling his brother in his arms.

Charon reached up to Phaidros, pain in his eyes as he finally managed to speak, voice barely a whisper. "We just wanted to live without suffering."

"I know," Phaidros answered. Behind them both, all of the bodies began to collapse without the potential to fuel them. Dom and Zenovia were released from their bonds, but to Phaidros the whole world around him and Charon disappeared. He gripped his brother tighter. "It is not your fault, Charon."

He smiled weakly at that, coughing out more blood as his eyes started to glaze over. He mouthed out words but Phaidros couldn't hear them. "Our… choice…" is what he thought it might be. The next words were unmistakable however. "Goodbye."

Phaidros watched as the last of his potential left him with a puff, before his soul gently drifted off into the heavens like a feather on the wind. The world around them was silent as Charon's body went limp. Phaidros stared up at the soul in horror through his tears. The fire in his body raged to new heights yet he could barely feel it through the pain of loss.

He hunched over, covering his brother's body as he held him close, then screamed in anguish into the air with nothing but the dead, silent jungle around him to answer.

CHAPTER 21

Remember those who are no longer with us. When their
body dies and soul moves on, all that we have to honor
them is their memory and the lessons they gave us.

-COLLECTED TEACHINGS OF THE EXALTED SOVEREIGN

PHAIDROS DID NOT leave his brother's side. His cries echoed throughout the quiet jungle. Dom and Zenovia did not feel it was right to interrupt him after they had both managed to recover. They stood nearby and watched Phaidros mourn the death of his brother by his own hand.

A flood of emotions raged within Phaidros, currents violently pulling him this way and that. What did he do now? How could he go on? All of his family were dead. The fire raged within him but what was the point of keeping such a fire if it led him to killing his brother? A hollow pit sat in his chest as despair overwhelmed him. It distracted him too much to notice the rolling smoke that began to fill the clearing.

Zenovia and Dom noticed it though, lifting their weapons weakly as they looked around for potential threats. "Phaidros," Zenovia said, trying to cut through the young Ignited's numb hearing. The smoke became so thick that even the trees were no longer visible from their position. They both switched to life sense and were near blinded as what was hidden in the smoke shone as bright as the sun, the flame that accompanied them filling all of their vision until they forced their perception back. "Ash and cinders..." Zenovia muttered.

Two, glowing, blue feline eyes stared at them through the fog, getting closer. Zenovia immediately took a knee and bowed their head. Dom stood a moment longer before saying something in a language that Zenovia did not understand but sounded an awful lot like buzzing before he too dropped to a knee. It was a sight each Ignited usually only saw once in their lifetime, the day that they ignited. The Exalted Sovereign.

Phaidros finally looked up from his brother to the approaching figure, peering through the fog as he wiped at his eyes and blinked away tears. The Exalted Sovereign? Here?

Do not kneel to me. Just as before, a gust of wind carried sounds that made out a voice when focused upon. *Stand tall.* If the three squinted they could make out a silhouette through the fog in the shape of a man only a little taller than Phaidros was with ram-like horns on either side of his head. His eyes were fierce, like a predator's. Even Dom, who was taller than the silhouette, seemed wary to size him up as both he and Zenovia stood.

The Exalted Sovereign did not look at the other two though, his eyes were focused purely on Phaidros. The tone of the wind sounded mournful. *You have achieved a great victory today, Phaidros, yet the cost of such a victory was equally great.*

Phaidros frowned deeply, looking back at his brother's body. "It doesn't feel like a victory," he replied softly. "It feels like I have lost everything. Why? Why couldn't you stop this? You're a god aren't you? Why would you let this happen?" His voice began to tremble, edging towards anger. "If this is such a threat you could have stopped it with a wave of your hand, why didn't you? Why did my brother have to die?"

Dom and Zenovia shifted uncomfortably, but did not dare speak to interrupt. The Exalted Sovereign's eyes closed, the silhouette of his head dipping low as if in apology. *For life to thrive, it must be given freedom to grow. Your brother was a victim to my counterpart. He who seeks to control everything to his designs.*

"If we had known," Phaidros barked, "then this could have been avoided! If you told us about this threat, everyone about this threat, then we could stop it. No one would have to die like this." He was barely attempting to hide his anger now. "My brother would still be alive if it weren't for you."

The Exalted Sovereign's eyes opened again; they did not return Phaidros' anger and resentment, only pity. *You had spoken to the Suneater. They spoke the truth. Should the masses know of this threat, then people would seek it out. If given the chance, they would openly throw themselves into shackles if it meant that they were long and gilded in gold compared to others.* Phaidros was still torn, looking down from him again and squeezing his eyes shut. "Why are you here?" he asked, tone defeated.

Your potential burns hot enough that your soul has become malleable. This made Dom and Zenovia perk up but they still did not speak. *You are ready to be Shaped.*

Phaidros had barely noticed the intensity of the heat within him; he had been so preoccupied with Charon's death. He did not look in awe like the others did however. He only looked confused. "I... am? Defeating the Shaped creature did not earn it but killing my brother did? Is this some kind of cruel joke?" he asked bitterly.

The Exalted Sovereign's gaze remained somber. *It is a common misconception that you must face great odds that might end in your death to become Shaped. The impossibility of the task is a part of it, yes... but it must be a defining moment. One that shows the world, life, me, a piece of the true shape of your soul within, by finding what keeps you moving forward against all odds.*

"Then please, enlighten me," Phaidros said, looking down again. "What is it you see? Because all I see is a murderer and someone who failed his family."

I do not blame you. Even if you are blinded by the despair you feel, it does not change everything that has happened until this point. A silhouette of a hand was raised, one finger lifted. *When your father died your fear of being alone is what made you take your first steps on the path.* Another finger lifted. *Through that desire for the bonds that surround you, you set yourself before an impossible task, not only earning powerful new friends in the process, but leading those friends.* Dom perked up further at the Exalted Sovereign calling him powerful before the god lifted a third finger. *With your newfound bonds that you created, you managed to stave off the beast before you, personally, were ready and sprang into action to defend innocents despite it meaning you would most likely die.* A fourth finger. *You did not give up on your bond with your brother until the very end, and in the end chose the bonds that you had forged yourself through blood and toil. You stood up, against pure, unfiltered fear, because you wished to see the bonds you formed thrive.*

"All I wanted was to save my brother," Phaidros said, beginning to feel fresh tears form in his eyes.

The Exalted Sovereign stepped up to the two of them; even this close he was only a silhouette, crouching down beside him now. *Your brother was gone and it was his own choices that led him down that path. You, however, have so much room to grow.*

Phaidros could not meet his eyes. When he put it that way it did seem to be the case didn't it? Yet out of all the ways to be Shaped, this was the last thing he wanted. "Must I? Must I etch this event into my very soul? Let it help define who I am? I don't know if I want killing my brother to be the reason I am Shaped."

It must be now, while your fire burns hot. Otherwise you may never get another chance.

Phaidros hesitated. This was something that most Ignited sought their entire lives.

Dom spoke up first. "Be reasonable here, Phaidros. You did a good thing here, no matter what way you spin it. It is a difficult path you have walked, you have earned this power."

Zenovia then finally spoke. "Remember what I said back in the Lion's Share? Don't let your brother be the one that rules your life. This is your chance to not only gain true power but to be able to use it so that what happened today doesn't happen elsewhere."

The Exalted Sovereign did not look to his companions as they spoke, only keeping his eyes on Phaidros. The young Ignited looked between them all. He would give up his Shaped soul if it would bring his brother back. That's what he thought at least before he finally looked at the book that had been dropped by Charon as he died. He stared at the leather-bound tome, the thing that had given Charon his power, who made him raise the dead and steal the life from all around him. From what the Exalted Sovereign and Suneater had said… there were more out there. He was then reminded about whatever it was that Charon talked to. Whatever it was that was feeding him lies. His grip tightened on his brother. "If I became Shaped… would I be able to find more of these books? Hunt whoever it was that made them?" He looked to the Exalted Sovereign.

The being that holders of the book speak to is one of dozens. Even an Ideal alone would struggle to truly kill one. That is if they go through the rest of their servants to begin with.

"But it isn't impossible," Phaidros pressed.

From the Exalted Sovereign's eyes it was clear he was smiling. *No. If you dedicate yourself to it, I'm sure one day you could. You may disagree with my methods, Phaidros, but my inaction is not without reason. It is a part of life and the rules that even I am bound by. You now know the truth of the greatest enemies that exist beyond our reach. If you wish to stop them, it will have to be by the hands of you and the other Ideals to rise up against them in this secret war.*

"I don't see how that would be possible without telling everyone the truth."

Then so it shall be. If you tell everyone, I would not stop you, but the consequences of such an action are yours. The Exalted Sovereign stood once more, looking down to Phaidros. *Now then…* The smoke began to thicken, making it impossible to see anything around the two of them save for the Exalted Sovereign's eyes. *Do you accept the shaping of your soul?*

Phaidros' eyes looked deep into the Exalted Sovereign's. He was still torn, his emotions in flux as he had to make this decision right here and now with his dead brother still in his arms. "I accept," he finally said, closing his eyes again.

Then by the might of life itself and the potential in all things. I shall bring forth the true shape of your soul. The god lifted a hand and everything went white. To Zenovia and Dominik they saw Phaidros' soul explode into fire, unable to be seen as the flames of potential manifested into the real world, enveloping Phaidros in his entirety.

It did not hurt as Phaidros thought it would yet it felt odd, like being in the center of a fire where the flames could not touch him. Yet at the same time he felt uncomfortable, like he was wearing too many layers of clothes and he had only just now noticed.

With this shaping you become a piece and manifestation of what set you on your journey. The **bonds** *of life that you seek to keep close at your fingertips.*

Phaidros felt his body shift and change ever so subtly while a hand reached into his very soul and struck away the imperfections until the shapeless ball of white of his soul molded into a new shape. Gone was the shapeless ball of white, an unknowable star among a vast sky of souls. Now, there were hands, all linked together and clasping one another by their wrist. There was no discernable start or end as they wrapped around each other. His body felt lighter, stronger, like some of the layers had been shed away by the Exalted Sovereign's power.

Many find comfort and strength in your connection to the world around you. Let all within the Ignited see you for what you are. You are He who Bonds, let none alive be beyond your grasp. The light began to fade, the smoke retreating with it.

"Wait, you're leaving?" Phaidros asked. "There is still so much more to say!"

My duty here is done. Should you seek direction, He who Bonds, speak to the Suneater. I will return once you are ready to ascend further.

"Wait!" Phaidros called after him, finally moving away from his brother yet the smoke had completely cleared, the light fading, leaving him alone with Zenovia and Dom.

Both of them were staring at him. "Phaidros..." Dom began. "You look..."

"Different," Zenovia finished. Phaidros' soul was not the only thing that had been Shaped. As Phaidros took a step closer to becoming idealized, his physical features also shifted as well. He looked at least five years older, his face well defined with sharp edges and intense eyes. All of his injuries had been healed.

However, on the inside, Phaidros slowly felt that pit return in his chest. He had agreed to become Shaped, he had become a manifestation of the bonds between all life, and he felt numb to all of it. He didn't respond to them, instead walking past them both to finally pick his brother up in his arms and turned back to them both. "We must speak to Sacred Suneater. One of you take the book."

Dom and Zenovia looked to each other again, not sure how to feel about all that just happened. Phaidros had been Shaped but... Phaidros clearly didn't look happy about it. Dom went to go pick up the book while Zenovia walked up beside Phaidros. It didn't seem right to congratulate him, or ask him if he was alright. He glanced at her out of the corner of his eye, expecting her to say something, a light frown on his face, eyes still red from crying. "You..." Zenovia began, "did your best, Phaidros. If your father were still here, he would agree with your decision today." She tried to offer a comforting hand on his shoulder.

Phaidros looked at the hand, expression blank. "Forgive me, Zenovia," he said after sighing. "I appreciate you trying to comfort me right now, I just need time." Zenovia frowned, but nodded, not saying anything more.

Dom caught up to the two of them. "We should hurry back and let Dasos know where to find the bodies before the jungle decides to take them for itself." Phaidros nodded and there was a small silence that followed before Dom continued, "...so, your soul looks a bit different now. I couldn't hear the last part of your talk with the Exalted Sovereign, but you are... Hands now? Your soul has been shaped into Hands?"

Phaidros frowned again. "It's He who Bonds," he confirmed flatly.

"He who Bonds, huh? Yes I think this is a good word for you. Even if you are not feeling very friendly and bonding now. You are feeling angry now I am sure."

"That is one word for it," Phaidros mumbled.

"Well." He lifted the book up. "I think I know what might make you feel better, sticking that blade of yours into whoever made this thing."

Phaidros didn't respond, though there was a look of cold determination in his eyes.

The trip back to Dasos remained silent, save for occasional attempts at levity by Dom. At some point both him and Zenovia began speaking encoded through their helmets in a private communications channel. Phaidros didn't mind, he didn't feel up to casual conversation as is.

The three entered the city; normally when a new Shaped would arrive there would be celebration, but people saw the body in his arms and wisely stayed quiet. They bowed their heads respectfully as the three passed and nothing more.

Suneater was where they always were, atop the great root of the tree that burrowed through the temple. The three Ignited entered with Phaidros at the head. Suneater was silent as they walked until they reached the base of the root. Phaidros knelt down and gently rested his brother on the floor in front of them, remaining on his knees.

"So it is done," Suneater said. "The book?" Dom approached the root and held the book up to Suneater; a branch reached down to take it and lift it up to the Ideal. They examined the cover briefly before grabbing it by its spine and unceremoniously ripping it in half, leather and all, as if it was a piece of discarded paper. There was a brief gout of flame and the book was gone, the magic keeping it together dissipating in its entirety. The Ideal's gaze then drifted to Charon and Phaidros. Silence lingered before the Ideal spoke again. "We failed him, Phaidros."

Phaidros blinked, not expecting that answer as he looked up at Suneater. The Ideal stepped down off the root to stand before the two of them, then bowed as much as their armor would allow them. "It is the duty of the Order of the Ignited to care for and ensure that the Cindered do not feel isolated and that we provide them the means to live a normal life. Charon was... difficult, but in every other regard the Ignited are supposed to embrace difficulty. Instead we isolated him. I can only beg for your forgiveness in this regard."

Phaidros wasn't sure how to take that. He sat there stunned that the Ideal of all people was apologizing to him. His fists clenched, he remembered when the Ideal spat on Charon's very idea at attempting to help Phaidros with his rite. Somehow it felt wrong for the Ideal to try and apologize to him, like they didn't have the right to even speak after they openly participated in his brother's downfall. He opened his mouth and closed it, grinding his teeth before finally some of his anger bled away so he could reply. "The last thing Charon tried to say to me was that it was his choice..." Phaidros sighed. "I believe it, but... we allowed him to get so far to make that choice. Thank you, Suneater, but I just wish to see that he is buried now." He hesitated. "...and that we speak to our next move."

Suneater stood upright again, nodding. "You are Shaped and thus your time in this city will be at an end soon to make room for other Ignited who struggle to maintain their fire. I know that you have spent most of your life here and your first few weeks of being ignited have been... eventful. However, we must follow our laws here." Phaidros nodded slowly, bitterness mostly hidden. That was what he expected. He was about to speak when the Ideal continued. "As for your next move. Unfortunately... the forces of life are more splintered and fractured than you may believe. The strength of the Amaranthine Planes is unified and mighty and without the full strength of the Ignited, it will inevitably succeed in any war it is pushed into."

That made Phaidros shift uncomfortably. "Why hasn't it just out-right attacked us?"

"The answer to that is hidden within the lands without stars," Suneater answered. "All I know is that for millennia they have slowly crept from system to system. I have only seen the denizens of their worlds several times in this age and the last."

"Surely the Ideals will see this threat? Isn't there the Council of Ideals?"

"Yes. They are the main people knowledgeable about the threat of the Planes. However… many have been stuck in their own affairs… As am I."

Phaidros hesitated. "Not even you can help me?" he asked, voice sounding pained.

"My city has failed your brother and that is a fault on my part, no matter what he says. I cannot leave Dasos unattended," Suneater said, a hint of apology in their tone. "If you manage to convince the other Ideals to join you in your crusade, I will vouch for you, but until then my place is here."

Phaidros' fire within made all of this sound way easier than his mind truly knew it was. He just needed to convince the most powerful people in the galaxy to trust him on a quest of vengeance. The anger bubbled in him more but the fact that there was a path at all soothed him. It would be a good distraction from everything that had taken place in the past few weeks. Where he didn't have to think about what he had done. What he had become. "What can I do to convince them?"

"A starship will be made ready for you that will take you to the Order's headquarters, The Cathedral, far from here," the Ideal answered, gently kneeling down and picking Charon's body up in his arms. Phaidros fought back the urge to lunge for the body. "There you will be able to do commissions for the Ignited and perhaps earn the audience of one of the Ideals. There is a civil war on Rodina, where the ruling Empress sits on the council and manages the war effort. If you wish for an easy way to make a name for yourself, start there. Bring whatever you need from your home here. You will not be returning."

Phaidros nodded then Dom took a step forward, sounding more rushed than Phaidros expected. "Wait, what about us?"

Suneater turned towards Dom. "What about you? You have not become Shaped. You are still welcome in this city and may stay for as long as you wish."

"Oh no. I am coming too," Dom said, arms folding. "I helped kill the big beast and I helped him take his brother. We are hunting partners now. Where he goes, I go." He looked to Zenovia as if waiting for her to back him up.

She looked from him to Phaidros and Suneater, folding her arms and drumming her fingers along one bicep. "You made a promise to me, Phaidros. I'll be damned if I let you go back on that promise for the sake of revenge. I'm coming with you too."

Phaidros froze. "You both want to come along? Dom, weren't you trying to get away from the civil war for a vacation?" he asked.

"You thought we were just going to let you go on an adventure hunting undead on your own? Nonsense. You are stuck with me. Besides, now that you are Shaped we will need a rematch soon. One with less one-sided win conditions. As for Rodina, seeing you has inspired me." He opened his mouth as if to add more before he just settled on grinning.

A smile managed to creep through onto Phaidros' face, though it was muted. "It will be nice to have company," he admitted.

Suneater nodded. "It is settled then. Now go, you all have preparations to make. I need to reach out to the port for one of their ships and have a burial made for Charon." All three nodded before leaving Suneater to their duties. As they were leaving the temple however, Phaidros paused. "Wait… there's one more person we should bring along."

"…Please tell me we are not bringing the dragon?" Dom asked meekly.

"Daxia made my armor, made new rounds for Zenovia to use on the beast *and* got you back up in fighting shape. She's earned a place, besides it would be nice to have a smith to make sure our gear is maintained."

Zenovia shrugged. "Well, you're Shaped, you would have been assigned one anyway so might as well." Phaidros nodded and was beginning to head towards the Merchant's District before Zenovia stopped him with a hand on his shoulder. "Don't go marching off," she scolded. "I know it's easy to just keep going even after you've experienced a loss, but you need to sit down and take a break. Go home, I'll go talk to Daxia. You've earned the rest."

Phaidros opened his mouth to speak but then closed it with a sigh. "I… alright. I'll try."

"That's all I ask." She clapped Phaidros on the shoulder. "See you tomorrow, Phaidros."

When Phaidros returned home, he stood in the entryway, eyes lightly scanning over the empty living area and kitchen. It was quiet. With no threat to his life hanging over the horizon, with all of his known family dead, he could truly feel how quiet his home was now. He was Shaped; with that came powers, he should be excitedly trying to figure out what it meant to be 'He who Bonds' but all he could think about was the empty spaces on the couch and the familiar faces there he'd never see again. He thought about the memories of the three of them all around the kitchen, talking about Charon's most recent victory or how well Phaidros was doing in his sword training. He stepped out of his armor, leaving it at the doorway as he walked further into the room and sat down at one of the seats at the kitchen counter and the moment that he had settled, the weight of everything that had happened settled with him.

He thought he had run through all of the tears earlier today, that he had been able to grieve enough, but he was wrong. Tears flowed freely from his eyes as he thought about all the things he didn't get to say to those he lost. The memories that would forever be memories, the happiness that he had once with them forever torn away by the cruel realities that all life must end. Never again would he see his father return home from another hunt with smiles and stories to share. Never again would he be able to sit with Charon about adventures they'd have once he also became ignited. No journeys into the stars awaited him for him and his family. For hours he sat there, crying alone, until inevitably exhaustion saved him from his anguish and lulled him into a deep and heavy sleep.

٭

The next day, Phaidros stood in full armor before two headstones, one bearing his brother's name, and the other his father's. His sword was slung over his back currently, with a large backpack and a few smaller bags hanging off of him with all of his essentials. Dom, Zenovia, and Daxia stood a little further away, Dom's armor still regrowing, all three of them were similarly packed as Phaidros.

"Goodbye, you two," Phaidros said, stepping forward to touch the headstones fondly. "I know I will not be allowed to come back here in the future so I wished to stop here and…" He trailed off. He wasn't sure what the proper words were. The emotions of yesterday crept back onto him. "Just say that I will not forget you both. It already feels like a lifetime since I've seen you, Father, and Charon…" He hesitated. "Charon, I will not let your death be in vain. I hope wherever you two are when you reincarnate… you will be living better lives than you did before. I will make the most of your memory." He lowered his head, fighting back the tears threatening to break free. "I miss you both. Please, if you ever do find Mother in your new lives, say hello for me." He pushed himself to his feet, taking one last look over to the graves before walking off towards his companions.

"You alright, Phaidros?" Zenovia asked.

"I'll be fine," he replied, though he was sure it wasn't convincing. Dom's hand found his shoulder and the new Shaped glanced up to see his friend smiling down at him.

"You are a bad liar, but that is alright"—the zhuk nodded sagely—"this is a hard thing to go through, but we are here to support you. Remember, you are not alone." The words brought a gentle smile to Phaidros' face. He glanced to Daxia, who seemed to be doing her best to try and give the three 'privacy' by looking anywhere but where they were.

She noticed she had been caught however and finally flicked her molten eyes back to him, "…don't look at me. I'm terrible at cheering people up." Her tail flicked in annoyance before she quickly added, "That one time a few weeks ago when you were really sad doesn't count." Phaidros' smile grew a little wider. "Thank you, all of you," he said, glancing between the three of them. "I don't know what we're going to face out there, but…" The words stuck in his throat, unsure of how to say what he wanted to say properly. He was scared of what lay ahead, what might be out there waiting for him. The Amaranthine Planes, the other Ideals. How would he try and prepare the others and himself for what he was leading them towards? "Just… thank you," his mind eventually settled on with a sigh.

"You need to work on your rousing speeches," Zenovia said, arms folding.

"It was touching!" Dom quickly interjected in his defense.

"I've heard worse." Daxia shrugged her shoulders. "Can we go now?"

Phaidros chuckled quietly then nodded. "Yeah... let's go." Dom shook his shoulder once in support as the four made their way towards the merchant's district and the starport that lay within. To leave the jungle behind and face new challenges in the stars above.

EPILOGUE

E XALTATION HOVERED IN a dark room, alone. An array of reflective mirrors stood before it, each showing different worlds, different faces, different pupils. The mirror in front of them suddenly cracked before shattering entirely. The sacrament did not flinch or show any signs of anger or disappointment at the shattering. It remained unnaturally still, single eye staring down at the remains.

Another falls,

it stated to no one in particular. With a single gesture of its hand, the floor beneath it opened and all the glass shards slid away before the hole closed back up. It looked to the other mirrors, seeing no one on the other side paying much attention to it. One hand lifted, and from the floor molded a new copy of itself to stand before the mirror while the being turned and floated out of the room it was in. The pupils would not notice the difference if this lesser puppet spoke to them or its main form. Two large, ornate double doors carved from bone opened into a hallway. It was open, with the wall facing towards the outside completely gone save for rows of pillars. From here Exaltation could see a vast city before them of twisting, macabre structures of bone and dead matter surrounding a mountain-sized archway with teal liquid trapped inside. It was only lit by the light of street lamps, unnatural fires, and the twinkling pinpricks of teal light like a sea of stars that came from the citizens down below.

It switched to soulsight to see the souls cast before it, seeing the light of the city shine brightly suddenly with clumps of souls bound together going about their business. Exaltation found what it was looking for and floated out the hallway and down into the sunless city. As it passed overhead, the creatures below averted their gaze, not wishing to garner its attention. Exaltation paid them no mind, should they anger the Father, they would see another sacrament, not them. Never them.

They floated to one of the nearby spires, towering far into the atmosphere. It was only slightly smaller than the sacrament's own tower. No one would dare try to think themselves greater than pieces of The Architect himself. As they approached the tower, the wall melted away like wet clay as Exaltation moved through the new hole in the wall before closing it behind him. It was eerily still as it moved through the air, arms behind it poised like an angel's wings as it descended from on high.

Inside was a throne room, massive pillars holding up the large chamber with a velvet red rug lining the center up the throne on the opposite side, perched upon a small set of stairs. The throne was made of polished ivory with countless, small carvings etched throughout the outside of its surface. At the throne's head was a single depiction of an eye, painted teal, situated so it stared down at all in attendance, a show that the sacraments were always watching. In the throne was a creature of bone, their body kept mostly humanoid in shape, like a mannequin, save for the six arms that sprouted from its shoulders. It was dressed in white silks embroidered with golden patterns across its entire surface. Mortals would consider it a masterpiece. Its face was the typical human skull, save for two larger sets of fangs and ridges carved into its brow. Two pinpricks of teal looked at the sacrament as it entered, calm, collected.

Arch Mortis,

Exaltation boomed, their collective voices making the entire room quake from the weight of it.

The time has come.

The Arch Mortis stood up, all six hands clasping together as they bowed deeply to Exaltation. "What does the Architect wish of us?" the Arch Mortis asked, their voice coming out as a choir of dozens speaking in perfect chorus. This Arch Mortis was more humble than some of the other ones Exaltation had known. Admiration had picked well.

The living will make war with us soon.

Exaltation answered.

You will gather a war party should this be the case, from the orders of death knights at your disposal.

The Arch Mortis tilted their head to the side curiously. "At once, Exaltation. They would be fools to try and attack us though, would they not? And they have not tried to make any incursions since the most recent ascension of Life." They raise their hands. "I do not question your decision, only seek clarification." The last thing they wanted was to make a sacrament upset.

We will not be caught idle, Arch Mortis. Praise be to the Father's wisdom that his flock has not been harried in many years. This is not all that we ask of you. We ask that another ten books be prepared and sent across the galaxy.

"Of course, Exaltation." The Arch Mortis bowed again. "They have already been transcribed and infused before you came here. It was coming close to around the decade you would make that request so I wished to be prepared."

Your diligence is praised by the Father, Arch Mortis. There is one more thing we require of you. You will find The Voices that Charmed The Stars' deeds have been noticed by The Father. We have a new task for them, one that suits their talents.

"It shall be done, Exaltation. What do you require of them?"

There is an opening within the Ghayr Muqayad region of space for the Father's will to be extended. They reject the teachings of Life but have not accepted the Father as their substitute. The Voices that Charmed the Stars will be our vanguard to lay the groundwork for further talks.

"You wish for diplomacy?" the Arch Mortis asked, once more sounding confused. "We have always expanded secretly, through the books on isolated worlds. It has worked for eons."

This is the Father's will. We do not ask why he wills it, we simply do as he commands, for his wisdom will grant us salvation, always, Exaltation answered, the two free hands it had raising as if addressing a congregation. *Such will bring glory upon us all. As it always has.*

It lowered its hands again. *As it always will.*

The End

For now…

Thank you for reading.

If you enjoyed this book, please consider leaving a positive review on Amazon/Goodreads/IngramSpark or wherever you happened to pick this up. I'm an indie author so reviews are very important. Of course, if you didn't enjoy it, please still leave a review and I will take what I learn into the next book which you will probably see around the same time next year.

If you wish to contact me directly, my business email is drewgoodman369@gmail.com. If you want to follow me and my writing journey, you can subscribe to me on "The Shaped Author" on YouTube, TikTok or the site formerly known as Twitter.

www.ingramcontent.com/pod-product-compliance
Lightning Source LLC
Chambersburg PA
CBHW022200170626
46807CB00005B/2287